The Fault Line

The meltdown of a marriage and a career

to Cecilia –
girl of wine,
with love

Pia Helena Ormerod

& friendship
Pia Helena O.

Men at some times are masters of their fates;
The fault, dear Brutus, is not in our stars,
But in ourselves, that we are underlings

Julius Caesar, William Shakespeare

Published in 2024 by FeedARead.com Publishing

First Edition

A CIP catalogue record for this title is available from the British Library.

This book is dedicated to Stephanie Stones – my daughter, who is showing that you can combine marriage and a career

Chapter 1

Bitch, bitch, bloody bitch. It felt good to spit out the words and swearing made it feel even better. Bitch, bitch, bloody bitch. She never thought she could hate someone so much; she just did not think at all. But she knew at that moment that her life would change and, strangely enough, it had nothing to do with her. It was, after all, not her fault.

Chapter 2

One year earlier.

The car stopped outside the Dorchester Hotel and Robert jumped out to open the door for Ruth. The door-man rushed forward to tell Robert where to park the car. The rain was light, still Ruth pulled her woollen cape tighter around her shoulders. She turned at the entrance and admired the myriad of tiny lights that covered the tree next to the car parking area. It looked magical and Ruth promised herself some tree-lights for their garden in Sussex.

The lobby was full of men in dinner jackets and women in silk and satins, all looking expectant, knowing that there would be a good dinner – and free. Ruth saw some of her colleagues near a grand piano in the large lobby area. She waved and they waved back, turning away as if hiding something under the piano. Her PA, Sirita, graceful and long-limbed, rushed forward and grasped both Ruth's hands.

"Are you excited? Nervous? You look great in that dress, it really suits you. Have you got your speech planned – just in case, but of course, we know you'll win." Sirita giggled as she saw Robert coming up behind. "You do have a very clever wife, don't you?"

Robert put his arm around Ruth, she could feel his warmth through the blue silk, and she turned to him, waiting for his affirmation.

"I had to park the car around the corner, no space left outside, and I forgot my umbrella. I'd better disappear to the gents to dry off. Will you wait here?" She looked at Robert with a downturn of her mouth.

Put off by Robert's lack of support, she joined Sirita and followed her down the room towards the others. She saw now why they had turned away. Larry from accounts lifted from the floor a gigantic basket filled with pale pink and blue hydrangeas, the blooms as big as cabbages.

"This is for you. Whatever happens tonight you'll always be the Businesswoman of the Year for us."

Larry blushed as he handed over the flowers. She wanted to hug him but the basket was in the way, so big that she could hardly hold it. There was a pink silk ribbon tied around the handle with some words on it. Ruth turned to Sirita, who grabbed one side of the basket and Ruth smoothed out the ribbon to read, *Good Luck from all of us at Babylove.*

The noise from the crowd around her disappeared and Ruth felt as if she were in a warm bubble, tears burned behind her eyes and she knew she could not be happier than this. Her staff loved her, she could feel it, and they wanted the best for her. This was going to be her night.

She had worked since she was seventeen when, with nothing but some rather undistinguished O-levels, she got her first job at a chemist's shop in Crawley. She hated the town, she hated her job but she knew even then that work was the only way out of Crawley and the cottage she shared with her angry mother. Her father had left her mother when Ruth was just a toddler and he had disappeared out of their lives for good. Ruth somehow always felt the mother held her daughter responsible for her own miserable life: one child, no husband and a dead-end job as a teller at a local building society.

Her mother took no pride or pleasure in the fact that her daughter, at the age of thirty-eight, was the managing director of Babylove, one of the fastest growing companies in the UK with a staff of over four hundred producing feeding bottles, changing mats, sterilising units and everything a new mother thought would make mothering easier. All the products were covered with an intertwined blue and pink heart, the logo of Babylove.

When Ruth came to Babylove, then called Watson & Rubens Ltd, there were sixteen people working there. She had secured a job as secretary to Mr Watson, a taciturn, red-eyed old chemist, who had invented a new procedure for sterilising hospital instruments. It was Ruth who saw the potential for sterilising feeding bottles and a subsidiary was set up to sell the equipment. Babylove she called it, always having loved the old favourite sung by The Supremes. Mr Watson left her to run it under his occasional guidance and gave her a room at the back of the laboratory.

She was on her own in her grey little office with a grey steel desk and a filing cabinet. "You make of it what you can, dear," said Mr Watson in a tone Ruth could not decide was filled with envy or encouragement. He was close to retirement and his partner Mr Rubens was already in his pre-paid grave in Surbiton. There was talk of finding a new director for Watson & Rubens Ltd but so far none of the applicants had appealed to Mr Watson who soldiered on spending fewer hours at his desk and more at the golf course.

He was a true gentleman, as far as Ruth could judge. She had not encountered all that many gentlemen when she first met him at the interview. He had obviously seen something in her and employed her even though she had only just finished a five-month course at Pitman's in shorthand and typing. She had speeds well below average – and also below what was asked for in the recruitment ad.

Now at the age of thirty-eight, she had been nominated for the Businesswoman of the Year Award. She was one of three finalists and the publicity had already given Babylove more space than hundreds of thousands of pounds of advertising could have secured. Ruth loved the interviews. She had often been on television to discuss the role of women in industry. On the first occasion someone had been taken ill and the BBC phoned her only hours before a programme on gender equality in business was to be broadcast. She had quickly washed her hair, something she seldom did herself but it was too late to get hold of Tony, her hairdresser. She worried about the unprofessional look but compensated for it by wearing her best Armani suit in pale pink, what else?

The BBC had offered her a car to pick her up and Robert came with her. He was left in the reception when a young girl came down to take her to a studio. "It's my first time," confessed Ruth as she jumped over cables in a studio, not much bigger than her bathroom. A man in glasses and thinning hair came over and introduced himself.

"I'm Charles Butterworth and you must be Ruth Farringdon of Babylove. Babylove," he seemed to suck the word through his thin lips. "Odd name that for a company."

"Not at all," answered Ruth and went into her PR mode. "We are here for all the mothers who love their babies and want to give them the best. We make sure that Babylove is safe love."

Charles Butterworth looked at Ruth for a second. "This is not a programme for commercials Mrs Farringdon, I just want to stress that now. We're not live, there's a five-minute delay, so I can cut out any answer that smacks of advertising. You do realise that? We're here to talk about women's role in industry, not your industry in particular." Ruth felt her cheeks burn. What an arse, she thought.

Ruth's nerves disappeared completely as the cameras lit up. She answered Butterworth's questions coolly and clearly and even managed a smile now and then, as if they were in sweet agreement. The five minutes seemed like one and suddenly the cameras were off. "Thank you, Mrs Farringdon. You're a natural. And I gather from Lizzie that this is your first time. Did you enjoy it?"

Ruth smiled. "Loved it," she said. "It's a bit like losing your virginity. So much worry and nerves beforehand and afterwards you think, was this what all the fuss was about?"

Butterworth and Lizzie giggled politely looking at each other. With a lopsided smile Butterworth gathered his papers on the desk and said, "Well, I seem to lose mine every night at nine o'clock."

After that Charles Butterworth had come back several times when he wanted a woman to give a view on anything from glass ceilings to sexual harassment at work. She had already promised him an interview if she won the Award tonight.

And this time Tony had done her hair and she knew she looked her best as she walked into the Dorchester Ballroom and saw that the basket with flowers was already on the Babylove company table. The room was humming and there must have been over five hundred guests. Ruth recognised several female politicians, some famous woman journalists and was that not the Duchess herself in a rather too deep décolletage and some stunning diamonds around her neck?

The lights dimmed until it looked like stars were glittering through the ceiling in the darkened room. Ruth's pulse started throbbing and she hardly knew what she was eating. The prize ceremony would take place after the dinner. To win would mean so much. She still remembered how her mother upbraided her for leaving the safe job with the chemist in Crawley in order to take the Pitman course. This would show that it had been worth it. Ruth would send her cuttings from the press tomorrow, just as she had always let her mother know when she would be on television. Her mother never made any comment.

A rather plump stand-up comedienne with a crew cut embarrassed most of the guests with some crude jokes. All eyes were on the Duchess, would she laugh? Diplomacy must obviously have been taught to everyone who marries into the Family as the Duchess seemed to be in a deep discussion with the organiser and appeared ignorant of the flat-lining jokes.

Now, finally, the organiser, a bejewelled woman of a certain age, took the microphone and turned to the Duchess to thank her for coming before she went on to introduce the three finalists. Ruth did not hear a single word of the nominations, her mind like an antenna which could only tune in when she heard the word Babylove.

"…And last, but not least, Ruth Farringdon, the managing director of Babylove, who set up the company as a subsidiary of Watson & Rubens Ltd fifteen years ago. Since then, the subsidiary has grown and taken over its parent company and today Babylove has a turnover of thirty-two million pounds. There is hardly a baby in this country who has not been brought up with their products. The company has also set up the Babylove Foundation, which so far has donated six million pounds for research into cot death." The applause was ringing in her ears as Ruth stood up and walked to the podium.

The three finalists were now on the stage staring at each other while pretending to smile. The organiser beckoned the Duchess to join them on stage and handed her a golden envelope.

She opened it slowly and waited for a second or two. Had she been told to do so in order to make the ceremony more exciting, Ruth wondered? It seemed like minutes to Ruth and the smiles of the other finalists stiffened like hers. Finally, the Duchess spoke.

"It is with great pleasure that I announce the winner of the Businesswoman of the Year, sponsored by The International Women's Association and Lambert Champagne. The winner is… Ruth Farringdon of Babylove, who has managed to combine sheer commercial success with charitable aims. Congratulations! And, may I add," said the Duchess, with a rather conspiratorial wink, "that all my grandchildren have been pacified by Babylove dummies, a great help to preserve the sanity of any mother."

Ruth grabbed the envelope from the outstretched royal hand and wondered if she should curtsy or not. She did not have time to worry as the sponsor came forward with a jeroboam of champagne. "Don't drink it all at once," whispered the Duchess.

The room erupted in applause and laughter as the microphone had picked up her remark. The laughter felt like a release for Ruth and the tears she felt behind her eyelids dried up. She stepped down from the stage, clutching her envelope and the large bottle as the band played a cobbled version of Babylove. Ruth returned to her table, glad that she did not have to make an acceptance speech apart from a thank you. Now everyone at the table patted her on the back to congratulate her.

Robert was the first to hug her. "I am so proud of you, Ruth darling. We'll celebrate later, but I've got Charles Butterworth upstairs with his camera team. You promised him an exclusive, remember?"

Later Ruth would remember that night as the happiest of her life. That was before it all changed.

Chapter 3

Charles Butterworth must have had some useful contacts at the Dorchester. He and his team were installed in a suite on the first floor and had obviously been treated to a bottle of champagne as well as jugs of coffee and sandwiches. Crumbs covered the glass-topped sofa table.

"A suite! Not bad, Charles. How did you manage to wangle that?"

"Don't get too impressed, Ruth. All these luxury hotels are desperate to get some decent publicity. Having a name check and flash of their stylish interiors on the BBC News does not exactly hurt their image. But enough of that. Congratulations. I somehow knew you'd win. It's that combination of profit and charity, it always works, especially when you can show pictures of healthy smiling babies."

Charles patted her naked shoulder. "Let's get cracking. We'll do the interview here on the sofa." The cameraman turned on some bright lights behind an up-ended white umbrella.

"This will be a short one for the news bulletin, Ruth, but I want to do an interview for 'Business in Depth' with you later this week. I've told my current affairs editor that you are the perfect role model for women in business. And that you've reached the top without any fancy business degrees or being the daughter of some mega-rich tycoon. Would that be OK with you?"

Ruth smiled. "Of course, Charles. It would be a pleasure. Come down to Caterham and we'll do it in my office. You can finally see the factory."

The item for the news bulletin took five minutes to record. "It'll probably be cut to a minute and a half when it goes out," warned Charles. "Or scrapped if some minister has been caught with his pants down or there's been another pile-up on the motorway."

Ruth thanked the cameraman and the sound engineer. Charles got a hug. "I'll be in touch with dates for that longer interview you want. Now, though, I'm off downstairs to drink my champagne with the rest of my gang. Didn't dare to have even a sip before my interview."

She called out to Robert who had been waiting in the bedroom of the suite. He came out, still holding some glossy magazine.

"Charles wants to do a proper interview for the 'Business in Depth' series. Isn't that great?"

Robert made a mock salute to Charles.

"Fantastic. Why don't you come down and share a glass of that jeroboam of champagne Ruth has just won?"

"No, it's back to the studio for me and the guys. Thanks anyway. You two go down and celebrate. You deserve it, Ruth."

For a second, a shadow crossed Robert's face. Charles looked intrigued as he watched Robert following his wife out through the door, two steps behind her.

Next day, a Saturday, Ruth stayed in bed longer than usual. The Lambert champagne bottle had not lasted for long and more bottles, although smaller than her jeroboam, were ordered to their table, many by people who wanted to be seen with the winner. By two o'clock Ruth and Robert were still in their seats. The organisers and the Duchess had left hours before but Ruth wanted to enjoy her success to the last drop. And it was those last drops that gave her a hangover that Saturday morning.

Robert must have gone up hours earlier. He had been out and collected all the newspapers from the newsagent as well as a bunch of tiny pink roses wrapped in cellophane. Coffee and croissants were ready on a tray.

"Thought you might need a bit of a lie-in after yesterday's celebrations. Look! You're in both *The Daily Mail* and *The Times* with pictures. And *The Telegraph* interviewed the organisers. Very good publicity for both you and Babylove. Anyway, darling, when will you be ready to go down to Hicks? You remember I've invited the Callanders over for supper. I did tell you that I also asked Mandy Richards, you know, my old mate from Leeds. They're all coming at seven. No, you don't have to worry. I've got everything planned and we can set off whenever you're ready."

Hicks was Hicks Manor, a house with more aspirations than class. It was not really a manor, but a large Victorian villa in a tiny village just outside Horsted Keynes. The red brick building could not be seen from the road, nor were there any neighbours close enough to overlook the untended gardens. For Ruth this was more than a house, it was the symbol of what she had achieved. A house with history and with rooms she had never even heard of when she grew up: breakfast room, boot room and butler's pantry. Every space held a special magic for her. There were no fancy rooms in the cottage in Crawley where she and her mother lived before Ruth got married. They ate all their meals in the kitchen or on trays in front of the television. And there was certainly no wine cellar like at Hicks; wine was never drunk at her home, it was sherry for Christmas and whisky for medicinal purposes.

Robert was not keen when they first saw the house. He found it dark and old-fashioned, but that was just what attracted Ruth to it. She loved the corridors, dark even on a bright summer's day and the top floor, which had been a nursery floor with several small rooms. Soon after they moved in, they tore down the walls on the top floor and turned the space into a gym for Robert and a small study for each of them. On the first floor there were four decent-sized bedrooms, with old-fashioned large bathrooms and dressing rooms. The house was spacious enough to have some guests, but not too many, as Ruth was quick to point out.

There was no real garden, just lawns with brownish patches where the sun never reached. The trees, which had probably been planted when the house was built, had grown high putting the house in eternal shadow. The windows always looked black, whatever the time of day. The slate-covered roof had a small open turret in the west corner reminding Ruth of illustrations in her childhood's fairy tales. In the summer it was used for pre-dinner drinks. There was no room for any chairs and their guests would pant heavily after having climbed the narrow steps from the top floor. "But look at the view," Ruth would say, grateful that Robert had carried the drinks and glasses all the way up. And it was a view to behold. Rolling fields of yellow and green and copses dotted with tiny clapboard houses and in the summer, they could even see the Bluebell Railway train chuffing along carrying train enthusiasts and excited children.

"It's not a cosy house," Robert complained, when he and Ruth saw it for the second time. "I expect to find a colonel with a dagger through his heart on the library carpet. There is something spooky about this place."

Ruth pretended not to hear his objections. She had fallen in love with the house the moment she stepped in through the double doors into a dark oak-panelled hall, made even darker by the stained-glass windows on either side of the door. The light from outside was cut into slivers of green, red and yellow as it hit the tessellated floor. "Of course, you find it gloomy, but just you wait until we fill it with our own furniture. You will love it as much as I do and this is exactly what I've been looking for." She did not add, and it is my money buying it, but she thought it.

It was not expensive; obviously everyone else who had looked at it found it as gloomy as Robert did. Ruth had managed to get the price down even further, thanks to the help of the estate agent who had almost given up hope of ever seeing it leave his books. In order to placate Robert, she had put him in charge of renovations and that included a complete state-of-the-art kitchen, which with the rebuilding and redecorations cost almost as much as the house. And he had grown to love it; maybe because when they were there, Ruth relaxed as her colleagues seldom disturbed her.

Through Robert's rounds at the golf club, they had made some friends locally and sometimes they would invite them over for dinner on Saturday night. Dinner was always served in the dining room, "What's the use of having one, if we don't use it?" Ruth said. Robert who did all the cooking did not agree. He wanted to show off the kitchen with its gleaming metal and marble just as he loved taking them down to tour the wine cellar.

* * *

Ruth packed a few things for the weekend; she wanted to give Marcia Callander a Babylove soap, a new line she was hoping to introduce, not for babies but for women who wanted a "skin as soft as a baby's". As an afterthought she put in one extra, for Mandy Richards, the other guest Robert had invited. "At least I don't have to give one to Dick, he hasn't got an ounce of vanity and would not know what soft as a baby's skin means." Robert ignored her remark, he was busy clearing up after breakfast.

Robert put bags of vegetables and punnets of fruit in a basket. The local greengrocer in Sussex had admitted to Robert that there was not much demand for rocket and aubergines in the village. "This is more a cabbages and leeks kind of place," he had told Robert. Ruth put their books from the bedside tables into a bag. "I am ready when you are. And when we're in the car you can tell me more about that woman you've invited."

The engine purred as quietly as only expensive engines can. Driving through grey suburb after even greyer suburbs they finally hit the motorway.

"Now tell me about Mandy."

And that is when Robert told her that Mandy had been his first girlfriend.

Chapter 4

Ruth swallowed to give herself time to think.

"You never mentioned this Mandy to me before, was she a serious girlfriend?"

Robert's eyes never left the road but his hand squeezed the leather-clad steering wheel.

"She was my first proper girlfriend. Aren't the first ones always serious?"

Ruth suspected that Robert was playing for time.

"Not always, I can hardly remember my first boyfriend. Well, to be truthful I can hardly even remember Luke, my first husband." Her laugh sounded almost like a hiccup. "When I was young I think I was more interested in having a boyfriend than in the actual person." She did not mention that Luke had been her first real boyfriend, as Robert had never shown any interest in her former life.

"So tell me more about this mysterious Mandy."

"We met when I was in Leeds doing my accountancy training. I was just twenty and she was eighteen. She worked as a secretary for one of the local law firms and her boss taught us the rudiments of commercial law. I met her through him, well, I had to hand over some papers at his office and there she was. Pretty, I suppose you'd say. I don't know what gave me the courage but I asked her out and that was it. She lived at home and I had some grotty digs in Meanwood so it was all rather innocent, but then the second year she got promoted and could afford a bed-sit and I sort of moved in."

"So how long did this little romance last?"

There was a sharp tone in Ruth's voice. It was not the old romance that worried Ruth but the fact that Robert had never mentioned Mandy before.

"We were together for two years. It finished as I came down to London, and that's it."

"No, that's obviously not *it*, as you're still in touch."

"Yes, that *is* odd. A couple of months ago I got an email from her saying that she had found my address through an old friend on Facebook. I had no idea he had given her my email address – and without asking me. I e-mailed back and we talked about..."

"Talked, you mean you met?"

"Well, she insisted and I could see no harm in it after all these years. We shared a coffee at some place near Victoria Station."

"And you never saw fit to tell me?"

"Darling, you are always so busy, why should I bother you with things I do during my days at home?"

"So how many times *did* you meet?"

"Oh, a couple of times, that's all."

"A couple, if you met just a couple of times, surely you remember how many?"

"Ruth, aren't you being a bit over-dramatic now? You'll meet her tonight and you'll see that she's a rather lonely woman in need of friends. I hope you will become one of them. Had I known you were going to react like this I would never have invited her. I didn't even ask her to stay the night because I knew you were tired, so she'll drive back to Orpington tonight."

"I am sorry I grumbled. You are right. I am tired. I even brought a small present for her, a soap."

They were both silent for the rest of the drive and Ruth could not wait to get out of the car as Robert parked it in front of the porch.

"Finally, home, my beloved Hicks," Ruth whispered as she put the key in the mortice lock.

The guests were expected at seven. "Why do they always eat so early in the country?" Robert grumbled as he sliced the onions. Ruth had insisted that they should eat in the dining room; she wanted to show Mandy that Robert had not married just anyone. Silly to worry, she thought, as she pulled out the damask linen and folded the large napkins, then with a cloth polished the glasses and buffed the silver. She liked a proper table with candles and flowers. The pink roses looked just right in a crystal bowl. For a moment she forgot about the guests.

Suddenly Ruth found that it was quarter to seven. Having rushed upstairs she put on black crepe trousers and a pink polo neck. A quick dab with the powder brush and lipstick, some scent behind the ears and she was done. She looked at herself in the mirror, her hair still in shape after yesterday's Dorchester party but her eyes did look tired. "I must take it easier, not allow Robert to organise dinners after a busy week. I would have loved a simple supper in front of the telly." The thought stopped there as Ruth remembered the sofa in Crawley with its springs gone and the tweedy material worn down at the armrests. "No, stop it! I'm going to enjoy my dinner in style," she said to herself as she heard the doorbell ring.

Marcia and Dick Callander were the first to arrive. Robert served them drinks in the drawing room. Ruth had always enjoyed their company in spite of them having nothing in common. Maybe that was a comfort in itself? Marcia, a former schoolteacher, was helping out at a sports centre in the next village. She did not work every day as she spent most of her time playing golf and tennis with other neighbours. Dick was a lawyer and commuted a couple of days a week to London. He never discussed his work but Ruth suspected that as he had not been made a partner of his firm he had more or less given up. He, too, played a lot of golf. Often with Robert.

Ruth knew that Dick had taken an almost paternal interest in Robert. At the end of a round they would sip a beer or two in the clubhouse and discuss whatever they had read that week in *The Financial Times.* Ruth suspected that Dick was secretly in awe of her, but she pretended not to notice and treated him kindly, like a favourite uncle. She admired his style, always so dapper and envied the way Marcia and Dick spoke to each other, as if they had just been introduced and still felt they had to be on best behaviour. Ruth and Robert had stopped saying please and thank you to each other years ago.

Marcia was in her late fifties. Maybe she had passed sixty, Ruth would not dare to ask, but she looked much younger than Dick. She had that kind of glow that only hours on the golf course and tennis court give you and her svelte figure was probably due to the fact the Callanders had no children. She dressed well and safely. This evening she was wearing a long skirt in blue and green check with a matching green scoop-necked jersey. And her eternal pearls, a wedding gift from Dick's mother, "as she was so pleased to get rid of him," Marcia told Ruth when she had once complimented her on the pearls, the size of walnuts.

Robert was just about to top up the glasses when the doorbell rang again. Before anyone could say anything, he put down the bottle and sprinted towards the front door.

"Robert has invited some old flame for dinner tonight. I've never met her, but according to Robert she is having trouble at work or something. Well, you know Robert, he loves a lame duck."

At that very moment Robert came into the room and Ruth shut her mouth quickly, praying that they had not heard her remark. She walked up to Mandy with a hostess smile.

"I am Ruth, Robert's wife, lovely to meet you" – there was a short pause – "finally. And this is Marcia and Dick Callander, old friends of ours, and this is Mandy, sorry I don't know your surname… ah, Richards, an old friend of Robert's."

Robert did not let go of Mandy's arm as the introductions were done. He offered her a glass of wine asking if she had found it difficult to find Hicks. Mandy just smiled and sipped her wine. Ruth looked at her. Next to Marcia, who was explaining to Mandy that they were neighbours of Robert and Ruth, she looked plump and dishevelled. Her woolly dress in some indeterminate colour looked in need of an iron and her blond hair had grey wiry streaks. She wore no make-up as far as Ruth could see. Could this really be a woman Robert had spent two years with? She seemed both awkward and shy.

Robert was still standing close to Mandy. "Would you like to see my wine cellar?" he asked.

"Come on, Dick and Marcia have already seen it, but you can help me to pick a wine for tonight's main course. We're having duck, no, not lame duck."

The Callanders laughed nervously. It was clear that he had heard Ruth's remark. Mandy seemed not to notice, she just looked happy to get away and the two of them disappeared. Soon their laughter was heard, coming up from the cellar.

"Do you think she heard what I said?" Ruth asked. The Callanders shook their heads and drained their glasses. The silence was uncomfortable for all of them and Ruth called out with a voice that sounded shriller than she wanted.

"Robert, have you two found a wine for dinner? Time to eat, I think."

She guided Dick and Marcia into the dining room and asked Dick to light the candles on the table while she poured the water.

Robert and Mandy entered the dining room holding two bottles of claret. There was white wine in a cooler on the sideboard waiting for the seafood salad. Robert turned his back to the guests and uncorked the wine leaving Mandy standing alone not knowing where to sit. "What a wonderful room, grand and cosy at the same time," she said waiting for Ruth to guide her to a chair. Ruth still had her back to Mandy pretending to be busy by moving the saltcellar and peppermill on the table like a general moves his toy soldiers.

"Come here, Mandy, and sit next to me," said Robert as he turned around. "And you, Marcia here on my right." Given their seating, the guests relaxed and waited for Robert to serve the white wine.

"I must be careful as I have to drive," Mandy said as she put her hand over the half-filled glass.

"Oh, don't worry. If you want to drink you can stay the night, no problem at all, we have a guestroom prepared. That's all right, isn't it Ruth?"

Marcia and Dick looked at Robert and then turned their heads to Ruth.

"Of course, no problem." She made a mental note that she had to speak to Robert not to invite guests to stay the night without discussing it with her first. Her muscles tightened and her lips stretched to a semi-smile.

Mandy did not say much during the dinner, seeming more interested in what was on her plate than in the discussion around the table. Robert tried to pull her in by asking her questions about her work but she mumbled monosyllabically. When Ruth brought in the coffee, her contribution to the meal, Mandy stood up and cleared her throat.

"I really must go. I've got quite a journey back home. It was lovely to meet you all and thanks so much for a fantastic dinner. You are a brilliant cook, Robert." She threw an admiring glance at Robert.

"Oh, do stay," he said. "I've got some lovely Armagnac for you to try."

"So kind, but I really must…"

"Well, thank you for coming. We might meet again, who knows," said Ruth as she stretched out her hand. Mandy took her hand in hers and looked at it as if she did not know what to do with it.

"I'll take you to your car, it's quite dark outside." Robert put his arm on the small of Mandy's back as if to guide her. Dick and Marcia exchanged some lukewarm goodbyes with Mandy before Robert led her to the front door.

Ruth turned to Marcia and Dick, who stood up to leave as well.

"Please don't you go yet. There's that wonderful Armagnac Robert would like you to try." Ruth needed the Callanders to be there. She poured the golden brandy into two glasses and handed them to her guests.

"Well, it's only ten, we're not in a hurry." Dick sat down in front of the fire and sipped his drink. Ruth thought he looked like one of those old-time advertisements for fine brandy, so elegant next to the open fire. Not a word was said as they were all waiting for Robert to return. They waited for more than ten minutes in silence, pretending to be lost in their brandy and thoughts.

Robert stomped on the floor in the hall as if he wanted to make sure that they heard him arrive. "Poor girl," said Robert when he entered the room. "Quite a drive for her back to Orpington. I told her to go by the motorway, not much traffic at this time of night, but she would rather not, so I spent some time with a map to show her the quickest route."

Ruth looked at Marcia. Did she raise her eyebrow for just a second, or did Ruth just imagine it?

"I'm so sorry. It was quite a party last night with the celebrations at The Dorchester and I'm exhausted. Would you mind if I left you in Robert's capable hands?" She kissed Marcia and hugged Dick before giving a small wave to Robert. "I'll help you clear up tomorrow." Both knew that she wouldn't and that Ruth would be awake when he finally came to bed.

Chapter 5

"What an evening. I don't think I want to go through that again," Dick said as he opened the car door. Marcia smiled, this was her general response when she didn't know what to say. She was tired; nothing is as tiring as pretending that nothing is going on. Marcia felt the tension from the moment Mandy had entered the room.

"I think it was wrong of Robert to invite— a woman Ruth didn't even know, for dinner the night after she'd got that major award. Poor Ruth, she looked exhausted. And who was this woman anyway, coming all the way from Orpington? Funny person, didn't say much for herself, did she? And I thought she looked rather scruffy, too," said Marcia.

"Darling, everyone looks scruffy next to you. I found her rather nice. She was shy, that's all. And I hope by God she didn't hear Ruth's rather catty remark about lame ducks."

The hum of the motor grew louder as they entered the motorway. The rain had left a sheen on the tarmac reflected by the headlights.

Dick turned off the radio, some ghastly modern music, and wished he had not had that last Armagnac.

He turned and glanced at his wife. Marcia was still a most attractive woman he thought, a figure that a woman half her age would envy but he also knew that she spent a lot of time and money on looking good. It was a great disappointment to them both that they never had children. He had been told some thirty years ago that something with Marcia's tubing had gone wrong. He had never discussed it with her since the final pronouncement from her gynaecologist after a messy miscarriage.

They had a beautiful home, not a dark and sinister house like Ruth and Robert's. Money was no problem. Whatever Marcia earned from her part-time job at the sports centre she spent on clothes while he was very happy to pay for their expensive golfing holidays in the Algarve and Jamaica. Marcia did not like windy winters in Sussex and sometimes they would go on a cruise with some neighbours. Luckily, Dick's parents had left them their house and those stocks and shares Dick liked to discuss with Robert. "They seem to lose value day by day," Dick often complained.

"I'm very fond of Robert," Dick said suddenly. "We always have so much to talk about. He's bright and talented in his way and I don't think it's easy to have a wife like Ruth. She is rather a cold fish, don't you think?"

"Not at all," said Marcia. "I admire Ruth immensely. Look what she has achieved coming from absolutely nowhere. There she was last night getting a wonderful award and chatting to the duchess and look what she's done for charity. I don't think you can run a company of that size and be just a sweet homebody. Just think of it, if she doesn't succeed, all those people at her factory will lose their jobs. A terrible responsibility. Not only that, she has to come up with new ideas all the time. If I were her mother, I'd be terribly proud."

"Well, her mother isn't. Do you remember how we met her the first time just after they had moved in at Hicks? She complained about everything. What was it she said, do you remember? Something about it was time Robert took over and that a man should be ashamed to be supported by a woman. I couldn't believe it."

Marcia nodded.

"It's an arrangement that suits them both. Poor Ruth, it can't be easy to have that added pressure. And I happen to know that Ruth is very generous to her mother. She gives her a hefty monthly allowance."

"I don't know if I told you, but I've asked Robert to help with some of our investments. The shares are sitting there doing nothing for us. He had some good ideas for investing in commercial properties in Scotland. It feels right to do something with our money and also to be able to help him in a way. A win-win situation I call that."

Marcia smiled again. She never talked about money; she was not interested as long as there was enough for the cruises and holidays.

"You're a good man, darling."

Dick turned off at the motorway junction, only two more miles and they would be home.

Chapter 6

There are many ways couples can quarrel without using words. Robert showed his anger by staying downstairs for more than an hour. He banged doors, the plates clattered as he put them into the dishwasher and all the while he hummed loudly and out of tune. Ruth heard it all though she tried to shut her ears as tight as her eyes. When Robert finally came upstairs, she pretended to be asleep. Her breathing was out of control and she knew that she could not fool him. With a heavy sigh she turned and glowered at him. Robert ignored her and started undressing, letting his shoes drop one after the other noisily onto the wooden floor. Bang went the wardrobe door as he closed it but only after having made the clothes hangers rattle. Ruth turned with another theatrical sigh, still not saying a word, pulling the corners of her pillow around her ears like a muffler.

Through her half-closed eyes Ruth saw him putting on his dressing gown and as he passed her on his way to the bathroom, he looked straight at her, it was a cold stare, like her mother used to look at her when she had done something wrong. Contempt mixed with anger and disappointment. Ruth wanted to stop the charade and apologize but she was not sure what for. And why was Robert angry? She had been perfectly polite to Mandy.

Ruth wanted to say something but by then Robert was already in the bathroom running the taps.

Their double bed had always been a non-combat zone. Even after a long hectic day at Babylove, Ruth knew she could curl up next to Robert in bed, all tension melting away. It was not just a question of sex, no, it was a silent togetherness that spread warmth through her tired limbs and helped her to sleep. Most nights she would fall asleep with her head nestling on his shoulder. Often Robert would stay awake and read, it never bothered her. The turning of the pages of his book had an almost soporific effect on her. She had given up reading at night years ago.

When she heard that Robert was finished in the bathroom she turned towards his side and stretched out her hand. Robert yawned loudly, climbed into the cold sheets putting out his light. He immediately turned his back on her. She was too tired, too upset to do or say anything.

She twisted the hem of her nightdress into a ball and moved back to the edge of the bed. Two can play at this game, she thought. Her mind was clear and an image of Robert with his hand on Mandy's back, as he guided her out to her car, was ingrained behind her swollen eyelids. She prayed for sleep but it did not release her until she had heard the grandfather clock in the hallway strike three.

When Ruth woke up next morning, she was alone in their big bed. There were no sounds from downstairs. Usually on Sundays Robert would give her breakfast in bed. Where was he? Ah, maybe he had gone to get the Sunday papers to see if her award had got another mention. She rose from the bed, still feeling drowsy, and walked downstairs. The kitchen was empty, looking like a showroom in its tidiness. The dining room showed no signs of yesterday's dinner. Where was he? Ruth suddenly felt nervous, what if something had happened to him? She grabbed her coat and put it over her nightdress and rushed out to the courtyard. The car was there. She looked closer and saw Robert sitting in the driver's seat holding his mobile to his ear.

The gravel hurt her bare feet as she ran up to the car and opened the door. The phone slipped from his grip and quick as a flash he gripped it with his other hand and touched the screen to turn it off.

"Morning, darling. You're early, it's only eight. I thought you might like a lie-in. You were so tired last night. Are you ready for breakfast?" His usual smile. She did not smile back.

"Who were you talking to at this time of the day?"

"Just testing the battery, I forgot to charge it last night. Thought I'd better charge it in the car as I can't find my normal charger. Have you seen it by any chance?"

Robert turned and looked at her, still holding the phone in his hand. He looked at her naked feet.

"You have no shoes on, you'll catch a cold. Come on. Let's go inside and I'll make some hot coffee and toast."

He put his arm around her and suddenly she felt warm again. Until she saw that he was still clutching the phone.

The rest of the Sunday was like so many at Hicks. Robert pottered in the garden while Ruth scoured the business sites on her laptop. For lunch Robert prepared a Sunday roast and as usual they shared a bottle of claret. Afterwards they took a long walk through the forest down to the bottom of the valley. Ruth loved these afternoons. They did not talk much, and for her these few hours were like a mind-wash. She went through her plans for the coming week, making mental to-do lists and prepared any discussions she was going to have with her lawyers or bankers. When they got back to Hicks, Robert prepared tea and sandwiches. Ruth was burdened with the sadness as always when leaving her beloved house. The weekends were too short. And last night's silence still hung over her like a miasma.

They would talk on the drive back to London, the way they always did. By the time they had packed the car it was dark. A chilly rain was pitter-pattering on the windscreen.

"It was nice to meet your friend Mandy yesterday. I hope she enjoyed herself and got home safely. The Callanders and I agreed that she didn't have a lot to say for herself, did she?"

Robert did not turn to look at her, his eyes fixed on the road. Without a word he turned on the radio.

"We don't want to miss the six o'clock news now, do we?"

Ruth said nothing, and for the rest of the journey they listened to the news followed by some comedy programme that they both pretended to laugh at.

Chapter 7

Charles Butterworth was an urban man, although he would rather be thought of as urbane. The country held no thrall for him, he wanted concrete under his feet. And London meant inner London, his bachelor flat in Chelsea was surrounded for him by unknown territories.

"Why could this woman not have come up to London? There's nothing interesting about a factory spitting out dummies for babies, is there?" his cameraman grumbled.

Charles felt like agreeing but out of loyalty to Ruth Farringdon, newly elected Businesswoman of the Year, he swallowed and kept his silence.

The suburban streets had given way to sprawling roads with tarted-up pubs and farm shops boasting about their organic wares and Kiddies Play Areas. Only forty-five minutes from London and Charles already felt out of his depth, certainly not ready for running an in-depth interview.

Ruth was waiting for him in the reception of the Babylove office building next to the factory. Charles noticed that she was, in his view, wearing far too much make-up but he also knew that the camera could take it. Ruth's thick hair had that lacquered look which meant she could shake her head but the hair would remain immobile. He put a hand through his own thinning hair and allowed himself a scintilla of envy.

"Ruth, finally we're here and ready to go. Where can we put down our stuff?" He pointed to the cameraman laden with canvas bags and light fittings and, just behind him, the sound engineer with even more bags. The driver had already gone back to the car, hoping for a couple of hours with his crosswords and Radio 1 before the journey back.

"Why don't you bring the equipment over to the factory? I think it would be nice to have me on camera at the heart of our organisation. Then we can do the actual interview in my office." Here was a woman clearly used to taking the decisions, Charles thought.

They walked across a paved area, where Charles noticed a bright new red BMW with a personalised number plate, RF1. He disliked that kind of snobbery, yet he thought it was perfectly all right to have his own initials embroidered on his shirt pocket.

Ruth opened the double doors to the factory and the three men followed her. They had all expected it to be full of noise but apart from a slight metallic sound from the conveyor belts, all they could hear was some bland music, the type you usually hear in hotel lifts. Ruth insisted that they wore protective clothing and paper hats to cover their hair. "We pride ourselves on our cleanliness here," she said as she put on her own pink coat with her name embroidered under the Babylove logo.

There must have been at least sixty women working at the belts. A few men were rushing around lifting heavy cartons on to electric trucks which were driven down to a large opening covered in heavy rubber strips at the other side of the factory.

"We are completely automated in our processes. The staff you see here are quality controllers. Unfortunately, we can't automate quality, not yet." Ruth smiled and walked on.

"And here the logistics chaps pick up the goods and they go straight from this station into the holding bay. Each carton is marked with a code of a customer. Our logistics department then loads our lorries with the cartons according to the area where our customers are situated and off they go. We deliver to roughly sixty wholesalers each day. Any questions?" Ruth was met with silence.

"I would like to show you our new range. We don't only manufacture products for babies, our product range is growing. We are about to branch out by making products for the mothers as well. We're starting with soaps and cleansers. Babylove is such a strong brand, we thought it would be silly not to utilise it to its full potential. My board has given me full support. Anyway, the staff are now going on for their tea break. Fancy a cup?"

"Ruth, sorry love, but we have to get on. Can we just take a few shots of you once the girls are back at their work stations and then start the interview?"

Charles was bored. He had seen enough of factories during his stint as business editor. At first, he had found it fascinating but the enthusiasm soon wore off. Greg, the cameraman, put up his equipment next to the baby bottle conveyor belt. Once the girls were back, Charles directed Greg and his sound engineer to take a few shots of Ruth while he asked her to give some figures of annual output and the number of products they had in production.

Ruth rattled the figures off, not even breaking for breath. She knew it all by heart.

"I'm proud of every bottle, every dummy that leaves the factory. The product range is growing each year. You ask if there have been any mistakes? Not really. Our inflatable changing mats never caught on. Still, our baby mugs in the shape of polar bears and penguins have won design awards all over the world.

Once back in the office Ruth offered bottled water and coffee as they sat down on the easy chair covered in pink velvet.

"Not too girly for you, I hope. You see, today most of our wholesale buyers are women. It used to be only men some years ago."

The interview took two hours and Ruth felt drained afterwards. Charles had not only asked about Babylove but also personal questions on how to combine a career with marriage.

"I gather your first marriage did not work out. Was that due to pressure at work?"

Ruth was so taken aback, that her lipsticked smile just vanished.

"Probably," she snapped and Charles knew he had hit a soft spot.

"But you're happily married now," he said with a placatory smile.

Ruth found her composure again and within seconds she was back on track telling Charles about her greatest triumph, the reverse takeover of Watson & Rubens Ltd.

How could she tell the In Depth viewers that she actually loved the rough and tumble of business, that she enjoyed the pure power of it, although she always thought of herself as a fair boss? The excitement she felt at pulling together a deal was almost sexual. The money was an added bonus, though the thrill was not in increasing her salary but in taking on more staff, pulling in new clients, coming up with new ideas.

She loved dealing with the firm's bankers. When she first stepped into the local bank manager's office with Mr Watson, they treated her as his secretary. They directed all their questions to him. Now she saw the managers at the bank's head office up in London. It had taken some years but she had earned their respect and now they often asked her to speak at their staff conferences. Ruth did this with pleasure, not just for the crate of fine wine they offered her.

When they finished Charles thanked her and told her the programme would be aired three weeks later.

Ruth was happy to see them go. "How did Charles know about my first marriage? I've not given Luke a single thought for the last two years," she thought as she returned to her desk. "And this is in spite of still signing letters every day with his surname." That was a lie.

Chapter 8

Ruth often thought about Luke. She did not want to, but images would pop into her mind whether she liked it or not. A scent could bring back memories or a tune she heard through an open window. She was twenty-two when she married him, her first serious love. Her mother was delighted that she had managed to land one of the Farringdons. His family, though, was not, something they made perfectly clear to her in many ways.

She had met Luke in the waiting room of the local vet. Ruth had gone there with her mother's sick cat Lucille, a mangy animal of unknown parentage. Ruth was still working at the local chemist. Next to her sat a young man with a smug-looking King Charles spaniel. Ruth eyed him furtively. He seemed roughly her age and was very good-looking with his dark crop of hair and open face. He turned and smiled at Ruth and she blushed. Just then the door of Lucille's travelling basket slipped open and the cat jumped out. The dozy spaniel reacted quickly, cornering the poor cat behind a display unit full of dog treats and de-lousing sprays. The hissing and growling rose to a crescendo and the cat jumped up on one of the top shelves followed by the less agile dog, who put his front paws on the lower shelf. The weight of the two fighting animals was too much for the flimsy display unit and it came crushing down, spreading boxes and spray bottles all over the floor.

The girl behind the reception desk dropped the telephone and screamed. The vet opened a door and seeing the destruction burst out laughing. "I knew it. It had to be you and that uncontrollable dog of your mother's. I think I must insist on home visits in future." He was still laughing but the young man's face reddened. Together they managed to put the shelving system together while the vet held the spaniel on a tight leash. With the help of the now calm receptionist, they returned all the goods to their rightful places.

"Mr Chisholm, the vet, knows my parents – and Buster. I'm so sorry about him attacking your cat. Is she all right? I'm Luke Farringdon by the way."

"Lucille's fine, thank you. I must say Buster looks cute, not like a cat-killer at all. And I'm Ruth, Ruth Green."

When Lucille had been given her pills by the vet, Luke was outside waiting for Ruth.

"I'm so sorry, can't I at least drive you somewhere. That basket looks heavy to me."

Luke drove her home – and Ruth was happy not to have to lug the heavy basket all the way. She did not invite him in, she never asked anyone in, feeling slightly ashamed of the old-fashioned and well-worn furniture. She had also seen his look of surprise when she mentioned her address, not the best part of Crawley. He carried the cat's heavy basket to the door and smiled before returning to his car. Next week to her great surprise he telephoned.

"I remembered your surname and I half remembered your address and there weren't all that many Greens in the directory," he said sounding relieved that he had got it right.

He was everything Ruth had ever dreamt of; tall, dark, well-mannered and he knew how to impress her. There were flowers and dinners with wine in dark-panelled pubs. And he had his own car. Ruth had never had a boyfriend before with his own car. He was polite to her mother, sometimes bringing her flowers, too. He was just perfect and Ruth loved him in a way she had never loved before.

After a few months they became lovers. Ruth's mother must have known but she pretended not to. This was a Farringdon after all. Almost everyone in Crawley knew who the Farringdons were.

Ruth did not meet his parents until the day of the engagement. And even then, she was not invited to their home. A dinner was arranged at some manor house hotel not far from Sharpthorne and Sir Alexander and Lady Farringdon hosted the meal.

"So, this is Ruth. Finally, we meet," said Julia Farringdon and moved her cheek towards Ruth without touching hers. "I must say this is a total surprise to us, this engagement, but we will of course make sure there are announcements in *The Times* and *The Telegraph*. Won't we, Alex?"

She turned to her husband, who did not say a word. He just grabbed Ruth's hand but kept his eyes on his wife.

Ruth had bought a new dress, pale blue linen, which she thought looked absolutely perfect in the shop, but as she stepped out of the taxi with her mother, she saw that the dress was covered in crinkles.

"You look just fine," her mother assured her but Ruth could feel that even she was nervous. Her mother had also bought a new outfit for the occasion, a dress with a matching jacket, which made her look like the old Queen Mother. Ruth had tried to steer her away from the brocade, but to no avail.

Luke and his father wore dinner jackets, something Ruth had only seen before in movies. Lady Farringdon was very elegant in her ice-blue silk and pearls. "And this must be Mrs Green," she said as she stretched out her hand to Ruth's mother. "I suppose you're as surprised as we are about this engagement. Don't you think they are both far too young for such an important step?"

"Not at all," answered Ruth's mother. "They are both old enough to know what they want and they're very much in love. Luke's a fine young man and I know that they'll be very happy together."

"Well, if you say so," Julia Farringdon sighed and turned to her husband. "You haven't offered Mrs Green a drink?"

"A glass of orange juice would be lovely, thank you."

"No, for goodness sake, this is meant to be a celebration. Do at least have a glass of champagne," snapped Lady Farringdon. Her ice-blue eyes matched her dress perfectly and she could turn her mouth into a coil of scorn, something Ruth had never seen before. Luke did not seem to notice the chill in the air.

Mrs Green resisted and the atmosphere cooled even more. Ruth wanted to drain her glass and just leave. The conversation limped as there was no subject they could discuss except the coming wedding. It ground to a halt when Lady Farringdon leant over the roast pheasant and said with a rather harsh voice. "Tell me, Mrs Green, we have wondered about Ruth's name, are you by any chance Jewish? Just so that we know, I mean… about arrangements for the wedding…"

Marjorie Green dropped her fork with a loud clonk on to the gold-rimmed plate.

"I am *not* Jewish, nor is my daughter. It is just a name we liked, my former husband and I. It's from the bible, you know." The last said with a sneer.

Luke tried his best to get the conversation back on track but everyone must have felt nothing but relief when Alex Farringdon sent for the bill and organised a taxi for Ruth and her mother to get back to Crawley.

Ruth finally saw the Farringdon home, a Georgian house near Crawley. It was a couple of weeks before the wedding and Luke's parents had offered to host the reception at their home after the wedding ceremony. It was what her mother called a grand house. The reason for the meeting was to discuss the final wedding plans. Julia Farringdon had already dealt with all the details for the reception and had generously also added Mrs Green's name on the invitation.

"I'm sure your mother doesn't want the bother of organising the church and the reception." Mrs Green, though, was allowed to pay for the flowers in the church but it was Lady Farringdon who decided which florist to use and the actual flowers. Ruth had no say at all.

She knew hardly any of the guests at the reception. Her mother, two of her cousins and a few friends were kept to another room as if there were two different parties only gathering to hear Luke's speech and the one from his best man. No one else spoke. Her mother decided the occasion demanded champagne and after two glasses she got tipsy and complimented Lady Farringdon on the lovely "canejps". Ruth could not wait to get away.

The wedding might not have been the perfect start to married life, but they were happy. A honeymoon-week in Paris and then home to a small flat in Battersea filled with wedding presents from people she did not know. Luke had just qualified as a surveyor and worked as an estate agent specialising in commercial properties. It was not a job he enjoyed, but his father had arranged it through an old school friend. On Sundays they would drive down to Sussex to have silent lunches with his parents, a task they both saw as a duty and the price they had to pay in return for the deposit the Farringdons had paid on their flat.

By then Ruth had left the chemist and worked hard at Watson & Rubens. She often stayed late to make sure that everything was the way Mr Watson wanted it. The journey from Caterham to Battersea added an hour at the end of her working day and often when she came home Luke would be down at the pub or club with his colleagues from the agency. Ruth was always too tired to come with him during the week, her mornings were earlier than Luke's so they hardly saw each other until the weekend.

What are the first signs when a marriage crumbles? Whatever they are, Ruth never saw them, never realised what it meant when Luke got home later and later. They had been married for three years when Luke took Ruth to a fancy restaurant in Chelsea, a treat she thought. Over coffee he told her that he had met a girl, the daughter of his manager at the estate agency, and they had fallen in love. As simple as that.

Although it wasn't as simple as that. The girl was two months pregnant and Luke wanted a quickie as he called it. His boss had warned him that no grandchild of his could be born out of wedlock.

The flat in Battersea was sold and, with her share of the money, Ruth bought a small flat in Crawley and put the rest into a building society. It took her years before she trusted a man again. Still, she would often think of Luke, handsome Luke. She never heard from him. And their short marriage seemed just like a dream. All the memories of their three married years had faded like linen in the sun.

A couple of days after the interview had been shown on the television, Sirita called her in the office and told her that a Mr Farringdon was on the line. At first the name did not click, she just took the telephone and answered with her usual, "Ruth Farringdon speaking."

"And this is *Luke* Farringdon speaking." It was his voice rather than his words that made her drop her pen.

"Luke?"

"Yes, Ruth, ages since we talked. How are you? I saw you on the box the other night, a great interview by the way, and I thought I must get in touch. Maybe we can meet up or something." The words poured down the line like honey and gave Ruth some time to collect herself. What could she possibly say to this man, who had caused her so much pain?

"Luke, how lovely to hear from you," she heard herself saying and it was not at all what she had meant to say.

"How are you and how are your family and your parents?"

"Family is fine. Rose and I have two daughters. She's…" There was a pause. "Well, we're divorced. She's remarried and I see the girls most weekends, probably less than that, actually."

He paused again. "Mum died five years ago, cancer, and Dad never really coped on his own and two years ago he married a neighbour, a widow, and he seems to have the time of his life."

"What about you, have you remarried?"

"God, no. Two marriages, that's quite enough for me, but I gather you haven't either as you're still Mrs Farringdon."

"Well, I have. Some years ago. I am really Mrs Robert Nieder now, but as I am known professionally as Farringdon, I kept the name. So sorry to hear about your mother, I had no idea."

She did of course. She had read the obituary in the paper, all that good work with the local charities paid off in a glowing tribute, which Lady Farringdon would have loved to see. Ruth had read it again and again and wondered if she should write to her former father-in-law but she did not know what to say, and, after a few days, it seemed wrong to write about a woman she had never liked and who had never contacted her after the divorce.

"Why don't we have lunch one day, for old time's sake? I would love to hear about your company and what you're doing. Me? Oh, I had to leave the estate agency for obvious reasons when Rose and I got divorced. I am now a commercial property consultant, running my own show. That's what I always wanted to do. Now what about lunch?"

Ruth could feel her pulse quickening. Luke still had that deep expensive voice that used to make her womb shrink.

"Yes, why not. I have my diary in front of me." She clicked on her computer and waited.

"What are you doing tomorrow? I know where your factory is, down in Caterham, isn't that right? I could pick you up at twelve-thirty and take you to lunch. I know a special place. What do you say?"

There was an unexpected enthusiasm in his voice and Ruth thought she should say no, it was too soon, she should let him wait but she heard herself say, "Great, see you tomorrow then."

Chapter 9

As soon as Ruth put down the phone Sirita put another call through. "It's John Barley at the bank, he says it's urgent."

Ruth's thoughts of Luke faded away.

"Hi, John, what can I do for you?"

"No, Ruth, it's rather what I can do for you. I've some great news. You know Pink's, your competitor in baby creams and lotions, they're having some difficulties and it wouldn't surprise me if they'd be willing to sell. And, as you know, they've got a very lucrative contract with a major supermarket producing their own-branded baby-goods. I've been going through their figures. They're not bloody brilliant but they could be with the proper management, like in the hands of The Businesswoman of the Year," John Barley giggled as if he knew he had already secured a nice fat fee for the bank and a bonus for himself.

Ruth had never really liked John Barley but he had been very helpful when she had done the reverse takeover of Watson & Rubens Ltd. He had secured a deal that pleased both Mr Watson, as it would keep him in green fees for the rest of his life, and it also pleased the jolly widow Rubens, who could finally afford a new husband.

"This is the deal. Pink's are in trouble and we must attack before others get to know the facts. Are you free this afternoon?"

Ruth sighed. John Barley always talked in gladiatorial clichés. There were attacks, counter attacks, forays and blitz offensives and, if really inspired, he'd plan a dawn raid. She thought of it as a Napoleon complex as Barley was short and stubby with youthful pimples and thinning straw-coloured hair. Yet, she had to admit that he knew his business.

"Fine, John, I'll look forward to seeing you at 3 o'clock this afternoon."

She re-arranged a meeting with the production manager to the following day and then tapped in lunch with Luke Farringdon at 12.30 onto the next day's agenda.

Sirita must have seen it on her linked computer as she immediately emailed Ruth: IS LUKE YOUR BROTHER? Ruth quickly typed back, JUST A RELATION. No one in the firm knew about her first marriage and she still did not know how Charles Butterworth had found out for the interview. She had never mentioned her short marriage to any journalist nor in any CV.

Luke had always wanted children but Ruth had found excuses. "Let me just finish the course I am doing, or, just give me time to settle in with Watson & Rubens, then we can think about it," she said. By the time she had settled in, Luke was gone and the marriage over. Now he had two daughters. Would she have been happier if she had children with Luke, would that have saved the marriage? The childlessness did not seem to matter to Robert but it did to Ruth. With him she really wanted a child. Now when she was properly established, she would be able to take some time off. But nothing had happened and the doctors said, "Keep trying, there is nothing wrong with you or your husband. Just learn to relax." Each month brought pain and disappointment but she did not talk about it to Robert. She felt it was her fault being unable to relax as the doctor had recommended.

She was relieved when Sirita came in with some letters to sign. Ruth was not prone to think about her private life at work, but hearing Luke's voice had brought it all back – the sadness, the feeling of inadequacy. He had left her for a girl with money and a solid background; this had been a wife that Sir Alex and Lady Farringdon could finally approve of. And, no doubt, that girl had produced children without being told to relax.

Ruth might be the Businesswoman of the Year but she knew that it was all surface. Beneath she was still the deserted girl from Crawley. She had married Robert because he had insisted, pursued her until she saw no reason to say no anymore. And through their marriage she had learnt to love him and appreciate his way of looking after her. Her work had become a baby substitute and Robert understood that in a way that Luke would never have done.

One of the letters Sirita handed to her was her reply to a letter from a local hospital asking for funds for their baby-unit and its research department. The day before Ruth had talked to the treasurer of Babylove Foundation and they had agreed a sum of £50,000. Now, as if to prove a point, Ruth tore up the un-signed letter to the charity and said to Sirita that she was going to increase it to £75,000. "We can afford it and it is a local hospital after all." She smiled, knowing full well that the extra money was not for charitable purposes but to make her feel better. She made a note to phone the treasurer as soon as the bank meeting was over.

"Ruth, that's a lovely thing to do. I know the hospital well, it's where my sister had her little boy last year. She loved it there and the doctors were brilliant." Sirita's warm smile made her cringe, but not for long.

At three, John Barley turned up. At first Ruth did not recognise him, there was something different about him. He was still dressed as he always was, wearing a colourful tie with a matching silk handkerchief popping out of his breast pocket. Dark suit with a hint of a pinstripe and a pale blue shirt with a white collar. What was different? His hair. The thinning hair was replaced by a bushy mat, which covered his former balding pate.

"You look well," she said, as she stood up from behind her desk.

"Do you like it?"

"Like what?" She'd hoped she would not have to answer his question.

"My hair transplant. Had it done when I got my last bonus. It looks OK, don't you think?"

"Looks great – and very natural," she added after a pause. Ruth averted her eyes from the blond tufts, as she knew that her eyes would betray her.

John Barley sat down and pulled out some papers from his enormous briefcase in silver metal.

"As I said, this is the deal. Pink's are in trouble and we must attack before others get to hear the facts. I think we can get most of their shareholders on our side as they haven't seen a divi for the last three years. And the best bit of news is that the MD, who sits on thirty-eight percent of the shares, is just going through a rather messy divorce – don't ask me how I know – so he'll need some dosh pronto to buy out the missus."

Ruth looked at his beautifully tailored Savile Row suit and wondered if he spoke to his tailor with the same mock cockney language, or was it specifically to her?

"What price do you think they will accept?"

"I think we start by offering 12 mill and then stop at 16 mill, that's what it's worth. Not a penny more."

"And where do I find 12 million, let alone 16 million?"

"That's where we come in. No problem, not with your debt-free balance sheet and great cash flow. Come, let's sit down here on your sofa and go through the figures on my computer."

John Barley stood up and walked over to the sofa table. He was never comfortable sitting on the chair covered in pink velvet.

"Any chance of some coffee and those lovely cream bickies you usually offer?"

For two hours they looked at the profit and loss account and balance sheet of Pink's. They calculated the cost of borrowing, the added bonus of the supermarket contract, the savings from moving some of the manufacturing to Caterham and selling excess space that Pink's leased in Basingstoke. It all made sense.

John Barley left with Ruth's request to find out more about Pink's while she would have a word with her board. Her head was still buzzing with figures and she felt a certain unease about the size of the loan she would need in order to be able to take over the company. In her mind she added the fees to be paid to the bank, the lawyers and to City PR firms. The sum was huge. So far Babylove was clean of debts and she liked it like that. There had been some re-organising of assets when she took over Watson & Rubens, but no heavy loans. It worried her, but then she knew Babylove could not grow any further without outside capital.

"I'll speak to Robert about Pink's tonight," she thought as she walked down to her red BMW.

* * *

Robert was still not at home when she finally reached their house in London. It had been a wet, boring drive; the traffic had slowed down to a standstill in Purley. She had listened to the news while her foot was tapping impatiently just above the accelerator. She phoned Robert from the car asking him to hold dinner but there was no reply. She sent him an irritated voice mail, which she regretted as soon as it was made. To calm her feeling of guilt she would ask him to open a nice bottle of wine for dinner. Then they could discuss the Pink's purchase.

The house was unwelcoming, not a single light was on. They usually switched on the light in the hall as soon as it got dark. It could only mean that Robert had been out for some hours. She looked for a note on the hall table, checked her mobile again but there was nothing. Ruth walked into the kitchen looking for an answer. Had he started to prepare their dinner? Robert would always start by laying the table, but the kitchen table was empty apart from a vase with rosemary and sage. Robert liked the smell of fresh herbs, said it kick-started the appetite. Absentmindedly Ruth opened the fridge, looking for something to nibble and saw a bottle of champagne in the door. There was a container from the supermarket with prawn salad on one of the shelves and that surprised her, Robert knew she hated prawns. In the bread bin she found a small baguette and gnawed at it without thinking. She was hungry and looked for some cheese.

"It's odd that I don't know where things are in this kitchen, I just eat here," she thought to herself as she rummaged around in the cupboards. She found a small tin of French paté on a shelf, opened it and dipped her bread into the tin. There was some sherry in another cupboard and with her hastily prepared sandwich and a glass she moved into the living room. The telephone was blinking indicating a message. She lifted the receiver and dialled 1571. There was her own message, but also an earlier one.

"Hi Robert. Can't make one o'clock as my boss suddenly wanted some work done urgently so I'll take a later train. I'll be there at three. Let's not bother with the picnic and just have a quick bite on the station. See you at three, platform 3. Till then, bye."

Ruth knew that voice. It was Mandy with her Leeds accent.

Ruth bit into her bread. It suddenly made sense, the champagne, the prawn salad and baguette; it was not meant for her and Robert, it was meant for *them.* She stood up, went to the fridge and took out the champagne. She threw the rest of the bread into the waste bin and looked for a flute, opened the bottle, poured herself a full glass and took a deep draught of the harsh bubbles.

It was nine by the time she heard his keys in the door. By then she had already drunk most of the bottle and was lying on the sofa.

"Hello darling," he said as he entered the room. "I've tried to phone you at home, your office and on the mobile to say that I would be late and that maybe we could go down to the pub for a late dinner, but I couldn't get hold of you. Where were you?"

"No, Robert, where were *you?*" She sat up, rather gingerly, looked at him and tried hard to focus. The combination of sherry and champagne was not a good one.

"With a client, a new one, and we had rather a lot to discuss. It took longer than I thought. He's a friend of the Callanders. They recommended me. Nice guy, he's the managing director of a PR company in Chiswick, very successful and he needs help with his pension planning. These guys in PR all want to retire early as they burn out quicker than the rest of us." He looked at Ruth for a moment. "Pub's a good idea, don't you think, or have you had enough?" Robert glanced at the almost empty champagne bottle.

"Listen, Robert, there was a phone message for you on the answering machine. From Mandy. What's this picnic nonsense, I want to know what's going..."

"Oh, that. I promised to help her with some tax advice and she only had time during her lunch hour so I suggested that I'd bring some sandwiches, but, as you heard, she missed her train or whatever, so we just had a burger at Victoria Station. That's all."

"Well, what about the champagne? And the bloody prawn salad?" Her voice was brittle.

"The champagne was for tomorrow. I put it in the chiller in order to pack it for Hicks. And the prawn salad was for my lunch, but then I had the burger with Mandy. I don't know what you're on about. Anyway, I am hungry and I'm going to devour that prawn salad with some bread – and I'm glad you saved at least some champagne for me."

He smiled at Ruth and left for the kitchen. She could hear him opening the fridge, pulling out drawers and after a few minutes he came into the living room with a tray.

"I suggest an early night tonight. We're both tired." Robert downed his glass of champagne and quickly finished his salad. He did not mention the bread.

That night they made love with an angry intensity that frightened Ruth, but she also knew that she had reached the best time to try for a baby. As for Pink's, she would speak to Robert about the deal tomorrow.

Chapter 10

The taste in her mouth was metallic and Ruth crawled out of bed to brush her teeth. She knew she deserved the dull pain behind her temples and stopped herself from feeling any kind of self-pity, but then she remembered the lack of a message on her mobile from Robert. This left her feeling both angry and sad. And what was all this about Mandy? Why had he not mentioned their planned lunch?

"I'm not going to tell Robert that I am having lunch with Luke today, she thought to herself. No, and that's for several reasons. I don't want him to feel jealous, and anyway why should I keep him informed of my lunch dates when he clearly doesn't inform me." She spat out the toothpaste and felt slightly better.

When she came down to the kitchen Robert had prepared a pot of strong coffee. He leant forward and kissed her on the cheek.

"You were on heat last night, maybe we should have champagne more often." His remark made her feel cheap and she ignored him.

"I want to talk to you about a deal John Barley at the bank has come up with. He thinks we should buy Pink's. You know, the firm that makes Pink's Baby Lotion among other things? They have a great contract with a major supermarket producing own-brand baby lotions and talc. Just the kind of breakthrough we can do with. But, and it's a big but, it could cost anything from twelve to sixteen million pounds. Should I even consider it? I can bring home the papers tonight and show you, but first I have to talk to the board."

Robert put down the coffee pot and rubbed his hands.

"That's just the kind of deal you need in order to grow. Go for it. The bank, no doubt, will provide the money, otherwise they wouldn't have suggested it, but let's analyse the figures tonight."

Robert served her a cup of steaming coffee and they both sat down to read the morning papers in silence.

By the time Ruth left for work, she had still not told Robert about her lunch with Luke, but he had complimented her on her outfit, a plain navy-blue suit which she knew suited her. She wanted to show Luke that she had moved on.

The morning went in a rush, there were phone calls with two of her board members who both made positive noises when she mentioned the deal suggested by John Barley. They wanted the company to grow and maybe one day get listed on The Stock Exchange. To sit on the board of a listed company had a proper cachet in their eyes. Ruth was not so sure. She enjoyed the freedom to act without having to listen to advisers, shareholders and analysts.

She also talked to the trustees of Babylove Foundation who agreed to the increased offer to the local hospital. "Good piece of marketing," said one.

At noon Ruth closed her door, applied fresh lipstick and dabbed some Joy behind her ears. That had been the perfume Luke had given her on their first Christmas, "the most expensive you can buy," he had added as he handed her the white box with its gold print. He had not even bothered to wrap it. She still wore it although it was no longer the most expensive scent money could buy.

She looked at herself in her compact mirror and, although no beauty, she knew she looked good.

Her intercom bleeped. "I've got Mr Farringdon on the line. Do you want to take it?"

"Yes," and there was already a sigh in her voice. Luke was always late, as if he wanted to prove that he was above such silly conventions as having to be punctual, not a virtue in his eyes.

"Hi honey. Got caught up in a meeting and should be with you at 1.30. Don't worry I have warned the restaurant. See you soon." He rang off with a kissing sound. Ruth sat with the receiver in her hand. She had not uttered a word. Things have certainly not changed and Luke is still Luke, she thought as she put back the receiver.

It was quarter to two by the time Luke turned up. Sirita giggled as she brought him into Ruth's office. "That's what you mean by a relative," she said with raised eyebrows as she looked admiringly at Luke. He put his arm around Sirita's narrow shoulders and laughed. "Yes, and that's the best wife I ever had. Oh, Ruth," he stopped, looked at her and let out a slow whistle of approval. "You look great, a million dollars, no, a million pounds!"

And, without a word, he took her by the hand and pulled her out through the door. "Don't expect her back too early," he said to Sirita, who actually waved to them as they stepped down the corridor.

A racing green convertible was parked just outside the entrance and Luke jumped into it having opened the door for Ruth. She knew very little about cars, that was Robert's domain. She had never seen the logo adorning the steering-wheel. Luke started the car and with a roar drove off, the wheels spitting gravel as they left the factory gate.

"I've booked a table at Honington Manor. Do you remember? We had our first dinner with my parents there."

How could she forget, she had never been back since. That awful evening when Lady Farringdon had looked at her as if she was one of the waitresses and that worried face when she asked if Ruth was Jewish. That night Ruth realised that she would never be accepted by her mother-in-law.

The manor house looked just the way it had all those years ago and Ruth felt her midriff tighten as she walked into the gloomy reception area. There were still those dark stained panels and rather dusty flower displays.

"Oh, Mr Farringdon, how lovely to see you again," said a pretty girl behind the counter. She lowered her mascara-laden eyelashes and then opened her eyes wide and smiled. "Quite some time since we last saw you, sir." She added the "sir" as if it were an intimate pet name.

A maître d' came forward and brought them to a table in a bay. The dining room was as dark as the lobby but the table was lit by several tea lights in crystal holders.

"Champagne to celebrate that we finally meet again." Ruth realised it was not a question so she just nodded. And in no time at all, an ice bucket arrived. Luke held up the bottle and nodded approvingly to the wine waiter.

"Well, honey, haven't you done well. Who would've thought? Well, I did think you would go far, I really did. You worked so hard. My other ex never worked at all, not once."

"But she had young children," Ruth protested while wondering why she defended the woman who had been the reason for the break-up of her marriage.

Luke ignored her reply and unfolded a massive leather-bound menu.

Afterwards Ruth could not remember what she had eaten, only that she had drunk far more than she usually did – and she would never normally drink at lunchtime during the week. She found it difficult to keep her hands still and she could hear her own voice as if it came from someone else. She talked about Babylove, the profit they made. He had not asked her, but she wanted him to know that she had done well. She mentioned the house in Fulham and Hicks Manor, "a modest manor," she added so as not to boast too much. She did not mention Robert, her marriage was private. And she was still angry with Robert. Sitting in a luxury restaurant with *her* former love and drinking champagne was her sweet revenge.

And she *had* enjoyed herself. The candles made her forget the gloomy interior and Luke still had that boyish charm that had made her fall in love with him years ago, an easy charm and confidence helped by money and expensive schools.

It was past four when she returned to her office and only after having promised to have another meal with Luke, and soon. It's such a joy to see you again and *a propos* joy, I like your scent and I'm glad you still wear it." He had leant forward and kissed her lightly on the lips before he revved up the engine and drove off. Ruth stood in the doorway and only turned when she could no longer see his car.

Chapter 11

"John Barley has phoned twice already." Sirita's comment sounded like criticism in Ruth's ears as she entered the office. Closing the door, she sat down to think about the deal. She was relieved that Robert had agreed it was a perfect way to expand Babylove.

Ruth thought that in certain ways she was still a novice; grateful to Robert, she trusted his advice. At the board meeting she was going to suggest that he deserved a small retainer for his professional advice. It did not feel right that she used him as a sounding-board for most decisions and all he got was the right to cook her dinner, organise her social life and act as her chauffeur when she had late meetings. Not surprising that he was willing to help Mandy and her so-called financial problems. A retainer would give him some form of recognition. With these thoughts still in her head she wrote a note on her pad to remind herself to talk to the chairman of the board about Robert at the meeting she had organised to discuss the Pink's deal.

"John, you phoned. No doubt you want to know how I feel about Pink's. I think we should go ahead and make them an offer."

"I thought you would come to that conclusion. It's a cracker of a deal. I'll talk to my boys and we'll go from there. As it happens our investment arm has already bought some Pink's shares quoted on the AIM on the sly. We've acquired about one percent for roughly £13 per share but as soon as the sharks can smell blood the price will rocket, so we'll continue to grab as much as we can until we are forced to show our hand. Hold on, girl, it's gonna be a rocky ride."

"Well, don't go crazy John. I haven't had the approval from the board yet. I'm seeing them tomorrow for an extra board meeting to discuss the Pink's opportunity. So hold your horses." Dear God, I'm even beginning to speak like him, she thought to herself. "And John, is this not insider dealing? Highly illegal as far as I know. I don't want Babylove involved with anything like that."

"Don't worry girl. We all do it. Later we will either sell the shares to you, or if you don't want them there will be others begging for them as soon as it's clear that Pink's is a juicy take-over object. We're just taking precautions." John let out a cackling laugh. "I'll await your orders tomorrow afternoon, madam, and good luck with your board." Ruth put the phone down and tapped her red nails absentmindedly on her mouse mat.

Sirita knocked and entered carrying a steaming coffee. "You looked as if you need one." Setting down the pink mug she looked at her with a quizzical smile.

"Something's going on, I can feel it. What's happening? You usually tell me."

John Barley believed in secrecy, it was in his blood. He had warned her not to divulge their plan to anyone but the board. "A word in the wrong ear could be the end of this deal."

Ruth sipped her coffee and smiled at Sirita. "Nothing serious, we just want to consolidate a few of our short-term trading loans into one loan to minimise our interest payments. It's just like cleaning out one's cupboards." Sirita looked unconvinced and with a sigh she turned on her high heels and stepped out without closing the door.

The next morning was spent preparing for the meeting. Not once did Ruth think of Luke, nor of Robert. In John Barley's parlance, she was preparing for battle. The board of Babylove consisted of ten members: three from the company and seven non-executive directors. She knew which ones she could persuade. At least four were grateful for having been offered a seat on the board. The unknown one was the chairman.

Sir Rupert Cherlow was a retired banker who had left the City in a huff long before it was time to collect his pension. John Barley had suggested him as it was always a good thing to have a baronet on the letterhead – and Sir Rupert knew everyone in the City. He had lost out in a bitter takeover battle when a US investment bank wanted to buy the two-hundred-year-old bank he headed. The Americans won the battle and Sir Rupert left clutching a very large golden handshake.

Ruth admired him but not his big ego. He was used to butlers serving tea from silver trays at board meetings, not to Sirita with her Habitat tray and chocolate biscuits. Sir Rupert might have lost his powerbase but still managed to convince himself that he was a VIP who deserved special privileges, like a permanent car parking space next to the entrance with his name on an engraved sign. He had to give in on that as he seldom visited the factory and Ruth had in turn offered to make sure there was a sign with *Reserved for the Chairman* in the car park every time he visited. He would often argue with the board about unimportant details. Ruth suspected it was just so that he could push his own will through. Would he play games?

She would have to cajole him, pandering to his vanity, and offer him something extra.

She had already telephoned three of the board members to secure their approval. She had learnt early on that private networking before an important meeting helped to secure the outcome. She was not shy in appealing to her board members, all men, by pleading that she needed their support. Sir Rupert would not fall for a trick like that and she knew it.

Then there was Bill Bradshaw who was the director of the local Chamber of Commerce. Ruth often spoke at his conferences and had also taken on some interns in the administration office. This was in order to help some of his members, whose children could not find summer jobs. She would not need to convince him. She was not so sure of Dan Higgins, an angry man, who was an accountant and with the soul of one. He always had a point of view and knew each and every rule in the book by heart. He loved referring to paragraphs and sub-clauses. He also urged caution at every opportunity so how would he react to taking on loans of twelve to sixteen million pounds? Not without a fight, Ruth feared.

She told Sirita to take out the "Reserved" sign and place it on the parking space next to the main entrance. "And if there is a car there already, make the owner move it as soon as possible." Well, that was one way of making Sir Rupert feel important – and maybe more willing to listen to her proposal.

At five minutes to three, Sirita and Ruth were ready in the boardroom. Cold mineral water bottles were on a tray and in each place were new note pads and Babylove pens next to a hastily prepared agenda. There were only two points on it. The company's proposed takeover of Pink's and a retainer for Robert Nieder for general financial advice given to Babylove.

Not everyone on the board was able to attend. Sirita had noted three apologies. Ruth had already discussed the matter with these three, managing to secure their approval of the deal.

Ruth usually enjoyed the board meetings. They often ended with congratulations on her ability to increase the profits. As the only woman, apart from note-taking Sirita, Ruth flirted mildly with all of them and Sir Rupert in particular. Some of them, apart from Andrew Miskin, a young management consultant, were old enough to be her father. Today she was not looking forward to the meeting, she already felt out of control. She would have liked more time to prepare, but John Barley had insisted that time was of the essence.

Sir Rupert was the last to arrive. He always was and Ruth suspected that he made his chauffeur wait until he had seen all the other cars arrive. The other members resisted the urge to stand up as he entered. It was the size of the man that impressed. He was probably fat but his tailor had managed elegantly and discreetly to minimise the damage done by many, heavy City-lunches. Sir Rupert sat down at the top of the table and formally opened the meeting.

Sirita read the apologies and Sir Rupert turned to Ruth with a smile. "Now tell me, dear Ruth, why we have been summoned here – and at such speed?"

Ruth explained the deal as well as she could, now and then turning to her Powerpoint presentation, hastily prepared.

"I would not propose this deal if I didn't think we could manage the debt burden. We calculate that the extra cash flow we would achieve after the merger would cover the interest payments and that the loan itself could be paid off in seven years maximum. Pink's is not well run, the managing director I gather, due to some personal problems, is ready to let go of most of his shares. At present he has thirty-eight percent, and, if he sells us enough of his shares, this would give us leverage required to bid for the whole company. The golden egg laid by this goose is the contract with a big supermarket. We have been trying for years to get a foothold at one of the major supermarkets and this would open the door."

Ruth looked around the room and all eyes were on her.

"John Barley, our banker, suggests that it would cost us in total twelve to sixteen million pounds to take over the company. Add to that legal, PR and special audit fees for due diligence and we're talking another couple of million." The men around the table all took a deep breath at the same time and looked at each other. She could see that they had not suspected a price as high as that for Pink's.

"There will not only be the profitable supermarket-contract. There will be several other benefits. We can move some of the manufacturing to our factory here and sell their Basingstoke premises. We can merge such functions as advertising, PR and HR and save money that way. Distribution is becoming more and more costly and there will be benefits in merging logistics as well."

Dan Higgins was the first to speak. He tapped the Babylove pen angrily against the teak table.

"And who says that the supermarket will uphold the contract if the owner changes? I think it is far too much money to gamble on one contract."

Ruth knew her board: if the first comment was negative, others would follow.

"I quite agree with Dan," said David Hofmeister in the stentorian voice he used to great advantage as a commercial lawyer. "How could we ever pay back that kind of sum in seven years?"

Andrew Miskin and Michael Dinnage both nodded approvingly.

"Well, I think this is just what this company needs, a way to grow," said Bill Bradshaw. "I think we should ask John Barley to provide us with more facts as soon as possible and that we suggest to him that the bank tries to buy some shares immediately. If we choose to go ahead, we have a foot in, if we don't want the deal we can sell the shares, and if it is such a good deal, there will be others willing to buy those shares, and who knows, we might even make a small profit. And as for the supermarket, I am sure that they will be interested in giving us a chance – I think that our Babylove Foundation charity will be an asset in securing the contract."

"Hear, hear," said Ian Shield, a sallow man, who had once tried to seduce Ruth before she had married Robert. She had never wanted him on the board but he was running the Babylove Foundation and was an important link in the organisation. "I give my vote for a deal."

With four "No"s from the board Ruth offered the three approvals from those absent. Now it was up to Sir Rupert to give his casting vote. Ruth knew that she had to offer him something, a bait.

"The best thing with this deal is that it opens the possibilities of listing the merged company on the London Stock Exchange."

Sir Rupert pondered. Was he seeing himself back in the City as chairman of a quoted company? He hummed, touched his immaculately white cuffs and looked straight at Ruth.

"I suggest we go ahead cautiously and buy shares for the time being and then see where it leads us. We must have a closer look at their books before we make a final bid. We have expanded our business as much as possible, we are debt free and have a very positive cash flow and enough money in the bank to cope and our best asset is our management."

He looked at Ruth with a smile. "Our MD, as we know, was recently voted top of the game, so our congratulations to Ruth, who obviously is willing to take on a new and greater challenge. It is, after all, her work that has led us to where we are today."

He nodded graciously towards Ruth and then looked down at the agenda. "But as for the retainer to Robert Nieder, I am afraid that's a no. It would be seen as nepotism. He did work for this company years ago and chose to leave when he married Ruth. I am sure he's successful in his new career and doesn't need a handout from his wife. Sorry Ruth."

The others nodded and agreed. The thought of debts totalling up to sixteen million pounds was enough to get on with. The meeting ended and Ruth felt flat in spite of getting the deal approved. It had been too simple. Back in the office she phoned John Barley to tell him the news.

Chapter 12

Christmas was coming and, although Babylove was not dependent on seasonal trade, Ruth was more occupied than ever due to the planned deal. She hardly saw Robert. Weekends at Hicks were cut short and Robert seemed busy with his new client in Chiswick, who in turn had recommended him to his business partners. It was mid-December when they finally sat down in the kitchen at Hicks to plan for their Christmas break.

They knew they would have to ask Mrs Green. Ruth seldom saw her mother but this was an invitation that was expected, not because she wanted to see her daughter. Ruth suspected that it was only so her mother could show her neighbours that she had a family of her own to visit.

Last year Mrs Green had stayed for three days and even Ruth had to admit it had been hard going. Her mother had complained about the food, calling it over-fussed. Ruth had invited the Callanders for Boxing Day hoping they would provide some leavening of the atmosphere, but Mrs Green thought the Callanders stuffy and snobbish. Ruth could only guess what the Callanders thought of her sour-faced mother.

Robert had done his best to entertain his mother-in-law with visits to the local pub. "Can't stand people drinking so much early in the day, and what happened to proper pub food?" was Mrs Green's reaction as she rejected anything with the word *jus*. He had bought a collection of DVDs with musicals from the sixties hoping it would amuse her. Finally, with lights dimmed, she smiled while humming out of tune along with Gene Kelly or Doris Day. "They don't make films like this now, do they?"

Robert was standing by his new coffee machine, all hissing steam and polished steel. "Ruth, why don't we make up a party this year? This new client of mine, Paul Gallagher, is incredibly nice and he has just got divorced. His ex-wife's going off to the Caribbean with his kids for Christmas – and the new boyfriend, so he is at a loose end. Then there's Mandy. No, don't look like that. She's a very old friend, and I stress *friend,* and I would like you to get to know her better. I think she and Paul – and he is an important client – would get on well. Then we can have the Callanders for Boxing Day. It would be so much easier to deal with your mother if she had others here to entertain her. Mrs G. isn't exactly easy to please, is she? What do you think? It's just a suggestion, they might not be able to come at such short notice."

Ruth twiddled with her wedding ring thinking of the retainer she had not been able to secure for him. He never complained, always thought of her and her needs first – and she had to admit to herself that sharing a house with her mother for three days was not easy.

"Fine, darling. You arrange it all."

Ruth was tired. The deal with Pink's was off the boil but only temporarily. John Barley had discussed the matter with Pink's owner and director, who seemed willing to accept the deal but insisted on remaining as the managing director of the merged company. This was not something that Babylove's board could accept. The negotiations had stalled but John Barley thought it was just a bit of gamesmanship, a distraction in the hope of getting a higher price in lieu of the directorship.

The coffee in her mug had cooled and, without being asked, Robert collected her mug and refilled it with fresh coffee. It was as if he were able to read her thoughts. Handing her the drink he leant forward and kissed her on the forehead. She thought how lucky she was to be married to him.

"Don't worry darling, I'll deal with it all and we'll have a great time."

Ten days later they were down at Hicks and this time for more than a week. The car was stuffed with food and presents. Ruth had bought an extravagant wreath with berries and cinnamon sticks, the smell had almost overpowered them on the way down. Robert had freezer-bags full of game, salmon and turkey – Mrs G. would not consider it a proper Christmas if there weren't a turkey – and The Wine Society had already delivered crates of wines – as Robert would not consider it a proper Christmas if there weren't good wines to lift the spirit. Ruth had bought presents for everyone, admittedly with some help from Sirita. A coffee table book for Paul on advertising through the ages and a cashmere scarf in silver-grey for Mandy. An enamelled Christmas box for Marcia and fancy driving gloves for Dick. For Robert she had bought a set of expensive kitchen knives as well as tickets for a cruise down the Nile for their February vacation.

It was dark when they arrived at Hicks and the air in the house felt cold and unused. Ruth shivered as she put the central heating on maximum before rushing out to help Robert with all the shopping bags and their luggage. There were two large bags from a designer store on Sloane Street. "No looking," said Robert and held the two bags behind his back.

"I can't help it, but I just love Christmas," said Ruth hugging Robert. "I still get all excited." Hands still behind his back, he did not hug her. "And *I* love seeing you so excited. Let's make this a happy Christmas."

By Christmas Eve, the house was dressed for the festivities. A fir tree bought from the local nursery was covered in white and red glass baubles, fireplaces stacked with drying wood. In the kitchen Robert had marinated the venison, prepared the turkey and steamed the Christmas pudding, again a nod to Mrs G.'s wishes. Ruth had crisscrossed the Brussels sprouts and peeled the potatoes. There was a satisfying smell of stock boiling on the six-burner range and all was ready for the arrival of the guests. Robert had picked up his mother-in-law from Crawley in the early afternoon and Paul was going to collect Mandy in Orpington on his way down. "That's the least I can do," he'd said to Robert.

Ruth had prepared the bedrooms. There were flowers, fresh towels and mineral water in each room. They really look nice, she thought to herself, enjoying a surge of unexpected house-pride. Each room had a different colour scheme and, as they had started from scratch, everything matched. The sales assistant at John Lewis had worked with a mood-board helping Ruth and Robert to pick curtains, bedspreads, lampshades, towels and bed linen. A local carpenter had built wardrobes and shelving units on which Ruth had put popular novels and ornaments, also chosen with the help of John Lewis. Robert had once said they looked like bedrooms in a better class B&B but Ruth loved the fact that everything matched. Nothing looked wrong.

She had put her mother in the pink room, Mandy would be in the pale green one and Paul was destined for the one with dark blue curtains, a more masculine look. In each bathroom there were new soaps, shampoo and expensive bath oils. She noticed that every time her mother had stayed, the shampoo and bath oil had disappeared. Ruth smiled at the thought but realised that in a way it was a compliment.

Mrs Green had unpacked her suitcase and drunk her first cup of tea by the time Robert started preparing dinner.

"I brought a cake we can have for afters," said Mrs Green, unwrapping a lemon drizzle cake with a cracked surface. "Made it myself."

Robert looked at it and smiled. "Thank you Mrs G. That's great, but I have already planned some panna cottas with a raspberry sauce for tonight. What do you say if we save this lovely cake for afternoon tea tomorrow?" They smiled at each other, both enjoying the diplomatic way Robert had dealt with her gift.

Chapter 13

Paul and Mandy arrived in time for dinner on Christmas Eve. Ruth had lit lanterns out on the porch to welcome their guests. Paul parked his expensive-looking car close to the house. He opened the passenger door for Mandy and carried her bags into the porch before returning to fetch several carrier bags stuffed with parcels. From the backseat he pulled an enormous bright poinsettia, large as a bush.

"So glad to finally meet you," said Ruth to Paul at the same time as she turned to smile at Mandy.

"Nice to see you again, Mandy. Welcome to Hicks."

Paul tried to hug Ruth but it was impossible with the plant. "This is for you," he said as he handed over the heavy porcelain pot with its vibrant bush.

"I've never seen one as big as that," said Mandy. Both she and Ruth giggled.

"As big as what?" asked Robert, emerging from the kitchen, still wearing his apron.

He hugged both of them and somehow Ruth knew that with, Paul's help, it was going to be a fine Christmas.

The guests were led upstairs. Ruth showed Mandy to her room and Paul was taken by Robert. Mandy loved the pale green decor. "Oh, I could stay here for ever," she said as she put her suitcase on the bed.

"And here's your bathroom and if there's anything you need, just let me know."

Ruth could see that Mandy was impressed as she looked at the white marble.

"It's like a five-star hotel. You really have the most exquisite taste. I can't tell you how grateful I am that you and Robert invited me for Christmas, so kind of you. I should have gone to my parents in Leeds, but they won a holiday in Italy so they've gone. Anyway, you must let me know if there's anything I can do. I really want to help."

"Thanks, but you know what Robert's like. He's in charge and I think everything is more or less ready. Once you've unpacked, you might like a bath or just relax. When you're ready, come down and have a drink in the living room. We don't dress up. You'll also meet my mother, Mrs Green. No doubt she'll tell you to call her Marjorie, but we all call her Mrs G. See you downstairs."

Mrs G. was sitting on the sofa in front of the fire reading last Sunday's magazine supplement. "There's a fantastic musical on TV with Bing Crosby and Rosemary Clooney at eight. You remember White Christmas, don't you? We mustn't miss that."

"Well, I think we'll be sitting down for dinner at eight but we can always see it later on iPlayer."

Mrs G. sighed. "It's not a very long film."

Ruth ignored her sulk and left for the kitchen, where Paul and Robert were drinking red wine, while Robert basted the venison with the remains of the bottle

"That venison doesn't know how lucky it is to be soaked in this fine claret," said Paul with a smile. "What a way to go."

Ruth immediately liked Paul. He had that bouncy Irish charm that made everyone feel at ease. He was not very tall and his body was almost square, as was his determined jawline. His eyes were a muddy green and his hair a robust brush of reddish brown. Ruth was never good at guessing ages but thought he must be in his late forties. She knew from Robert that this was his first Christmas without his children, both teenagers, and that his divorce had been amicable. The thought crossed her mind that maybe Mandy and Paul would get on.

At that moment Mandy appeared, dressed in the same woollen dress she had worn when she last came to Hicks. Ruth decided on the spot not to change into the black trousers and the cashmere top she had planned. Mrs G. was saving her brocade outfit for Christmas Day, the one she had bought for Ruth's engagement so many years ago. It was only worn for Christmas Days, or "for best" as Mrs G. said.

During the evening Paul flirted outrageously with Mrs G. who giggled, drunk as she was from both his compliments and her one glass of claret. Mandy and Ruth found they both enjoyed the theatre. They talked about some of the plays they had seen. Mandy seemed happier with Shakespeare and Chekov while Ruth preferred comedies and plays dealing with the City – and of course she loved musicals as she had grown up with them. Paul and Robert talked wine and it turned out that Paul also was a keen cook. They had already agreed that Paul would cook scrambled eggs to go with the smoked salmon planned for next day's lunch.

"I am so pleased to finally meet you, Ruth," said Paul as he lowered his empty wine glass. "Robert always talks about you and how successful you are. So, please let me add my congratulations on your being awarded Businesswoman of the Year. I remember seeing the interview on the BBC some months ago. Little did I know I would spend Christmas with this very clever woman!" He smiled and then turned to Ruth's mother.

"You must be very proud of your daughter."

Mrs G. stiffened and raised her shoulders. "Of course I am. Girls nowadays have so many more opportunities than I had in my day. There were no openings for women in the building society where I worked. Oh, no, the men just saw us as cashiers or secretaries." She sniffed as if there was a bad smell. "No, Ruth was given every chance, thanks to a proper education."

"What do you think, Mandy? Have girls got more opportunities nowadays?" Paul put his hand on her arm as he gently refilled her glass.

"Yes, that is true, but there are also more demands. We must be able to run a home as well as doing a fulltime job. I've seen so many of my women colleagues more or less collapse under the pressure. Ruth is very lucky to have such support from Robert."

Mandy smiled at Ruth. "And, another thing, Ruth and Robert don't have any children, that also helps." It was said in a low voice, almost a whisper but it hit Ruth like a whiplash. Had Robert mentioned anything to Mandy?

"Ruth was never very maternal," Mrs G. piped up. "Of course, I would have loved to have grandchildren, but when she was married to Luke Farringdon – you've heard of the Farringdons, I suppose – she was far too busy thinking about her career. In the end he skedaddled and married another girl and promptly had two children." There was a slight pause. "And now, when she is so secure in her job, I can't understand why she can't take time off to start a family. Robert has a job after all…"

"Mum, let's not drag up old history."

"I didn't know you'd been married before, Ruth," said Mandy.

"Oh, it was a long time ago. I was very young and so was he. Yes, I did put a lot of effort and time into my career. Yes, I am indeed lucky to have Robert, who not only supports me but also understands that Babylove in a way is our baby. Robert worked for Babylove before we married and his work helped to lay the foundation for the company's success."

Robert turned to Ruth and pecked her on the cheek. "Well, that's an exaggeration, but we had some fun years back then..."

"Before we married, you mean?" Ruth said with a laugh.

"Do you mind working from home now?" Paul asked Robert.

"Not at all. We came to an agreement of what would be best, both financially and personally. It's as simple as that. And I have a perfect office in our London house."

It was past midnight when Mrs G. stumbled up the stairs with one last wink at Paul. She had completely forgotten Bing Crosby. In the living room the fire was low and Ruth re-lit the candles as they sank into the large sofa for a last glass of brandy. Ruth was happy, the evening had been a success. She hugged Mandy saying, "Let's all have a lie-in tomorrow. Breakfast at ten for everyone?" Robert put the screen in front of the fire and blew out all the candles as Ruth and the guests went upstairs.

* * *

When Ruth woke up next morning Robert was already up and she could hear voices from the kitchen. She looked at her bedside clock, it was only half past eight. She put on her dressing gown and slippers and brushed her unruly hair. In the kitchen she found Paul, Robert and Mandy, all dressed and drinking freshly brewed coffee.

There was a smell of toast. How long had they all been awake?

"Happy Christmas and good morning, darling," said Robert and kissed her cheek. "Fancy some coffee?"

"Morning and happy Christmas," echoed Paul and Mandy in unison.

"I thought we'd agreed we'd meet for breakfast at ten," said Ruth. "That's what I told Mrs G."

Robert brought her a cup of coffee and a glass of orange juice. "Well, it's such a fine morning and we thought we'd better have an early breakfast as we're going to have some champagne and open presents at midday. Don't you agree? We've already had our breakfast, but I'll fix you some toast now. Do you think we should wake Mrs G.?"

"No, let her sleep. I'll have a bit of toast and then go up and change. What are you all going to do now?"

"I thought I'd take Mandy and Paul for a walk down to the village as the sun is shining for once. We might pop into the pub for a couple of drinks before we come back for lunch. So there's nothing to worry about. It'll give you time to have an easy morning."

Ruth bristled. She did not want an easy morning. She wanted to go with them, not having that niggly sense of being left out, but they were already in the hall putting on boots and warm coats.

Robert must have sensed her unease. "We should be at the pub at about ten thirty if you and Mrs G. want to join us. If not, we will be back by noon." No, she didn't want to join them. She wanted them to wait for her, now. But the door slammed and suddenly the house was quiet.

She finished her coffee in the kitchen and chewed on her cold toast. How come they all had woken up at the same time? No, she mustn't let it get her down. There were things to do, but first a bath.

She was ready by ten and suggested to her mother that they might join the others down at the pub. Mrs G. refused. "What I want is to see White Christmas with Bing Crosby. I don't want some overpriced drinks in that pub full of smelly dogs and wellies." Ruth brought her mother a cup of tea and together they sat down on the sofa and watched a movie that was even older than Mrs G.

It was close to one when they returned from the pub, rosy-cheeked. "Your jolly publican served half-price drinks as it was Christmas, so we felt we had to stay to enjoy this seasonal bargain." Paul smiled at Mrs G. and added, "We missed you both very much and hope you've missed us."

Mrs G. blushed. "We've enjoyed a great movie, White Christmas with Bing Crosby, so much better than the pub. The film has put me in the right mood and now I'm ready for the Christmas festivities."

Paul took off his coat and put on his indoor shoes and then laced his arm around Ruth's mother and together they went into the living room. When Robert had taken off his winter gear he kissed Ruth on the cheek and put his arm around Mandy's shoulders.

"Let Christmas begin."

The Christmas tree was lit, and although the room was often rather dark, the rays from the winter sun mixed with the tree lights made the room look magical. The fire hissed as the champagne cork hit the ceiling.

"Time for presents," declared Robert. He bent down and picked a parcel from under the tree. "Here's one for you, my darling." Ruth opened the beautifully wrapped parcel and inside was a box with the name of a famous designer store. She tore off the ribbon and pulled out a soft felt bag which contained a black leather evening bag with a large gilt clasp. "It's beautiful, absolutely beautiful and just what I wanted." As she said it, she wondered if he had kept the receipt.

"And for you Mandy," he said and handed over a similar parcel, from the same designer. As Mandy unwrapped it all eyes were on her. Out came a simple black bag with no ornamentation at all. Just what Ruth would have wanted. Mandy rushed up from her seat and kissed Robert. "I have never ever owned anything so beautiful. I don't know how to thank you both." She turned and kissed Ruth and then, with reddened cheeks, said, "I've so little to give in return, I do hope you understand." She handed over a large parcel to Ruth. "It's for you both." Robert came up to Ruth and together they opened the parcel wrapped in shiny red paper. It was a teak board shaped like a fish with its tail and head covered in silver-coloured metal.

"It's superb, what a great gift, perfect for salmon. We will inaugurate it for lunch today. Don't you think it's beautiful, Ruth?"

Ruth had seen boards like this before and often thought of buying one for Robert, who liked kitchen gadgets. Now Mandy had done it and it irritated her. More champagne was drunk as they emptied the basket of presents kept under the tree. Robert was thrilled by the promise of a cruise down the Nile and Mrs G. was equally thrilled by a DVD set of Fred Astaire movies and a wine-coloured cardigan. Paul had bought them an antique wine coaster in silver and potted orchids for Mandy and Mrs G.

While Paul scrambled the eggs mixed with some fresh dill, Robert placed the smoked salmon on the new board. "I've always wanted one of these, just what this kitchen needed." He gave a hug to Mandy, who looked as if she had won first prize. "Isn't she clever?" he asked Ruth. She didn't answer but pretended to be busy with the cutlery.

"Yes, but with that fish head and tail it means you can only carve fish on it. A bit of a waste, isn't it?" Mrs G. was clearly not impressed by the board. And for once her daughter agreed but in silence.

They all had a siesta after lunch apart from Mrs G. who settled down to watch the traditional royal Christmas speech on the television. They had agreed to meet in the living room at seven for drinks, "and we do dress up slightly for Christmas dinner," Ruth explained to Mandy. She knew that her mother looked forward to the annual outing of her brocade ensemble. "We *all* meet up at seven," said Ruth with a rather sharp tone in her voice. She wanted to make sure that this time she was not going to be left behind.

Ruth was restless and could not sleep in the afternoon. She was glad that her mother had given her a new thriller by Donna Leon, a favourite of Ruth's since her first visit to Venice. The hours vanished in the delightful company of the Italian Inspector Brunetti and suddenly it was time to freshen up and put on her black dress with the jewelled belt.

Robert had gone down earlier to deal with the vegetables and gravy. Ruth and Mandy had laid the table before the siesta, so all was set for a festive dinner.

* * *

"Look what I bought at the pub," said Paul and held up a branch of mistletoe. "Have you got a ribbon or something so I can attach it to the door lintel?" He was dressed in a dark suit with a bright green silk tie and Ruth had to admit he was rather good-looking. Robert had also changed and had a rosy glow from the hot stove. Ruth had always admired Robert's looks; he had kept his shape and although his hair had some streaks of grey there was no sign of thinning. He looked just like the young Robert she had married and she hoped that he felt the same about her.

As she went upstairs to look for a ribbon, she remembered the early days. Robert had worked in the finance department, first with Watson & Rubens, later he followed her to Babylove after the takeover. He was married then and so was she. At that time, she saw him as a rather competent accountant, very punctilious and not very imaginative. Their marriages broke up at roughly the same time; Robert would tell her his story about his unfaithful wife and she would grumble about her equally unfaithful husband but that was as far as she wanted it to go. However, Robert was insistent and, in the end, she thought, against all wisdom, why not have an affair? The one affair she had after Luke left had meant nothing, it was more a kind of revenge; at least with Robert she could discuss the balance sheet, if nothing else.

They had some weekends away in second-rate hotels in second-rate towns just to make sure that their colleagues would not run into them. Ruth got used to his doglike attention, it was like a soothing balm after Luke. She felt in control as she was not in love, unlike him. If the relationship did not work out at least she would not be hurt. Robert proposed on a regular basis, and one day she found herself saying yes. It was time to settle down and she realised that Robert would always put her first, protect and love her. And soon after they got married, she knew that her respect for Robert had grown into love.

Their wedding took place in the register office in Fulham, not the most romantic of places, and afterwards they had a lunch in a restaurant in Kings Road. Mrs G. in her brocade smiled non-stop, glad that her daughter had finally married again. Robert had an elderly cousin, who welcomed her into the family and that was it. The honeymoon was spent in Venice and it rained all the time, so much that St Mark's Square was two foot under water. After five days she was glad to be back at her desk.

Upstairs she couldn't find a red ribbon but suddenly she remembered the black and white ribbon from the designer store the bags had come from. "How wonderful," said Paul. "Not every mistletoe has a ribbon from Chanel!" He managed to fix it to the door lintel between the dining room and the living room and immediately kissed Ruth gently on the cheek. "Now, Mrs G. Come here for a proper kiss." Mrs Green jumped up from the sofa, a slight creak from her arthritic knees, and rushed into Paul's strong arms. Then everybody had to kiss everybody and there were plenty of giggles.

The dinner was heavy and so was the claret, the Christmas pudding and brandy butter were hardly touched except by Mrs G. who liked things to be "proper".

"I'll make the coffee, darling, as you've been so busy in the kitchen. Mandy, maybe you could help me by clearing the table?"

"No, I will and I insist." Paul stood up gathering the plates. "Mandy, you and Robert and Mrs G. go and have a rest in front of the fire. We'll be with you in no time."

Paul and Ruth carried out the detritus of the meal while chatting about advertising and famous slogans. Mrs Green withdrew to the living room to settle in perfect bliss with Fred Astaire. From the dining room Ruth could hear Robert and Mandy talking in low voices. It had worked out well, Robert was right; having people to stay lifted the atmosphere.

Paul was filling the dishwasher when Ruth suddenly remembered the dirty napkins left on the dining table. Afterwards she would remember how Fred Astaire was singing, in his rather old-fashioned voice, an old standard called Embraceable You. It was then she saw them. In the doorway under the mistletoe; Robert and Mandy kissing, not a friendly peck, but a passionate kiss. Ruth could not move, her feet were stuck to the floor and she felt her own laboured breath but not a sound came from her lips. She had no idea how long she stood there, watching the two like a snake watches its prey.

Suddenly they parted and stared at her. Had they felt her presence? Robert still had his arm around Mandy. He looked sheepish but shook himself and let out a nervous giggle.

"This is what happens when you try out the mistletoe, you get caught by your wife." Robert pointed to the mistletoe hanging from its black and white ribbon.

"Suppose we got a bit carried away, must be all that claret and port. Come here darling, let me give you a kiss as well." Robert held out his hand but Ruth did not move, could not move. After a second or two she unfroze.

"Well, you two lovebirds, if you don't mind I'm going to bed. And breakfast will *not* be served before nine tomorrow. Good night."

"You're not going to bed already?" It was Paul standing in the doorway. "The night is still young."

"But I'm not," said Ruth and left the room.

* * *

"How could you embarrass me in such a way? How could you and in my own home? Thank God my mother did not catch you two snogging like teenagers."

Through her gritted teeth every word came out like a wheeze. Robert did not answer. He stood by the side of the wash basin and lowered his head, reading the label on an after-shave bottle. He looked at it with an intensity as if he had found the Rosetta stone.

"Look at me when I'm talking to you, you could at least show me that courtesy." Her voice was now shrill.

"Lower your voice, or do you want Paul and Mandy to hear you – and your precious mother if she has finally torn herself away from Frank Sinatra or whoever it was she watched all evening. I can't see why you're making such a fuss about a kiss under the mistletoe. Did I make a fuss when Paul kissed you? You're making too much of a simple kiss."

"That, Robert, was not a simple kiss. That was a lover's kiss, halfway to bed, that's what I'd call it. And don't you compare it to Paul. He just gave me a peck like any gentleman would, not a tongue halfway down my throat, thank you very much."

Robert looked up from his bottle and smiled. "You are determined to have a quarrel, aren't you? But I'm not going to give you that satisfaction. I'm tired, I worked hard to make this a happy evening and, if you don't mind, I'm going to bed and we can discuss this molehill that you see as a mountain tomorrow – after breakfast if you don't mind. Now, will you be first in the bathroom?"

Ruth knew she had lost the argument and she asked herself if, maybe, she had overreacted. Would she give Luke a peck or a proper kiss if she met him under the mistletoe after champagne, claret and port? She probably would like to give him a real kiss but, and here was the real but; she would not do it in front of Robert.

Ruth rested her head on her soft pillow and it was an image of Luke that she saw as she closed her eyes. Luke with his soft, caressing voice whispering to her how much he enjoyed their lunch. She turned off her bedside light and without opening her eyes she turned her back to Robert's side of the bed.

When he emerged from the bathroom ten minutes later Ruth was fast asleep. Her last thought had been that come tomorrow all this would be forgotten. She didn't know how wrong she was.

Chapter 14

When Ruth woke up, Robert had already left their bed. She stretched out her hand to his pillow. It was cold. He must have been up for quite some time, probably preparing breakfast she thought – and then she remembered. The image made her lose her breath. Mandy and that kiss.

She turned around in the night-warm sheets and wondered if she could pretend to be ill; stay all day in her bed until they'd gone. That bloody Mandy and Paul with his nice charm. "Go, go home and leave me alone," she whispered to herself. But then she thought of having her mother coming up to fuss, and what about the Callanders? That stopped her and she threw her legs out from under the duvet. A bath would put her right.

Dressed, she went down into the kitchen. It was just before nine and there was no sound of anyone but only a slight hiss from the coffee machine. Then she saw Robert standing next to the coffee machine with his back to her. He looked so dejected, his head down and his shoulders sloping. Ruth felt a pang of love, this was her man, her husband and that was what really mattered.

"Darling, I'm sorry about my outburst yesterday, blame it on the wine. I missed you this morning, so can I have my good morning kiss now, please."

Robert turned and smiled. He opened his arms wide and Ruth fell into his embrace.

"Darling girl. I'm sorry, too. Let's forget all about it. Now, what about a cup of freshly made coffee and some croissants before the others come down. A moment of peace for the two of us." He kissed her gently on the cheek and patted her back before turning to the machine with an empty cup.

At precisely nine both Paul and Mandy came into the kitchen. Paul, with a hearty smile, kissed Ruth on the cheek and thanked her for a most wonderful Christmas Day.

"I thought I'd miss my children, or maybe even feel envious of my ex-wife lording it in the West Indies but I couldn't have had a better Christmas. You really are such kind and generous hosts. And, then, of course I must admit that I've fallen in love with Mrs G. Your mother is very special but I could never compete with Fred Astaire and his twinkle-toes." Paul did a little turn and tapped his feet to an unheard tune. Mandy giggled and all the tension in the air lifted as she said "I quite agree with Paul, a most wonderful day. I couldn't have wished for a happier Christmas. Thank you."

Ruth looked at Mandy and noticed that the dark shadows under her eyes were deeper than before. She had obviously had a bad night. Her skin looked sallow and her hair was unkempt, a straw-like frizz. Ruth had washed her hair and she had put on full make-up before coming down, she had even dabbed a drop or two of Joy behind her ears.

"Did you have a good night?" Ruth looked at Mandy as if she knew the answer.

"Maybe not perfect, I think I might have overdone the port. The bed, though, is very comfortable and it's such a lovely room."

"Mandy, come and have some breakfast." Robert led her to the breakfast bar and offered her a glass of orange juice. "This will put some roses in your cheeks," he said as he bent forward and pecked her pale face.

Mrs G. entered the kitchen in a flower-bedecked bathrobe and matching slippers, a Christmas present from Robert and Ruth last year.

"Now, don't I look fine?" she asked and did a little twirl.

"Mrs G., you look sensational in your finery. If only I could get my feet to obey, then we could do a dance together but that's a pleasure that my clumsy feet deny me. So sorry, but maybe I'm allowed to give you a Boxing Day kiss?"

Mrs Green smiled and blinked flirtatiously at Paul. Ruth had never seen her mother so coquettish before. How little it took to make her mother happy, she thought.

"Now, what's on today's agenda?" said Robert as he poured a cup for his mother-in-law.

"We could go to Boxwood Forest for a walk and then end up at the Fox in Sharpthorne for fish and chips. The best in the county. I suggest fish as there'll be venison tonight with the Callanders." Robert turned to Mandy. "You've already met them, Mandy, do you remember, last time you were here?" Mandy looked up from her cup and nodded. Robert turned to Paul "They're our best friends down here in Sussex, older than us but you'll like them, Paul. Now, what do you all think about a walk?"

"I'll stay behind, if you don't mind. I want to see Funny Girl with Fred Astaire, oh, and that lovely Audrey Hepburn, far too young for him, could be his grand-daughter, but never mind, at least she can dance. It's such a good film, you'd like it, Paul," said Mrs Green maybe hoping that Paul would join her.

Mandy sipped her coffee with her eyes closed. She really did not look well. She had refused the offered croissant.

"Would you mind if I kept you company, Mrs G. I think I overdid it last night and I feel a good movie is just what I need."

"Of course, you can, Mandy, dear. You're sure you don't want to join us, Paul?"

Robert bent forward and touched Mandy on her arm. "I think a walk would do you good. This is real good country air and nothing is better for you than that when you feel you've overdone it."

"If Mandy wants to stay here with Mum, let her, for God's sake. She's a grown-up. Don't you agree Paul? I'll come with you two for a walk and then we'll come back here for a light lunch with Mrs G. and Mandy."

Mandy smiled weakly at Ruth. "Oh, don't come back for our sake. I'm sure Mrs G. and I can make some sandwiches for lunch, that'll be fine."

"We're coming back and that's it." There was a sharp tone to Ruth's voice and they all looked at her, knowing that this was the last word.

Paul finished his croissant and wiped the crumbs from his mouth.

"Do you know what? I think I'll join Mrs G. after all. Do you mind Robert? I think you and Ruth deserve some time on your own. So why don't you have lunch at that pub and I'll fix something for the girls."

At the mention of *girls* Mrs Green looked at Paul and tittered.

"That's fine with me." Ruth put her dirty plate in the dishwasher. "I'd love a walk and if you're still on, darling, let's go."

They left their three guests pottering around in the kitchen and by the time Ruth and Robert had put on their Wellingtons and thick jackets, Paul was in charge of the video recorder and Fred Astaire's elegant voice was singing the film's signature tune.

"Well, it seems we can't compete with Funny Face. See you later."

Robert looked disappointed but no one stirred on the big sofa, all three faces staring at the wide-eyed Audrey Hepburn.

It was a clear day. The lawn was covered in frosty lace and the dark firs looked ominous as if they were hiding a secret. The gravel on the drive felt slippery under their rubber-soled feet, but Ruth set off at speed, relieved to be away from the house.

"I think we'd better talk about Mandy," Robert said, panting slightly to keep up with Ruth. "There's something you should know. I should've told you from the beginning but I never found the right time and I didn't quite know how to say it." Ruth stopped mid-stride. "I'm listening."

"I was very young at the time and I didn't know any better. As I told you, she was my first girlfriend and I suppose I panicked."

"What, tell me what is it you want to tell me?" There was irritation in her voice and she stamped her foot on the gravel.

"She got pregnant the second year we were together." He stopped as if he wanted to see how Ruth reacted. She said nothing and that seemed to frighten him. She just looked at him with a stony face.

He broke the silence.

"I paid for her to have an abortion. In London. There was no way I could've supported a family. I was halfway through my degree."

"What happened then?"

"Mandy didn't want to do it, but there was no other way. And I'm sure in the end she realised that, too."

"You forced her, you mean?"

"That's putting it a bit strong. I acted sensibly and thought about our future. At that stage I still thought we had a future together, but she was all emotional and said she'd always wanted a child. She told me we didn't have to get married, her parents would understand. That was rubbish, of course, and I knew it. Her parents were very middle class and strict. They never accepted me and they hated the fact that we lived together. No, it was the only way. We lived in a one-room flat; well, it wasn't really a flat as we shared the bathroom with another couple. No way could we have had a baby there."

"Why have you never told me this before? Is that really the only reason you asked her to have an abortion?" Ruth turned to look at Robert.

"A good question. Maybe our relationship had lost its momentum. I wanted to get on in life, Mandy was happy to remain a secretary with that law firm. Happy in that crummy flat. I realised that we didn't have much in common."

"So how long did your relationship last?"

"The odd thing is that after we came back from London, after the abortion, she changed completely She asked me to move out. I never understood why and she never explained it to me. In a way I was glad to get out. Which meant that during my last year at university I lived again like a student, had fun and no responsibilities. You may call me selfish, Ruth, but I was young, very young."

"And after your university days, you never met again..."

"Not until she contacted me some months ago."

"I'm glad you told me. Now it makes some kind of sense."

Robert held out his arm to Ruth and pulled her to his tweed-clad chest. She could smell the scent of Hicks; smoke from the open fireplaces and the furniture polish that Mrs McCleeney sprayed on everything in the belief that it constituted cleaning.

"I suppose I felt some kind of guilt, although Mandy has never mentioned it since we met up again. But she did tell me that she didn't have any children during her short marriage, which only lasted a year or two. I think she's a lonely woman, no husband and a job she hates. We must be kind to her."

"And by being kind to her, you mean kissing her passionately and buying expensive gifts?" Ruth didn't look at Robert, her foot tapping the ground.

"No, darling. The kiss was a drunken mistake, you know that, so let's not start on that all over again. And the present, yes, I suppose I was trying to buy her forgiveness, but, as I said, there really was no other way, and besides, we would probably have been very unhappy together in the long run."

Ruth took his hand in hers and through her thick glove she could feel the warmth. No wonder that Robert invited her, it was all guilt.

"Now, Robert, let's go for a brisk walk and forget about our house guests. And I'm dying for some fish and chips!"

Chapter 15

Marcia and Dick packed their presents in the boot of the car under Robert's watchful eye. The night air was cold and the light emanating from the downstairs windows threw golden shards on the dark gravel. The house looked much bigger in the evening light, almost menacing. Marcia had never understood why Ruth loved this unforgiving Victorian monstrosity. All those gloomy corridors and dark, panelled walls. You needed the lights switched on all the time, even on sunny days. Yet, she had to admit, with the fires lit and the Christmas tree with its many candles, it had looked wonderful. Yes, it had been a happy evening.

"You have, as usual, given us a fantastic meal, Robert. Thanks to all of you. And great to see Mrs G. so cheerful. It must be all that attention from Paul. He certainly knows how to handle her," said Dick, laughing in order to hide his envy. He had never been able to get a smile from Ruth's mother, let alone a kiss.

Robert stood in the doorway and waved as Dick gently manoeuvred the car out of the drive.

Marcia put her hand on Dick's arm, admiring his new driving gloves. "Such an expensive present, but then Ruth has always been very generous." She thought about their gift to the hosts, a bottle of 40-year-old whisky, maybe not exactly what Ruth wanted, but then what do you give a woman who has everything?

Dick turned to face Marcia. "I thought Mandy had cheered up as well. I was a bit worried about having to spend another dinner with her. She didn't have much to say last time we met."

"And she looked so different, her hair was brushed properly and her dress, well that indigo colour really suited her and I could tell it wasn't from Marks and Sparks."

Dick nodded. "Do you remember the atmosphere last time? You could've cut it with one of Robert's fancy knives. Now this time Ruth and Mandy seemed almost friendly with each other. I think it's all due to Paul. That man could defrost anyone, must be all that Irish blarney-charm."

"Well, I'm glad. There was such tension last time we were there. I know Ruth has very few women friends, I think other women find her rather frightening. She's not an easy woman. I mean, I like and admire her but I can't imagine Ruth and me having a chatty lunch together. I'd have nothing to say, except talk about you and Robert..." Marcia touched his arm again. "It was a thoroughly happy evening, but now I long for bed. It's all that wine."

Chapter 16

Ruth was glad to be back at work. John Barley phoned almost immediately as she arrived. He told Ruth he hated the long break for Christmas and New Year, especially if there was a deal brewing. In his view what could be more important than business? He went on to say, "We've got to negotiate with Pink's owner, that tough Mr Parkin. He still insists on his role as MD of the merged company. I think it's his way of holding out for a higher price but according to my analysts the price we've offered is the right one. Twelve mill tops."

"And a happy new year to you, too," Ruth laughed. Oh, it was good to be back.

"I quite agree with you. Now, do you think it would help if I had a chat with him? Face to face? So far it's been your guys dealing with him. Maybe I can soften him up?"

"That's not really how it's done, Ruth. I should be there representing the bank, but if you want the rest of our people to be absent, sure, I'll see what I can do."

"No, John, I don't want you there either. I mean just Parkin and me. Remember it's my company and I'm your client."

"And it's our bloody money that will pay for the deal," he interjected. Ruth could imagine his face turning a boiling red.

They agreed finally that Barley and his henchmen would have another meeting with Parkin and his team and that they might be able to increase their offer another million or so. After all, the board had agreed to a maximum sum of sixteen million.

As Sirita was still on annual leave, Ruth put the notes from her discussion with Barley onto her computer to be re-written later and sent to Sir Rupert. Now it was time to open all the mail that had gathered during her break.

There were endless letters inviting Ruth to speak at Women's Institute meetings, all stressing what a role model she was for young business women. She had attended several of these meetings in her career and she remembered with a smile one Women's Club which had invited her as a guest speaker at their annual shindig some years ago. She had accepted because it was a local club in the neighbourhood of the Babylove office so she could pop in straight from work.

The event was held in the local village hall on a crisp autumn evening and Ruth had driven there hoping to be able to leave after an hour.

"Mrs Farringdon, I suppose," said a voice as she stepped out of her car. "I'm Laura Frith, the Chairwoman of Chessingham Women's Club. Welcome, we're so thrilled to have you here." The voice dripped with disappointment as Ruth climbed out of the car. She soon saw why. Ms Frith was dressed in a long purple gown with a generous décolletage on which rested some glittering stones. Her blue-streaked tight curls were held back by a purple pin.

"Did our invitation not state that this was a gala event?" The voice had lost its welcome. Ms Frith looked down her rather large nose at Ruth's perfectly serviceable tweed suit and leather boots.

For a short but uncomfortable moment – for both of them – they stared at each other.

Ruth broke the silence first.

"I'm terribly sorry. I never read the invitation myself. My secretary just mentioned that I was expected to give a talk. I'm afraid I live in London and it would take me hours to get there and back, so either I leave or you take me as I am. Let me just say how sorry I am for this misunderstanding."

Ms Frith pondered for a moment, obviously assessing which was worse.

"Well, of course we want you to stay, Mrs Farringdon," she said and handed Ruth a cup of what looked like cold tea but turned out to be a rather sweet sherry.

"The rules of the village hall say that no alcohol must be served on the premises unless a special licence is applied for, but I'm sure you won't tell anyone. You won't, will you?"

Ms Frith smiled conspiratorially. Ruth gratefully took a glug of the sherry and asked when and where she was expected to give her talk.

"We're having our dinner first and you're our guest of honour. Just follow me. Once we have finished our dinner we would love you to speak before the coffee is served."

"I really did not expect dinner, just to be here for seven to give a talk. Would you mind if I just gave my presentation and then left before your dinner? I'm so sorry, my secretary must have got it all wrong. I have another dinner appointment in London." The lie did not sound convincing even to Ruth.

Ms Frith gave her outfit another look. "In a tweed suit? I'm sure you can tell your other appointment that you have been double-booked and that you will come later. Our members have all been looking forward to this special evening for a long time with you as their guest of honour. You don't really want to disappoint them, now, do you?"

Suddenly Ruth felt as if she were upbraided by Miss Pownall, the dreaded headmistress of her school in Crawley.

"I'll make a phone call and, of course, I will stay for dinner."

Ruth would often think of that evening, seated between Ms Frith and Ms Braithwaite as she ate her standard conference chicken followed by apple crumble. Not haute cuisine but the sherry which accompanied each course did help.

After dinner Ms Frith stood up and introduced Ruth, "One of the local Farringdons and now a successful business woman in her own right. She will now tell us how she managed to make Babylove, a company we have all heard of, into such a success."

Ruth gave her speech, one she had given several times before. Facts about the business and the sector in general and how she had managed a takeover of her original firm. The applause was warm; Ruth thanked the audience and hoped that she could sneak away quietly.

"And now for questions. Any questions before we let Mrs Farringdon go?"

An eager hand shot up. It belonged to a woman in her mid-thirties.

"Can you really combine a demanding career like yours with a marriage? How does Mr Farringdon react to your success? I know my husband would be proud but he still would insist on his dinner on the table at 6.30." Her question was accompanied by several cries of "hear, hear".

Ruth smiled; she was certainly not going to reveal that Mr Farringdon had left her for a new wife who probably had dinner ready every night, nor that she had a new husband who had a meal ready for her.

"There'll have to be compromises. You can only get a balance that suits both partners in a marriage if you are open with each other and discuss what you both are willing to contribute to the marriage. Maybe your husband, who you say would be proud of your success, might be willing to share the dinner duties if there was more money coming into the household? And more money can also buy convenience foods, which means less cooking for both of you."

Ruth felt the last remark was frowned upon. Another hand was raised.

"I really must ask this. You have such a lovely blouse. Where did you find it?"

Ruth suppressed a giggle, so much for their interest in Babylove and women in business. She rose.

"I have already apologised for being underdressed amongst you all in your fine dresses, so I'm particularly glad you liked my blouse. It's from Jaeger and it's about five years old. It might still be in stock. And on that note, I would like to thank you for your interest in Babylove and also give my thanks for this gala dinner."

Ms Frith stood up, and from behind her chair she plucked up a bag from which she produced a set of purple towels.

"We really loved your talk, didn't we girls? And as a thank you, we would like to hand over this gift set of towels in our club colour." Ruth looked at them and knew they would go straight to the Oxfam shop.

"We were hoping that you would stay on after dinner. We usually have a dance or two and then some parlour games. There's more sherry, you know. But if you must go, you must."

From that day Sirita and Ruth checked all invitations very carefully. Ruth enjoyed talking to other women and although she was happy to leave Chessingham Women's Club, she felt a strange pang of envy. The women had fun together; the room was full of laughter during dinner, apart from the top table.

With Sirita away, Ruth looked at her in-tray. There were letters from young students who wanted job experience or trainee positions and those would be handed over to Anne in HR. The bills would find their way to Larry in accounts. Among the envelopes was one handwritten on woven stationery. Ruth immediately recognised the sloping handwriting. It was Luke's. She tore open the envelope.

Dearest Ruthie

It was such a pleasure seeing you and I would love to see you again. Fancy lunch at Honington Manor again? Or, what about The Griffin in Fletching? You always loved that place, even in winter. I have so much I want to talk to you about. You can reach me on my mobile at any time.

Happy New Year, sweet Ruthie

Your ever-loving ex

Luke

Without even thinking Ruth dialled his number.

Chapter 17

The Griffin; of course she remembered The Griffin in Fletching. She and Luke used to go there when they had something to celebrate. In the summer they would sit outside with a bottle of white wine in a ceramic wine cooler while taking time to pick their choice from the menu. Neither of them was particularly interested in food. Her own appetite had only been refined since she met Robert, who had made great attempts to inspire her with his own cooking, but in vain. She liked his dishes but had no wish to cook. Luke neither. They had lived on takeaways or ready-made meals, both of them dreading those long, boring Sunday lunches at her parents-in-law's, when an overdone roast was served with all the trimmings.

The Griffin was famous for its good pub-food but that was not what attracted Luke and Ruth. It was the unspoilt picture postcard village with views of undulating fields from the beer-garden. It took them just over an hour to get there from their flat in Battersea. Away from the dusty streets of south London Fletching seemed a rural idyll but without odd smells or frightening animals, just the undemanding vision of the pleasant countryside.

Yes, that would be the perfect place to meet up.

"I'm having my girls to stay with me for a couple of days this week, so what about lunch next week? You decide which day suits you." Luke sounded really pleased to hear her voice and Ruth picked the following Wednesday.

On the Tuesday he phoned to postpone, something about the girls again, and they picked the following Wednesday. Ruth did not even admit to herself how disappointed she was.

On the day of the lunch Ruth fluttered around her office irritating Sirita, who was back from her holiday in Bradford. John Barley was constantly on the phone, eager for a fight with Mr Parkin, who still insisted on becoming the managing director of the merged company and therefore John Barley demanded a meeting on that very same Wednesday to finalise their battle strategy.

"We're talking serious now, Ruth, we must be properly prepared. Every development now is vital and if they win this first battle, we could lose the whole war."

For the first time in years Ruth put her own wishes before that of Babylove. She wanted that lunch with Luke and the strategy meeting with Barley had to wait. She booked that in for Thursday instead. She was not going to cancel the lunch in Fletching, not like Luke had.

On Tuesday evening she watched the heavy clouds but the promised snow had not arrived. She worried that the unruly weather conditions might make it impossible for Luke to drive down from London.

She sighed with relief next morning as she opened the curtains. The weather had improved. She cursed herself for being so silly. This was simply a lunch with her former husband, who had left her for another woman and had not shown her any interest whatsoever in the meantime.

Robert stood next to her, still bed-warm and he tried to pull her closer. Ruth, not in the mood, guiltily suggested: "Robert, why don't you come down one day to Caterham and we can have lunch together? We haven't done that for years. Or I could drive up to London and we can go to that restaurant you always talk about, what's it called, Le Salon?"

"Oh, I know which one you mean. What a great idea. Let's fix a date. Do you have your diary with you?"

"Give me a call at the office."

Ruth was slightly embarrassed when Robert kissed her. Her wonderful husband was like a dog who'd been given a bone, she thought, but her conscience was cleared.

It was an easy drive to Caterham and, as always, Ruth was the first to arrive in her office. The factory staff had already been working since six when the first of the two shifts started. Ruth loved the soft hum of the conveyor belts mixing with the voices of the packers at the back of the factory. Even the muted music playing to cheer up the quality controllers had its charm at this time of the morning. It promised to be a glorious day.

The morning disappeared in a rush. Sirita was full of vigour after her extended break in Bradford, "too many meals, too many relations and far too many rules. So happy to be back." Together they cleared away last year's diaries and made plans for the new year. There were so many meetings, with the trustees of the Babylove Foundation, Ruth's membership of the committee for Women in Business, her speaking engagements and most important of all, the board meetings of the company. She also must set time aside for their Nile Cruise, her Christmas present to Robert. Would Egypt be too cold in February? Could Sirita google temperatures in Luxor?

At noon Ruth went to her private office and got ready. Fresh lipstick and a dash of Joy behind her ears. She expected Luke to turn up at 12.30 but knowing him he would probably be late.

And so he was. By quarter past one, she got worried and phoned his mobile.

"Ruth?"

"Yes, I wondered what had happened. I got worried", she swallowed her words as Luke sighed heavily and muttered

"Shit. It's today isn't it?"

"Yes, we were meant to have lunch today. At The Griffin, do you remember?" There was a sliver of ice in her voice.

"I'll make it up to you. I promise. So sorry, got held up in meetings and completely forgot time and all that."

But Ruth knew that he had simply forgotten. And suddenly she was that young woman Luke had deserted so many years ago and she was hurting.

That night she crept over and let Robert hold her tightly until she fell asleep.

Chapter 18

The roses on her desk were from Luke. Not the "I-love-you" kind of red roses but a deep coral; with them was a card asking for forgiveness. "Please phone me, so we can fix a new date". She dropped the card in her wastepaper-bin and decided that a call to Luke could wait, just as he had made her wait. Instead, she concentrated on the report that John Barley had sent her to read before their planned meeting.

He and one of his colleagues had visited Mr Parkin, the managing director of Pink's, and their discussion about the future of a merged company had stalled again. Mr Parkin agreed to sell, agreed to the price offered by Babylove but insisted on being made managing director. He even agreed that the name could still be Babylove, not that he liked the name.

Neither the board of Babylove, nor John Barley's bank, would agree to that and it looked as if the deal would collapse. The bank had bought as many shares as they could on AIM without making any waves in the financial press, therefore they were very eager that the deal should go through. John Barley's report suggested several ideas to "inspire" Eric Parkin to give in. By looking through the Court papers, some researcher had found that the reason for the upcoming divorce was that Mrs Parkin had found out that Mr Parkin was more than professionally involved with his secretary. Ruth did not want to find out how the researcher had come upon this information.

When John Barley appeared on Thursday for the meeting, he said he had no idea how the researcher had discovered the reason for the divorce. Instead, he suggested offering a few tips to some of the financial columnists, who loved nothing more than some tittle-tattle. Ruth was shocked, but then John Barley asked how she thought all these columnists got hold of what was always referred to as "City rumours".

For a managing director to be caught with his pants down could be seen as an embarrassment. John Barley explained to Ruth. "Especially if it's with his own secretary. Discretion is the key. Perfectly OK with someone else's secretary but considered bad sport with one's own."

There were also ways one could spread rumours of the company being in difficulties. "It would lower the price of the shares and that's a risk the bank doesn't want to take as we bought quite a few, but usually some well-chosen words and figures to a handful of analysts can make a lot of difference."

Ruth looked at John Barley, grinning under his new mop of hair, and sighed.

"Listen, John. I don't really want to be involved in anything underhand. I have an idea. Why don't I go and see him? I can take Sir Rupert Cherlow with me. He can sweet-talk anyone."

"You know I don't particularly want you to get personally involved, that's what you pay us to do." There was a note of petulance in John Barley's voice.

"But as you seem to have reached an impasse and your only advice is to darken poor Parkin's character, maybe even the reputation of the company, I insist that we try my way. I can invite him to a meeting over a drink and just see how we get on, nothing more. And I certainly don't need any bankers or advisers for that. I only suggested Sir Rupert because he is, after all, a City grandee and that might impress Mr Parkin."

"Ruth, in that case, I don't want to know anything about that meeting. It'll have to be something between you and Parkin." John Barley's lips narrowed to a mean line

"Can't see how people as stubborn as you two will get on, but that's not my business, is it?" He folded his file, put it in his briefcase and stood up. "Maybe you can inform me of the outcome of your clandestine meeting once it's over and then we can go back to discussing some proper strategy." Ruth swallowed hard and said she would be in touch.

When John Barley had left, she fished out Luke's card from the bin and straightened it out. She decided to phone, but not today. Instead, she phoned Sir Rupert and asked him to give her some dates for an early evening drink with Eric Parkin. "I'd be delighted. I would suggest my club but they're a bit fussy and don't approve of business dealings within their hallowed walls."

"Nor do they allow women, if I remember correctly."

Sir Rupert grunted. Ruth assumed it was a laugh. "Quite right my dear, quite right. I suggest we meet at The Goring Hotel near Victoria. Their bar is as discreet as it can be, but then they have learnt their lessons since dealing with the late Queen Mother and her camp entourage." There was another grunt.

She asked Sirita to phone Eric Parkin's secretary to ask her to put Mr Parkin on the line. Ruth had his direct number but this was all about game playing to show that she considered him important, as also was she. Eventually she heard his well-modulated voice. "I didn't think I would hear from you, Mrs Farringdon. I have had some dealings, not all pleasant, with your adviser Mr Barley. Very insistent chap."

"This is purely a social call, Mr Parkin. My chairman, Sir Rupert Cherlow, and I would like to invite you for a drink, just social chitchat, at The Goring Hotel in London on a date that suits you."

"Sir Rupert, eh. Well, that would be very nice." Ruth could hear him tapping the keys of his computer. "Just social chitchat, you said. Well, I am up in London on Tuesday as it happens. Would that suit you two?"

Ruth looked at the dates Sir Rupert had given her; his diary like her own was empty for that day.

"Perfect. Shall we say 6.30 in the bar? I'll get my secretary to confirm it by email with the full address to you today. Very much looking forward to meeting you, Mr Parkin."

"Likewise, and call me Eric. You did say it was going to be a social meeting."

Chapter 19

Robert waited for Ruth in the kitchen. He had prepared a warming goulash. In his hand an early glass of Hungarian Bikaver. He knew that Ruth would have had a few drinks at The Goring. She had been edgy in the morning, changing her outfit twice, a sure sign of nerves. Robert knew his wife.

He remembered their morning chat: "I'm not sure how I shall approach this man tonight. Do you think I should leave it all to Rupert?"

"No, it's you he's interested in, darling, and I think you should take the lead. Get him to talk about his company and how he secured the supermarket contract. Men like him adore talking about themselves, especially in front of someone like Sir Rupert. Throw in a few compliments on his management skills as well. You're usually so good at buttering people up, much better than that stiff-lipped Sir Rupert."

Robert had poured his wife another cup of strong coffee while staring at the bleak January sun reflected in the shiny coffeepot. Ruth watched his eyes following the captured light as it danced across the polished table. How they longed for some sun, which they had not seen since that Christmas walk down at Hicks. The winter gloom always affected them both. She was imagining they would feel better after the Nile cruise she had organised.

Robert had patted her shoulder as if he could read her thoughts, saying: "Anyway, you look great in that pale suit and how appropriate that it's pink. That man is probably more nervous talking to you than you are of him. Remember that."

Ruth had smiled. Robert knew how to make her feel that she could take on anything. She'd stuffed the unread newspapers in her briefcase and kissed Robert goodbye.

* * *

It was close to nine when Robert finally heard the key in the front door. As Ruth opened it, there was a flash of the red brake-lights from a turning black cab. Robert waited at the hall table and tried to read Ruth's face. It was inscrutable.

"How did it go? You said you'd phone." There was reproach in his voice as if he had been worried. "The goulash is probably overcooked by now."

"Give me a minute, pour me a glass of wine and I'll tell you." Ruth took off her heavy coat, folded her scarf, put it on the hall table and slowly slid her gloves into her capacious handbag. Her face was still a blank.

In the kitchen Robert poured her a glass of the dark wine. She sniffed it approvingly.

"It should really be champagne," Ruth said and her face broke into a large smile. "It all went fantastically well. Let me tell you over dinner. I'm starving. I was so nervous I could hardly eat or drink a thing at that fancy hotel. Oh, it was like stepping into a world I thought had vanished. All Madame this, white gloves and liveries."

"What was he like? This Pink's chap?"

"He's called Parkin, Eric Parkin, and he is a rather gruff man. I'd guess in his mid-fifties. Grey bristly hair and a rather military moustache. He didn't look like a man I could butter up with sweet compliments. On the contrary."

"So, what happened?"

"It turned out he was far more interested in Rupert than in me. Will you believe it, they'd been at the same prep school. No, it's true. And in no time at all they were busy discussing what happened to Binky and Fatty, you know all these silly names kids give each other at boarding schools. Over the second gin it was like a school-reunion and from then on it was plain sailing."

Robert smiled. "It never surprises me how the old school tie still rules the City, Whitehall and even, it seems, the management of companies producing baby talc."

Ruth put down her fork and looked at her husband. She knew that, like her, he still found the establishment a conundrum. They both wanted to be seen as part of it, yet at the same time they professed to detest its class-ridden rites and unwritten codes.

Robert's father, David Nieder, had fled to the UK from the Jewish persecutions in Germany in the late thirties and had spent most of the Second World War in a camp for enemy aliens. He had been a chemist working for one of the companies which later produced the gas that killed so many of his relations and he had promised himself never to work in the chemical industry again. After the war he married Danuta, a Polish girl, who had worked as a ladies' maid in London. They met in a pub and were married within weeks. Ruth had never met them as they had both died by the time she met Robert.

David and Danuta had opened a small boarding-house in one of the backstreets of Victoria with money Danuta had inherited from the couple she had looked after. They worked hard and their business grew. When David died, Robert, their only child, was in his teens, Danuta still worked and managed the half-dozen flats they had bought cheaply – or "for a song and dance", as Danuta said, always struggling with English idioms.

Robert's parents had sent him to a boarding-school in Devon, desperate for their son to become an English gentleman, but it was a school no one had heard of. It left Robert feeling that he was neither working class like his parents nor middle class which they so very much wanted him to become.

"Surely, there must have been more than chat about old school chums during the two hours you spent at The Goring?"

"Yes, yes. It all worked out well, but it's really thanks to Rupert. Did you know that he was called Rupsey at school?" Robert smiled. It was hard to imagine the impressive knight as a school boy let alone one called Rupsey.

"Once we started discussing business you could see that Eric Parkin was still as much in awe of Rupert as he had been at school. Rupert later told me in the cab that he hadn't recognised Parkin at all, nor did he remember him from school, but never mind, Parkin remembered him. So, after a lot of toing and froing, Rupert suggested that Eric and I should share the managing director post for the first six months. Then he would hand it over to me, telling the media that the company was now in good hands, as if it were all his doing, and then Rupert would appoint Parkin deputy chairman of the new company with a sort of semi-executive role. It would also mean a seat on the board of Babylove Foundation. He was thrilled as this would give him more time to settle his own affairs. I gather he has a rather messy divorce on his hands – and a young girlfriend who wants to travel."

"Fantastic news. Well done, this is one in the eye for John Barley. You're sure you don't mind sharing the job with Parkin?"

Before Ruth could answer the telephone rang. Robert leapt up from the table and lifted the receiver, turning his back to Ruth, as if he knew who was calling. Ruth attacked her lukewarm goulash without enjoying it.

"Hi. No, I'm sorry. Yes, I remember, the blasted battery on my mobile, forgot to charge it earlier, but it should be all right now. Have you tried? Could you do me a favour and try it now? I'll go and fetch it."

Robert left the kitchen and picked up his mobile from his jacket pocket at the same moment as it rang. He winked at Ruth and gestured that he was taking the call in the living room. Ruth could not hear a word he said, but, somehow, she knew it was Mandy. She took a great glug of her wine. The minutes did a slow crawl.

"Who was that, phoning this late?"

Robert seemed to hesitate. "It was Mandy. She was a bit unsure of some financial advice I'd given her and just wanted to make sure before she contacted her bank. I have suggested that she puts some of her cash in…"

"Robert, I'm not really interested in Mandy's financial affairs but I do think it's a bit much to phone you at home, on *our* line, at this time of night."

Robert put down the mobile on the table and looked at Ruth sternly. "God, you're unreasonable. Why is it that I'm always expected to show interest in your business, that I'm always there for you and Babylove – whatever time of the evening? You take it for granted that I'd pick you up after late meetings, accompany you to events in which I have no interest whatsoever. And now you make a scene just because I get one call, one lousy call from a friend who also happens to be a client."

"Client? Does she pay you?"

"No, Ruth," his voice fell. "She's after all a friend and I hope a friend of yours, too."

Ruth dropped her fork on the plate with a clang. She touched Robert's hand across the table. "I'm sorry, so sorry. Blame it on a rather tense evening with Parkin."

Ruth knew her anger was based on pure jealousy but somehow it was also directed at Luke for standing her up. There was no way she could say that to Robert.

Chapter 20

Robert was right, as always. John Barley had not been pleased when Ruth gave him the news about the agreement Sir Rupert had engineered with Eric Parkin. When John Barley turned up at her office on a frosty morning, his demeanour as cold as the January air, he looked sullen. He was in a dark blue pinstripe suit with a bile-green silk tie and matching handkerchief neatly folded in his pocket. He proudly opened his jacket to reveal a purple lining. Ruth was lost for words wondering if his Savile Row tailor really had suggested such a shocking colour combination.

"So that's it then, all done and dusted," he said and there was a sibilant sound in his voice she had never heard before.

"I'd thought you'd be glad. You always complained about the obstinacy of Parkin. Now we have an agreement and it's a good one. I have already discussed it with my board." Ruth drummed her pen against the side of her computer, hoping the rat-tat-tat noise would show John Barley how irritated she was.

Ignoring the drumming, John Barley raked his fingers gently through his expensive hair.

"If you're pleased, dear Ruth, so am I. Now, maybe you can leave it up to me to organise the actual deal. I'll schedule a meeting as soon as possible with our M&A department: that stands for mergers and acquisitions in case you wondered. When we've had our meeting, I'll send you a report. No doubt Parkin wants the deal to be closed as soon as possible. Still, before we make any moves, I'd like to hear what your board said to this solution of sharing the post of managing director, albeit for only six months. I bet that not all of them were pleased. Am I right?"

Ruth was not willing to tell him about the battery of persuasion, flattery, bribery and even threats she had used in order to get David Hofmeister and the other three board members, Miskin, Dinnage and Higgins, who had been against the deal in the first place, to agree. Again, it was Sir Rupert who had to step in and, in his words, talk some sense to the recalcitrant quartet.

The thought of a future listing on the Stock Exchange was one lure with an attractive allocation of shares to each board member. Another was the threat that some of Pink's people might come onto the Babylove board thereby forcing the chairman to ask some of the present members to leave. Parkin had not requested any of his board to be given a seat on the merged company's board, but Sir Rupert had not found it necessary to mention that. David Hofmeister was the first to change his mind and the others followed soon after. It had taken Ruth and her chairman several stressful hours to come to a unanimous agreement.

"I have the support of the whole board, absolutely everyone. You need not worry about that. I look forward to your report."

She rose from behind her desk and stretched out her hand to John Barley. He had already turned his back on her, fidgeting with the lock of his briefcase. It was the first time he had travelled to Caterham and not been offered a coffee.

As soon as John Barley had left, Ruth walked over to Sirita's office and whispered,

"I'm dying for a coffee, but I didn't want to share one with John Barley today. He was in such a sulk. What is it with men? If they don't feel they're in charge they play up and get surly."

Sirita was already busy at the coffee percolator, spooning in the ground coffee.

"Don't ask me, Ruth, they're a mystery to me. Let's forget about men – and diets. I bought some doughnuts this morning on my way to work. Come on, have one."

Sirita would never have to worry about diets. She was long-limbed and slim and her brown cheekbones threw becoming shadows on her unlined face. Long ago Ruth had set up a gym for the staff, but she had felt embarrassed about the after-gym showers with the other girls and preferred the rowing machine down at Hicks. Sirita, on the other hand, was a regular and liked the camaraderie in the communal changing room. And of course, she did not need to hide any unsightly ridges of belly-fat, thought Ruth, as she automatically pulled in her own stomach. Robert's cooking had left its mark and she knew she had to diet before going on the Nile cruise, yet she devoured the doughnut, greedily licking her sugary lips.

"It's funny how some illicit calories really do put the world to rights. Thanks, Sirita."

Ruth put her hand on Sirita's shoulder and walked back to her office with her half-drained mug.

Ruth had still not phoned Luke, a week since their aborted lunch. She tried not to think about it and with all the excitement about the deal she forgot her hurt at being slighted. She knew Luke was not trustworthy, that he lived off his charm and used it for whatever purpose he wanted. He had had everything given to him by his loving parents and the best of everything according to his parents – apart from her. He had taken a chance on marrying her, breaking one of those unwritten codes which mystified both her and Robert.

She had always adored Luke. Maybe it was her striving so hard for success that broke the marriage? All she had wanted was that he – and his parents – would accept her and notice that she had achieved something. The studies, the long hours, had it been worth it?

Maybe now we can be friends, remember the good times and forget the sad break-up, she thought as she pulled out his note which she had hidden underneath her mouse mat, before calling him.

He answered immediately, sounding glad to hear from her. "I was beginning to wonder if you'd ever phone. I didn't want to pester you, especially as I suspected I was in your bad books."

They picked a new date and Ruth couldn't stop smiling as she put the phone down.

She left the office later than usual. Robert had already driven down to Hicks and she was to follow. There were papers to go through, next week's agenda to prepare and also letters to write which Sirita would deal with on Monday morning. The office was quiet and all Ruth could hear was the slight hum from the factory floor. She loved these silent hours on her own, no telephones to interrupt her thoughts, no knocks on her open door with queries about staff, nor any calls from irritated wholesalers who insisted on dealing with the boss if a delivery had been delayed or gone astray. Robert had long since accepted her urge to clean the desk before the weekend. He knew it meant Ruth arrived in a relaxed mood.

It was close to nine when Ruth finally put the keys in the lock of the heavy door at Hicks. She had listened to Any Questions on the way down and as usual shouted at the politicians who tried to score party-political points for every question. Through her women's network she had met a few politicians and had, at first, been intimidated by their power until she realised that they were in the hands of their departments run by wily civil servants. She particularly remembered meeting the minister responsible for equality. Ruth had been called to her office at Whitehall and kept waiting in a corridor, while a young girl, who probably dreamt of a career in politics, offered her some coffee and rather stale biscuits with an apologetic smile.

"The minister had to take an important call. She'll see you soon." Her blond bob bounced up and down as if her hair was curtseying.

After twenty minutes the girl appeared again asking Ruth to follow her. She opened a door to another long corridor which had no windows. Dark oak-stained panelling covered the lower part of the wall above it a mossy green wallpaper with the parliamentary emblem embossed in gold.

The dim ceiling light could not brighten the dark space and Ruth screwed up her eyes to be able to see the names on the door plates. Under each name there was a title, Assistant Under-Secretary was one. No noise was heard from behind these doors as Ruth followed the clatter of the young girl's heels on the wooden floor. With a theatrical gesture, the girl knocked on the door at the end of the corridor and said through the half-open door, "Minister, Ruth Farringdon from Babylove to see you."

The room was enormous with windows on three sides. The sudden light almost blinded Ruth. The minister rose up from behind an over-sized desk and stretched out her well-manicured hand.

"I'm glad you had time to come and see me. I'm very interested in meeting women in business and I was given your name. What I would like to do is to sponsor a bill that forces companies to have more women on their boards, at least thirty percent. I've just come back from Scandinavia and it really seems to work there."

"I gather they also have representatives from the workforce on their boards, chosen by the employees. Is that also part of your bill, Minister?"

The minister froze for a moment. Then she smiled, a polished and no doubt often rehearsed smile.

"No, Mrs Farringdon. I don't think we're quite ready for that yet. But I have heard many positive things about you – and your company." The smile was switched on again. "Do tell me, how many women do you have on your board?"

Ruth looked at the tiny woman behind the desk, her short dark hair streaked in an attractive silver grey which belied the young face. Her eyebrows were dark and her lips were painted a strident red. Ruth wondered if she dyed her hair grey in order to achieve a look of gravitas.

"I'm afraid they're all men." It had never occurred to Ruth to look for a woman, just because she ought to have a woman on the board. She needed people who could help and support her.

"I'm surprised, well disappointed actually."

Ruth felt embarrassed, muttering, "I will look into it, when I have time."

"But your end customers are mostly women, are they not?" There was clear irritation in the minister's voice, as if she had been offered some shoddy goods. Her bright red lips narrowed. "I do find it so distressing that women aren't willing to help other women to get a foot on that vital rung which might lead to a seat on the board."

"I think most women want to reach those rungs on the ladder on merit rather than tokenism. What we do need, though, is to ensure that women are empowered to gain sufficient self-confidence to apply for top jobs. This must be true even in politics. How many women are there along this corridor, apart from assistants?" Ruth asked, with a smirk of a smile.

There was a moment of silence. Ruth could hear the gentle tick from a clock on the heavy marble mantel piece.

"None, you're right. And when we had our first woman prime minister there was not a single woman in the cabinet. But it's up to women like you and me to change that. Small steps to begin with. We have a lot to learn from those Scandinavians. The PM is quite taken by the Swedish way of dealing with the question of equality, rather than the quota system the Norwegians favour. I'm setting up a working group, mostly women, and I would like you to join this group. It'll not be too time-consuming and it is unpaid, but, as you know, 10 Downing Street has its way to reward citizens in other ways." The minister actually winked at Ruth and touched the side of her nose, like a second-hand car dealer.

A flush of pride warmed Ruth and she told the minister that she was only too happy to help.

One week later the minister was sacked from her post, having abused the parliamentary expenses system and furnished her lover's house in Clapham with expensive items from Peter Jones, while pretending it was for her own London flat. When Ruth contacted the new minister, his office said that the proposed idea of a working group had been shelved, for the time being. Ruth never heard a word from him. This time they had picked a man and a man of impeccable background and with no known lovers with un-furnished homes.

Finally home, Robert met her at the door. "Did you have a good journey down?" He must have heard her engine or seen the headlights from the hall.

"Fine, no problem. I listened to Any Questions and fumed as usual." Ruth handed her briefcase to Robert and took a deep breath.

"Oh, a whole weekend at Hicks, just what I need. It's been a tough week with this deal brewing. Now, what's for dinner? It smells delicious."

"And I've got some news for you. Good news. Dick and I played our usual round of golf today and it's now official. He has given me his entire portfolio to look after, says he's sick and tired of his so-called wealth manager, who seems more interested in creating his own wealth rather than that of his clients. I have some good ideas and Dick is looking forward to being a bit more adventurous in his financial planning. As he says, the money just gets eaten up by fees and inflation. Not that he needs to worry about his future, his parents left him a tidy sum and now it's up to me to make sure that it remains a tidy sum. You remember I mentioned this hotel project in Lithuania and I think that is something which will fit him perfectly, so we're both going in as shareholders."

Ruth hardly listened but she was glad that Robert had a proper project to get involved with. And it would keep him away from Mandy and her silly little ruses to get back with Robert. And maybe he would not mind too much if the Nile cruise had to be delayed because of the developments with Eric Parkin.

Chapter 21

Luke turned up with yet another bunch of roses. "Thought I'd demonstrate again how sorry I am."

With his arm cupping her elbow, Luke led her to his car. It was a chilly day. As Ruth had forgotten her gloves, she crossed her hands into the sleeves of her woollen coat. She did not know what to say as she put the flowers on her lap. Both were quiet as he drove swiftly through the bare winter landscape, the naked trees silhouetted against a grey sky. There were still clods of dirty snow on high-lying land and Ruth had a pang of regret for having delayed the Nile cruise. Robert did not seem to mind as he was very busy with Dick's portfolio. He would probably have to go to Lithuania as soon as possible to inspect the new hotel project.

"Busy times at Babylove? Or does it slow down after the Christmas rush?"

Ruth could not tell him about the deal. Nervously she fingered the edge of her coat sleeve.

"It's been very busy, very exciting times with new projects and products, so busy in fact that I had to cancel our planned holiday in Egypt."

"I hope that means things are going well."

"Yes, very well indeed and it's all great."

"Something you can speak about?"

"No, not really. It's not of any interest, just changes, but it's all going in the right direction."

She looked at Luke's strong hands gripping the steering wheel. Luke had always loved driving; during their marriage he had never let her drive. She remembered their first big holiday, soon after she had been promoted by Mr Watson. For the first two years of their marriage, they had stayed with Luke's parents in their villa in southern Portugal. Luke had pointed out that they got an almost free holiday, but for Ruth it was not a relaxing break. She tried to help his mother but a Portuguese girl both cleaned and cooked and neither of them wanted Ruth to interfere. Luke's father spent most of his time on the golf course. There was a man to clean the pool, another to look after the garden. Every time Ruth felt she could relax in the sun one of the staff turned up so she quickly retired to her room, feeling awkward lying around while others worked. At night, she felt equally awkward when Luke wanted to make love, imagining that Lady Farringdon listened for any squeak from their bed springs.

As Ruth was given a generous bonus with her promotion, she insisted that they should forgo the pleasures of Portugal and have a holiday on their own. It did not have to be expensive, she promised him. They decided to drive through France stopping wherever the road took them. It turned out to be the best holiday they ever had. Luke did all the driving, leaving it to Ruth to find suitable stops with the help of both red and green Michelin guides.

She had been so happy, the excitement of new places each night and wonderful food the like of which she had never had before. Frogs' legs with garlic and parsley butter tasted delicious, to her surprise, and the wine of each region they travelled through was a new experience as well. They had stopped in Chablis where they stayed in a small hotel surrounded by vineyards. How they laughed when they saw the wine list, thick as a telephone directory. The hotel owner, a jowly man, explained that he had to offer the wine from every local grower. "If I didn't, my life here would be hell."

Finally, they ended up in Avignon, where they rented a small flat. Ruth loved going to the *supermarché* preparing what she considered French meals in the tiny kitchen. Most days it was charcuterie and salad, but the leaves were different and there were ripe cheeses to follow.

During their long drives she had looked at Luke's hands just the way she looked at them now and her excitement grew as they drew nearer to Fletching.

Luke had booked a table close to the open fire, remembering how Ruth loved the smell of burning wood. Lamb shanks and a strong Barolo made her forget the chill outside. They talked about their French holiday, she had forgotten many things and Luke had other memories, as if they had been on different holidays. But they both remembered the saffron-scented fish stew in one of Avignon's many restaurants. It had been their last night in the flat and they were both dispirited at the thought of the long drive back to England.

At the end of their lunch, as coffee was served Luke took Ruth's hand putting it to his cheek. It was a gentle gesture.

"There is something I want to discuss with you, as a friend. I've come across an opportunity that is too good to waste."

Ruth nodded encouragingly.

"As I told you, I'm now working on my own, still in the property business. I love it because it's a sector where so much is happening and where one can make some real money. This is one of these fantastic opportunities I want to discuss with you. Through a contact of mine I've been offered the opportunity to buy a property in Brighton. It's a six-floor early Victorian house along the seafront. It's been used as a school, you know the sort: teaching English to foreign students. Well, the school has gone bust, or had to close due to some irregularities, so the property is going to be auctioned off if they can't find a private buyer. They want a quick sale and I've been offered it, but just now I'm a bit short of the readies so I wonder if you'd like to come in with me on this project. I can rustle up part of the purchase price but need another three hundred thousand. With the smallest investment, let's say another two hundred thousand, it can be turned into flats, I reckon at least ten of them with a market price of two hundred fifty thousand each. That means we can more than double our money. What do you say? I have the details in the car and I can show you the property any time you like. It promises to be a really good investment."

Ruth did not stir. She had often heard that kind of sales talk and she knew how to deflect it. When someone promised a doubling of your money, that was when to say no. Then she looked at Luke, his dark eyes focusing so intently on her face. Surprising herself she smiled and said "Luke, I'll think about it and talk to my bank. Why don't you pop out to the car and get the particulars and I'll come back to you when I have had time to read them. If, and I stress *if*, I'm interested we can go together to inspect this property."

Luke leant over the table kissing her on the cheek. "You'll love it, Ruthie, you'll just love it."

Back at the office, much later than she had told Sirita, there was an urgent message from John Barley. Could she phone as soon as possible?

Chapter 22

"You won't believe this. I had a phone call at lunchtime from your buddy-buddy Mr Parkin and he told me the managing director of Wonderdrug has been in touch and offered to buy Pink's for 18 mill AND to top it all, they have invited him to stay on as managing director of Pink's. The idea is that it'll remain as a separate entity within the Wonderdrug Group. And with the purchase comes a special contract for Pink's to produce own-label products for their chain of chemists. This has come totally out of the blue. I'm livid, livid on your behalf. I'm not sure we should go into battle with Wonderdrug, we must remember that they have a much larger war chest than you have. What I can't understand is, why now? I thought you had Parkin under control. I can't help wondering if he's trying to up the ante by using Wonderdrug as a stalking horse. Is he that kind of guy? You know him better than I do."

Ruth was speechless. She tried to collect her thoughts but she could feel the anger rise in her stomach, making her gasp with nausea.

"Don't ask me. I'd obviously got him totally wrong. And why has he not spoken to me?"

"He told me he was going to discuss it with you but he wanted to speak to me first. Quite right, too."

"Shall I phone him or wait for him to phone me? I thought his word was as good as a contract. As you know, we've already got going with the due diligence work and the lawyers have been working overtime in order to get it all done. I can't believe this man just ignores us. And how did Wonderdrug get to know that he was willing to sell? There is something fishy about all this. I think I'll ask Sir Rupert to contact him. Do you think that's a good idea?"

Her voice sounded nervous. She had put so much effort into persuading the doubting quartet of the board this was an excellent deal, and now she might have to tell them it was off – or even worse that it would cost more and their carefully prepared budget, showing all the synergy effects of the merger, would fall apart. She had never had to deal with a situation like this before.

"Yes, get Sir Rupert to talk to him and then come back to me. Remember, Ruth, we're here to help." His voice had an almost fatherly ring to it.

There was an hour of nervous waiting before Sir Rupert came back to her.

"I knew there was something not right about Parkin, I just knew it. Well, I have spoken to him and he says that Wonderdrug has presented him with an offer he can't refuse. If we want to proceed, we would have to raise the money. It's as simple as that. His board agrees. He is willing to share the post with you as we discussed, but he's not willing to negotiate on price. If we want Pink's we must meet or better Wonderdrug's offer. Deep down I think he'd rather go with us. I have a feeling he's not all that interested in being part of a large conglomerate and especially one owned by Americans. As you know, they can be pretty tough. Remember years ago, how Kraft dealt with Cadbury's after the takeover? Wonderdrug has already laid down some demands, that's what he said to me in confidence. The management expects a hefty increase in sales, costs to be cut and all marketing to be done from their HQ. What looks like a separate entity is in reality a toothless subsidiary. So, what we're talking about is more money and then Pink's will be ours, but this is a decision which has to be taken by the board and any higher bid must supported by the bank. The money *per se*, I think, is not a problem."

"That's a relief," said Ruth. "Do you think that it makes financial sense to increase our offer? But what if Wonderdrug decides to battle it out? It could be very expensive."

"This is something we have to discuss with the board. The budget we prepared must be redrafted, but I do think it makes sense."

Ruth sighed. "I'll talk to John Barley. He is eager to fight and he is very annoyed with Parkin and feels, like you, that the man can't be trusted."

Sirita had already left for the day when Ruth phoned Robert to say she would be home late but that she wanted to discuss the day's events with him as she trusted his advice. There was no reply.

Instead, she phoned Bill Bradshaw, who was still at his office at the Chamber of Commerce. He was a staunch supporter of Babylove and had been on the board since its inception. He was surprised to hear her news and offered to come and help with the redrafting of the budget.

"Is Larry still there? Good. Get him to pull out all the figures and then we can get going. And make sure there's plenty of coffee. I'll be with you within an hour."

Earlier, Ruth had spoken to John Barley, who'd said that pushing the price up to fifteen pounds per share would give Pink's the sum they wanted. As the bank was already sitting on quite of few of the shares they had bought for between twelve and thirteen pounds during the last month, they saw no problem in increasing their loan to Babylove, but they needed new forecasts and a redrawn budget.

"We're not going to let these buggers get away with it. Let battle commence!" John Barley had said in an almost gladiatorial glee.

A trader is always a trader whatever his business card says, thought Ruth as she put down her receiver.

Larry Fender from the accounts department had spent six years with Babylove and still looked like a schoolboy. His pale skin had red blotches that spread when he got nervous and his hair was lanky and ash blond, really more ash than blond. Ruth had always liked Larry. He worked hard and conscientiously, never ever clock-watching. Each week he produced perfect spreadsheets covering sales, outgoings and accurate forecasts. He had no family; in a way, Babylove had become his family. He took part in all the events organised by the staff. He ran the cricket team and was in charge of the gym. Ruth trusted him completely.

He had gathered files and reports and with his laptop by his side, Ruth knew that he would be able to give her and Bill all the figures they wanted and that they would have a new budget before the evening was out.

It was past midnight when she crept into the house in Fulham. On the hall table was a note from Robert. "Had a busy day, sorry to hear about Pink's. Let's discuss tomorrow. I'm sleeping in the guest room. Hugs R."

Her head was still swimming with figures and she was relieved to have the bed to herself.

Chapter 23

The particulars from the Brighton estate agent were at the bottom of her loaded in-tray. It was almost a week after her lunch with Luke before Ruth had a moment to look at them. The cover photograph showed a six-floor whitewashed Victorian building with an iron-railed balcony stretching the length of the façade. The sash windows were tall and faced the promenade and the sea. A perfect location. The interior photos revealed ugly new partitions obviously put up to make classrooms but the first floor still had a magnificent plaster ceiling, marble fireplace and French doors leading on to the balcony. It looked as if it had been used as a school dining hall. In that special language used by estate agents, there were three double receptions, eight double bedrooms, two singles, kitchen, larder, laundry room and a large basement with windows which could easily be turned into basement flats. The garden was small, not more than a courtyard, and looked full of fag ends. Along the dividing wall, a rather ugly brick extension had been built and used as a staff flat. That would have to go, she thought.

Ruth could immediately see the potential of the property. She would like to use her money and there was cash in the bank, as Robert was good at looking after her savings. This really could be a money spinner. She wanted to see it for herself, though. As soon as possible.

Luke sounded happy to hear from her and they decided to go to Brighton next day. She would take her car as he was staying on to do some other business in the area. With all the excitement of the Pink's deal, she could do with an hour or two by the sea.

It was almost impossible to find somewhere to park, so Ruth ended up in an expensive private car park and had to walk for ten minutes to get to the house. She was late when she knocked at the door having found the electric doorbell was silent. Luke opened the door accompanied by a young man with an elaborate quiff and a shiny suit.

"This is Mrs Farringdon, who might join me in this project."

The estate agent took her outstretched hand.

"Say, aren't you the Mrs Farringdon from Babylove? My sister works in your despatch department. Louise Wilcox?"

"Louise, of course. I'll tell her that I met you. Small world."

Proudly, as if he owned the property, Colin showed them around the building. She could see that once, stripped of the ugly partitions, the rooms had a certain grandeur. The fireplaces were untouched, just boarded up and the cornices would be beautiful when relieved of layers of paint and grime. The view, though, was the real selling point. Colin opened the double doors leading out to the balcony and, although the gusts of wind chilled them, they all agreed the view was spectacular. The steel grey waves were crashing on to the promenade below and angry seagulls shrieked as they swooped down looking for scraps.

They spent just under an hour with Colin, before going for a coffee in the small bar of a hotel next door. Colin left them with more papers and an outline of a survey. The house seemed to be in good order. Luke's enthusiasm was contagious and she forgot to think about the half million pounds she needed to invest. All she could think of was how much fun this project would be.

It was dark when she finally walked back to the car park. She had promised to come back to Luke within a day or two. She had never invested in property herself; that was Robert's domain. She looked forward to discussing it with him even though Robert did not even know she had been seeing Luke after all these years.

As she left Brighton on the A23 she felt tired of all the excitement of the day. Rather than driving back to Fulham, she thought she might as well spend the night in Hicks and go straight from there to Caterham the next morning. She left a message with Robert on his mobile and turned off the main road to Hicks.

It was the first time she had been there for a night on her own. A long bath, some coffee in front of a fire, then blissful sleep, that's what I need, she thought as she parked the car outside the front door. They always left some heating on as it would be too cold to heat up the house when they arrived for their weekends, but it was warmer than she expected. She touched the hall radiator; it was glowingly hot. She took off her coat and went into the living room. There was a comforting smell of wood smoke. Something was different, she could not decide what it was. She walked into the kitchen; that was fine, nothing there to disturb her. The dining room was just as she remembered leaving it last Sunday night.

Upstairs she went into their bedroom, thinking she must be imagining things. She filled the bath with steaming hot water. The bath calmed her down and, dressed in her thick robe and slippers, she went down to the kitchen to see if there was anything to eat. In the fridge she found a bottle of milk. Robert usually did not leave milk from one week to another. Had he been down here without mentioning it to her? Without thinking she ran up the stairs and looked into all the rooms, ending up in the blue guestroom, where she noticed the scatter cushions on the bed. They were not put in the pattern Ruth had taught Mrs McCleeney, the nickname they had given Mrs McQueeny a long time ago. Someone had been here. Why?

It was in the blue bathroom she found a small chemist bottle. Oil for Troubled Skin, it said on the label. Immediately remembering Mandy's acne-scarred face, she knew. Mandy and Robert must have been here. Bruised with anger she tore off the bedclothes, looked for any signs but found nothing. She rushed to the other bedrooms and stripped the beds of their linen. Piles of sheeting gathered in jumbled heaps on the floor.

Mandy had been in her house, with her husband. When the telephone rang some minutes later, she knew it was Robert. She did not answer. She had to decide what to say, then she would speak to him.

The anger was so strong she found it difficult to breathe but she knew she had to keep a clear head. Without thinking she returned to the bedrooms and mechanically remade the beds. The bottle of oil she threw away, not in the bin, but through the window she had opened. Her brain felt as if it had been frozen. Whatever she did the next day could decide the future of her marriage.

As she woke up, the pale sun was casting long shadows on the floor. The sleeping pill she had taken had not worked and she remembered hysterical tears at dawn. She must have fallen asleep after that.

Worried that Robert would phone before she had time to collect her thoughts, she turned her mobile off and went in search for some strong coffee. She had never used the espresso maker in the kitchen and after trying she thought that it was safer to fill a mug with the instant coffee they kept for Mrs McCleeney. The fact that she could not even cope with a simple espresso machine without Robert made Ruth think what a future life without him could be like. No one to cook for her, manage Hicks, give her financial advice, hold her when she needed to be held and who understood her so completely – and loved her. Or did he?

All she knew was that she loved Robert – and hated Mandy.

Chapter 24

As soon as Ruth reached her own office after having collected her mail from Sirita's desk, she telephoned her bank. She first had to answer all those irritating security questions about the brand of her first car, mother's maiden name and her favourite city. Her manager, who must have known her voice after several years of calls, was then finally ready to speak business.

"So, Mrs Farringdon, you want to sell some of your shares in order to invest in a property. Usually, we deal with your husband, Mr Nieder."

"Yes, I know, but this is a property investment that I am in charge of, not my husband." There was steel in her voice.

"How much did you have in mind, Mrs Farringdon?" asked the manager.

"To begin with I need £300,000 and, as soon as the purchase has gone through, I'll need a further £200,000 for the renovation work."

Ruth's voice sounded natural again as she described the property and its potential. The lack of enthusiasm in response quietened Ruth. Like a spoilt child she said, "It is my money after all," to counteract the silence. She could hear the manager tapping the computer keys with an angry clatter.

"When did you last see your bank statement Mrs Farringdon? I just ask because, as of the beginning of this month, you have a total of just over £130,000 in your investment account and another twelve-hundred in your current account."

"But that can't be right. There should be some £800,000 there at least."

"Your husband, Mr Nieder, withdrew £750,000 on the 24th of February. Like you, he mentioned it was for investing in a project. Wait a minute, I've got the papers here. Yes, here it is; a hotel in Lithuania, that's what he said." His voice was professionally cool.

"Hotel in Lithuania? Never heard of it."

"I suggest you speak to your husband."

His voice managed to combine both pity and contempt. He probably thought "So much for The Businesswoman of the Year", Ruth reflected then said rather sharply, "I will and I'll come back to you later. Good-bye!"

Slamming down the telephone, she picked it up again and dialled Robert's mobile number. But before the first ring, she put the telephone down as she suddenly remembered how Robert had mentioned something about a hotel in some Baltic country, could it have been Lithuania? And that he was doing it together with Dick. Maybe he had asked her to sign some papers, she really could not remember. She had always trusted Robert in his business dealings.

But what Robert did not know was what Ruth referred to as her nest egg. Part of the money she received from the Battersea flat after her divorce from Luke had gone into a special account. She had later added the generous bonus payments from Babylove into the local building society every year without telling Robert. She quickly phoned the building society and went through the security rigmarole again, but this time the voice at the other end was friendly.

"The amount in your account, Mrs Farringdon, is by today's date £412,693.62 to be exact."

"Wonderful, thank you so much. Now, I need to withdraw three hundred thousand very soon as I'm going to invest in a property." She told him all the details about the property and he sounded quite excited.

"I know Brighton very well and it's an area where prices have been rising faster than the rest of Southern England."

"Later I will need some more. Once the purchase has gone through, we will start renovations in order to turn the building into flats."

"But what you have left in your account can't possibly cover those costs?"

Ruth laughed. "No, I know that, but I'm sharing the project with a partner, a commercial estate agent. He's putting up the majority of the money."

"Oh, I'm glad to hear that. It's quite a sizable investment, but we'll have the money ready for you when you need it. Just give us a couple of days."

How fitting that the sale proceeds of the flat she had shared with Luke would now go towards a house to be owned by the two of them.

Ruth had told Sirita that she was not taking any calls, but Sirita could not stop her mobile pinging repeatedly with messages from Robert. "Phone me ASAP, love R."

With a cup of coffee in her hand, more as a prop than a drink, she walked around her desk, circling it faster and faster until she sat down and dialled Robert's number.

"Ruth, what's happening, didn't you get my messages?"

"Yes, but it has been a very busy day. I also had a bad night at Hicks, so I overslept, which is not like me."

"Darling, I don't really like you staying down at Hicks on your own. It's very isolated and I worried about you last night." There was a short pause.

"But everything was all right at Hicks? Not too cold?"

"No, fine, everything was fine. You must have left the heating on. And there was fresh milk in the fridge."

"Well, the milk is for Mrs McCleeney, you know she can't do anything without her cuppa. I wondered if she had left the heating on. She is getting more and more forgetful. I wonder if it's not time to pension her off. What do you think?"

She knew he was lying. Mrs McCleeney never turned the heating on. She kept warm by endless cups of tea or instant coffee. Ruth also knew that she did indeed bring her own milk, full cream milk, not semi-skimmed, which Ruth had found in the fridge. 'I want the proper stuff, not that blue-tinted milk you like.' Ruth had been told. She did, though, approve of the tin with Orange Jaffa cakes, always kept in the cupboard to accompany her drinks.

"There is something we must discuss tonight." Ruth heard Robert's intake of breath.

"What? What is it you want to discuss?"

"I spoke to the bank today and it seems you have withdrawn almost all the money in our investment account. I can't remember agreeing to that. It has left us with hardly any cash available at all."

"Darling Ruth, I told you several times about the hotel project Dick and I are investing in. We discussed it and you agreed, as you always do, when it comes to my suggestions. I don't think you can complain so far. Yes, it might leave us a bit short but you know we also have the student flats we bought in Leeds, they give us a steady income. If the worst comes to the worst, we can always sell one of them. This hotel project is just such a good deal, trust me. Dick is putting in ninety percent and we are responsible for the remaining ten percent."

Ruth did not answer, but decided to tell Robert about her own investment plans that night.

It was long after seven when Ruth finally put her key into the front door. The afternoon had been busy with meetings. She spent three hours with John Barley. Together they had gone through the revised budget to see if the board would approve of a higher bid for Pink's. John Barley hated to see a good deal wasted.

A scent of meat casserole met her as she opened the front door. "I'm in the kitchen. Want a glass of wine?" Ruth threw off her heavy coat, not bothering to put it on a hanger. She dropped her briefcase on the hall chair and went into the kitchen holding out her hand for the proffered glass. She looked at the man she had been married to for so many years and it was as if she saw him through someone else's eyes. She had forgotten how handsome he was as she let herself be enveloped in his arms. Mandy might try, but she was not going to get her husband.

Over coffee Ruth pulled out the estate agent's particulars from Brighton. She put them down on the table without saying a word. Robert leafed through the papers, then started to read them carefully.

"What's all this about? You're not investing in property now? Is it something to do with Babylove? And why Brighton?"

Ruth did not quite know where to start nor how to explain the reappearance of Luke in her life. Robert had never shown any interest in her former marriage, although sometimes she would have liked him to be at least a little bit jealous of her life before they met.

"A friend of mine, well, actually Luke Farringdon, my ex-husband, is an estate agent specialising in commercial properties. He saw this and suggested it to me as a great investment project. He wants to turn the old school into ten apartments and I think with that incredible sea view they should sell well. There are still the original fireplaces, the old ceiling roses and cornices and, really, once those awful partitions are gone, it will be very easy to turn the space into flats. Luke has some very reliable and cheap builders – and it will be my investment, you don't have to worry."

"How much are you thinking of putting into the project?"

"Three hundred thousand to begin with, just to purchase the building and then it'll be another couple of hundred thousand to deal with the renovation work."

"Three hundred thousand, but we haven't got that available. Is the company giving you a loan? Or where do you think that money will come from?" Robert sounded like a parent chiding his naughty child.

"As it happens, I have some money, money that I have saved during the years. Most of it is actually from the sale of the flat I shared with Luke while we were married."

"You never told me, and how much is this little nest egg then?"

"Enough to cover my part of the purchase, but not the renovations, so I would need to dip into our investment account."

"I don't know what to say. You have always trusted me to deal with our investments and now you come up with this poppycock idea of investing in a project that'll cost probably much more than you imagine. It also gives you no guarantee if or when you will be repaid. And how much does this Luke know about the property market? And why did you not let him discuss it with me?"

Robert took a sip of his now cold coffee.

"And another thing. You haven't even told me that you've met your ex until now. Since when have you been meeting and is it just business?"

"He phoned me some months ago to congratulate me on being Businesswoman of the Year and suggested lunch, that's all."

"What, you mean at the lunch he brings out a business proposal?"

"No, of course not. That came later."

"Oh, so there have been several little cosy lunches you haven't told me about."

"Now, Robert, don't be silly. You don't tell me about all your meetings with your old ex-girlfriend. You see a lot more of Mandy than I have seen of Luke."

"Yes, but my relationship is business."

"Just like mine with Luke. Now, what do you think about the proposal?"

Robert looked at Ruth then grabbed the particulars, going over them again.

"I see some definite possibilities but I want to speak to the agent. I also need to discuss it with Luke, then we can decide."

"Actually Robert, it's going to be my investment. I don't interfere with your plans whether it's a hotel in Lithuania or a guesthouse in Balham. This is my money and I can spend it on whatever I want. I just asked for your opinion – and access to some of the money in our investment account. That's all."

"Well, if that's the way you want it, that's OK with me, but don't come crying to me if this doesn't work out and you lose your precious money. I still can't get over the fact that you never told me about it. Don't you trust me?"

For a moment Ruth was tempted to say that she didn't and that she had all the reasons in the world not to. But trying to save her marriage was more important than any investment.

Chapter 25

Mrs Green never contacted Ruth at work, so she was surprised the next day when her mother phoned.

"Could you pop in one day soon? There is something I want to discuss with you. No, it can't be done over the phone. Nothing serious, I just want to talk to you. Is that so odd?"

Ruth knew that petulant tone only too well.

"As is happens Robert is seeing a client tonight," she hoped her voice would not betray the lie, "I could drop in on my way home tonight, if that's ok with you."

It would be a relief not to have to discuss the Brighton project again and she had not seen or heard from her mother since Christmas.

"That would be nice. Do stay for supper, I'll get some lamb chops. I'll expect you at seven." Her mother put down the receiver before Ruth had time to agree or object.

As always Ruth felt her chest tighten as she drove down the narrow road to her mother's bungalow. It was a small estate built in the late fifties with twelve homes gathered around a rather unloved patch of common ground. When Ruth grew up, the children played games on the rough grass but now most of the residents were pensioners, happy to remain in a house on one level and with a small garden. The common patch, always referred to as The Meadow, was looked after by the council, which sent a man twice a month to cut the grass. A bench was sited in each corner, two of them gifts in memory of past tenants.

Mrs Green had moved into the cottage straight after her marriage. She and her husband had planned to move to a bigger place in the centre of Crawley once they had saved up for a deposit. But when Ruth was three both her father and the money saved for the deposit disappeared. Mrs Green pursued him through the courts for alimony and child support, which she received for almost a year, but then he vanished and even the courts could not find him.

Ruth was really too young to miss him and Mrs Green always assured her that he had not deserted his daughter only given up on his marriage. Ruth trusted her mother although they were never close during her childhood. Mrs Green worked long hours at the building society while Ruth put all her efforts into her schoolwork. In the evenings Mrs Green would relax by watching soaps on the television. They never had guests, mainly because they knew very few people, but once a year there would be a communal party in The Meadow for all the tenants on the estate. Her mother would contribute an oven rack of freshly baked scones to the festivities. They both looked forward to the party, well aware that they would hate it on the day, feeling uncomfortable with their neighbours who all seemed to know each other so well. "Not our kind of people," Mrs Green muttered on her way back home, eager to draw the curtains so as not to see the end of the partying. Ruth never figured out who "our kind of people" were.

The cottage had not worn well. The fence along the path to the front door was grey with age and several of the wooden slats were missing or rotten. Ruth had not been to her mother's place for years and a shard of guilt pierced her. Since her mother's retirement, Ruth was not sure what her mother did with her time. She had never been interested in any hobbies, only films and TV, which provided her with spoon-fed entertainment.

The scent of cooking met her as her mother opened the door. Not only cooking, there was also that special smell that Ruth remembered from her childhood. The litter tray that Lucille had used was long gone but somehow that ammonia smell remained mixed with a hint of beeswax and bleach.

Mrs G looked well. Her hair looked less grey. Had she been colouring it? And her nails were painted a pale coral. This surprised Ruth as her mother had always seen painted nails as a sign of moral laxity. She did not know what to say, so with a chirpy voice she asked, "So, Mum, what is it you wanted to talk to me about?"

"Let's go to the lounge. Now sit down, dear, you must be tired after a day's work. Let's have a sherry, it's not often I have the pleasure of seeing you here."

Without waiting for an answer Mrs Green went to the teak sideboard in the corner and took out two small crystal glasses and a bottle of supermarket sherry. She filled the glasses and handed one over to Ruth.

Before she had closed the sideboard door Ruth noticed a bottle of whisky on the top shelf, malt whisky; another surprise. Her mother only used whisky in emergencies and certainly not an expensive malt. The bottle was half full.

"Well, cheers. And thank you for a great Christmas, the best I can remember. It was a real pleasure to meet your friend Paul, such a fine man, a real gent."

"Oh, Mum, you haven't fallen for his Irish charm, have you?"

They both laughed and for a moment Ruth felt close to her mother.

"Now, what's on your mind?"

"We'll talk after supper but first a top-up."

They brought their refilled glasses to the kitchen where Mrs Green busied herself over the stove. They talked about Paul, Mrs Green's new neighbours, "up all hours, no respect for others" and that Crawley was not like it had been, "looks like America now with all these shopping malls. Whatever happened to all our nice shops? You remember the one down the road, which sold everything and knew what you wanted. All gone now."

After Ruth had finished the rhubarb pie, sweet and rich, her mother suggested that they take their coffee in the lounge. On a tray she put her best cups and a cream jug, inherited from Ruth's grandmother, a set that Ruth knew her mother only used for special occasions.

"I wanted a chat with you because I hope you can help me. As you know, my pension from the building society is pathetically small and the state pension isn't all that much either. I don't think you have any idea of how tough life is, not you with your two houses, two cars and fancy holidays."

"But Mum, I give you five hundred pounds each month and have done so for years."

"For years, yes, that's it. With inflation and bills shooting up, it really isn't enough any longer. I haven't had a holiday for years, simply because I can't afford one."

"But you've never hankered for a holiday, I can't remember us ever having a holiday when I grew up. We used to spend a week every year with grandma in Cumbria. You couldn't wait to get back to Crawley."

"Well, I didn't see that as a holiday as I had to help on the farm. I want a proper holiday and I think I deserve it. What I wanted to suggest is that you double my allowance."

"But, Mum, that's a thousand pounds a month. I can't afford that. We have our money tied up in investments and to run two houses isn't that cheap either. But if you want a holiday, I'm willing to give you an extra five hundred, which would provide you with a good break."

"Five hundred. That wouldn't even buy me half a cruise down the Nile, would it now?"

"That's all I can afford, I'm sorry."

Her mother picked up the cups, although Ruth had not even finished her coffee, and carried the tray back into the kitchen. She could hear her banging cabinet doors, just the way Robert did when he was irritated.

Ruth took out her cheque book from her handbag and wrote a cheque for seven hundred and fifty pounds and put it on the coffee table. She joined her mother in the kitchen and took the old Buckingham Palace tea towel hanging on the cooker rail and started drying the dishes.

"And how is that husband of yours?"

"That husband of mine is called Robert, you should know that by now. We have, after all, been married for over eight years."

"Still at home, is he? What's it called nowadays, yes, still a househusband, is he?"

"If you mean, is he still working from home, yes, he is and he's doing very well. Paul, who you find so charming, is one of his clients and so are the Callanders. No, he's keeping busy and likes his job."

Her mother still had her back to Ruth, fiercely attacking the grease on a dish with a green scrubber as if she wanted to erase Robert from her mind.

"Don't you think it would be better if *he* worked so you could start a family?"

There was a short pause as her mother took off her rubber gloves with a snapping sound and turned to look at Ruth. "You'll soon be past it, won't you? When I was your age, you were a teenager. It's not good to wait too long, you know."

Ruth sighed and dropped the tea towel on the kitchen table.

"Mum, I've told you several times, we have no plans for children."

She picked up the towel again and scrunched it into a ball. How could she tell her mother that there was nothing she wanted more than to have a child with Robert, that they had both been to see specialists in Harley Street and even considered IVF. Ruth could feel her jaws tighten. This was something she did not want to discuss with her mother.

"And besides, if I didn't work, I couldn't even give you five hundred a month, let alone any extras."

"No, but you could give me something even more important; *joy*."

Her mother almost spat out the last word.

Ruth walked back into the lounge and picked up the cheque. She almost threw it into her mother's hand.

"Seven hundred and fifty. Oh, I see. Thanks, thanks a lot." But there was no gratitude in her voice, and the hug Ruth thought the increased sum would buy her was not forthcoming.

On the way home Ruth stopped in a layby and wept. She could not even buy love from her mother. If she was lucky to have a child one day, she would show her love every day without expecting anything in return. Suddenly she longed for Robert.

Chapter 26

Coming home, Ruth found that Robert had again retired to the guestroom. For a moment she thought she would leave him in peace and have an early night, but she was perturbed by her mother's odd behaviour; that new hairdo and those painted nails, also the fact that her mother had never before asked her for money. Ruth remembered how frugal she always was, never wanting something she could not afford and now she wanted Ruth to pay for an expensive holiday. It did not make sense. She needed Robert's cool, practical advice and she also wanted a hug.

She knocked at the door of the guestroom and found Robert in bed reading a heavy tome. Robert did not read much, but now and then he would come home with a book about the First World War, a part of history Ruth found totally uninteresting. Maybe it had something to do with Robert's German background, she thought.

"I'm still awake as you can see. How was Mrs G.? In one of her better moods, I hope."

Ruth looked at Robert, as always naked in bed, and could think of nothing more inviting than to lean her head against his chest and tell him about her evening.

"Shove over and make some room for me and I'll tell you."

Robert moved over lifting the duvet to make room for Ruth. She kicked off her shoes and got into the bed.

"Put your arm around me, please. I think I'm going mad. Mum wanted me to double her allowance which I can't afford *and* she wants a holiday! She's never wanted one before. Do you remember her reaction when we offered to take her to Paris for a long weekend for her 60th birthday? She wanted none of it. Now she says she *deserves* a holiday. And when I offered her five hundred pounds, she made some snide remark about it wouldn't even pay for a Nile cruise. And, you won't believe it, she had painted nails."

"Painted nails? What do you mean?" His eyebrows raised.

"Well, she has always been of the opinion that only loose women paint their nails."

"Ah," said Robert and raised himself up to a sitting position. "Do you think there's a man in the picture? Maybe a case of *cherchez l'homme?*"

"But Mum hasn't looked at a man for years, not since my father left."

Then she remembered the half-empty bottle of malt whisky in her mother's sideboard. Suddenly it all made sense. She looked at Robert and smiled.

"You think she's desperate to go off on some romantic tryst with a man? Who would have guessed?" He smiled back at her, saying "After all these years she does deserve to have some fun, don't you think?"

His smile warmed Ruth and she got out of bed and started taking her tights off, then quickly stepped out of her skirt. She lifted her arms in order to get out of her jumper. As she pulled it over her head she caught a glimpse of Robert's face. There was a second of disgust, just long enough for Ruth to catch.

"Darling, do you mind? I'm awfully tired and was just about to go to sleep, must have a cold or something coming on. No, don't kiss me, I don't want you to catch anything. Sleep well and see you tomorrow."

Robert turned his head away from her and took up his book from the bedside table. Gathering her clothes, she shivered; rejected for the second time that evening.

Next morning, she brought Robert a cup of hot honey and lemon, her cure for all ills.

He was just waking up and this time he did not refuse her hurried kiss.

"I feel so much better today. I'm planning to phone Luke Farringdon and see if I can have a look at this project of yours. Yes, I know it's *your* project but some of the money towards it is ours."

"Do you really feel up to going to Brighton? What about your cold?"

"Much better after a good night's sleep," he said and jumped out of bed as if to prove it.

Robert had never met Luke, never shown any interest in her former husband or lovers, not that there were many. But then Ruth knew very little about Jane, Robert's first wife, only that she had gone off with a married neighbour in order to fulfil herself as she called it. Ruth had never seen a photograph of her and all she knew was that Robert had once referred to her as a "temperamental redhead". Like Robert, she had not been very interested in his former life. Maybe that was the reason why he'd never mentioned Mandy either. And now Mandy was on her mind all the time, like a small ache at the back of her head.

Once at Babylove, she forgot about her mother and Mandy. She took an early tour around the factory floor. She loved watching the conveyor belts coming out of the expensive Swiss machines which were spitting out babies' bottles at speed. All now done by robotics. Ruth remembered when they bought the first one, how frightened she had been of spending so much on a machine. The bank had given her a loan and it was the first time she had borrowed money. Now there were sixteen of them on the floor, all capable of manufacturing different products in sterile plastic.

As soon as she arrived at her own office, John Barley rang. He was so excited that he stumbled over his words and Ruth had to ask him to repeat what he'd said. "The story's out. I don't know how. Someone must've got hold of the news because a chum of mine at *The Daily Telegraph* phoned to say he knew all about the take-over battle brewing between Babylove and Wonderdrug for Pink's. He said it would make a very interesting article. You know the sort of headlines these guys have in mind; *Businesswoman of the Year in fight with US giant.* Of course, with some good photographs of you getting your award from the Duchess. I think you can expect some calls today because if one guy knows the story, the others will quickly follow. These journalists do nothing nowadays but sit on their arses and read each other's tweets and blogs."

As usual, John Barley was right and before lunchtime Ruth had dealt with fourteen calls, one from Charles Butterworth, and again she promised him an exclusive if the deal went through, but asked him to keep it all quiet for the time being. She also received a call from Eric Parkin, who was not happy.

"I thought we had agreed that there would be no press involved until the deal was done. I haven't even spoken to Wonderdrug. How do you think they'll react? We're still negotiating for God's sake. And where did this leak come from? Your obnoxious banker, is he the one who let the cat out of the bag?"

Eric Parkin was almost fizzing with anger and Ruth tried to calm him down, assuring him that neither she nor her banker knew anything – it could even be Wonderdrug's management team who had informed some journalist in order to get the ball rolling. She could hear herself sounding more and more like John Barley.

Lunch was non-existent. Sirita had come in with a cup of coffee and asked if Ruth wanted a sandwich, but Ruth was on the phone again and this time it was Robert who was on the line. He told her that he had got hold of Luke and that they were meeting down in Brighton at three o'clock together with the estate agent. That must be Colin in his shiny suit, thought Ruth.

Sir Rupert also rang. He had heard from a former colleague at his old bank that Babylove was planning a take-over. He offered to deal with the press as he had the finest contacts, "on the top floor, of course," and he rattled off some names that Ruth knew were business editors.

"I don't think we should go out with a statement even mentioning that we are interested until we have Parkin's word that our deal is going through. And you know how much I trust that man."

She spent the rest of the afternoon answering several calls. By the end she had got the "no comment at this stage" to perfection. She was still at her desk at seven, when Robert phoned again.

"Good, you're still at the office. Luke and I are on our way back from Brighton and we thought we'd pick you up and take you out for dinner. What do you say? We'll be with you in half an hour."

She did not even have time to answer before he finished the call. Ruth had completely forgotten about their planned meeting in Brighton. Was that not meant to take place at three? It was past seven now. Whatever had they talked about for four hours?

She pulled out a mirror from the desk drawer and sighed as she saw her pale face, her eyeliner smudged and her lipstick more visible on her coffee cup than on her lips. She quickly freshened her make-up and pulled a comb through her hair.

It was almost eight by the time Robert came stomping up the stairs to her office, followed by the gentle footsteps of Luke. Robert took three long steps reaching her desk and then kissed her rather demonstratively on both cheeks. Ruth could smell alcohol. So that's the reason why they had been four hours.

They ended up at an Indian restaurant, not far from Caterham. It was a hangar of a place, almost empty. Luke and Robert ordered beer while discussing the much-thumbed menu with the waiter, who had probably never been to India. Ruth did not feel hungry at all in spite of not having eaten since breakfast and Robert seemed to have forgotten his cold completely.

"I'm quite happy with an omelette. I don't feel all that hungry," said Ruth as she unfolded her napkin.

"Nonsense, we're going to have an Indian Feast to celebrate this fantastic deal," said Robert in a loud voice. "It's a great project. Luke has very kindly offered me a third of the deal. He's also shown me a few other properties in Brighton, much better quality than our student flats in Leeds and cheaper than London prices."

Robert nodded knowingly at Luke, who seemed almost embarrassed by Robert's enthusiasm.

The food started arriving and Ruth toyed with her leathery omelette and drank her wine in gulps. She felt she was watching Luke and Robert as if they were in a play and she was the audience. She looked at these two men, who knew her better than any other people and it was wrong, totally wrong that she should be ignored.

Other diners were leaving and by eleven they were the only remaining guests. After a silly to-and-fro with the bill, Luke picked it up and insisted on paying.

"I've got an idea," said Robert, with a slight slur in his voice, one that Ruth recognised well. "The night is young and we have a decent bottle of Armagnac at Hicks. Why don't we go there, it's just a short drive. Luke and you can stay the night. I don't think any of us, apart from you Ruth, is in a fit state to drive. Luke and I can leave our cars here and pick them up tomorrow. What do you say?" Robert looked pleadingly at Ruth.

"I need some fresh clothes for tomorrow and really we should all go home to London." She could hear how prissy her voice sounded as she added a reluctant smile.

Luke looked at Ruth then at Robert. "I'd love to see Hicks, the place seems to mean a lot to you, Ruth."

"The least we can do after Luke has given us such a fine dinner. Come on, Ruth, cheer up."

When they finally arrived at Hicks, Ruth said no to a glass of brandy, and, saying she was tired, left them and went up to the bedroom. Tomorrow she would tell Robert about Pink's. For more than an hour she heard them laughing in the living room. Ruth stretched her hand out and patted Robert's pillow. "Oh, do come to bed, darling," she whispered in the darkness. Not quite sure to whom she was talking.

Chapter 27

Ruth often spoke to Robert about her longing for a child, an issue she never discussed with anyone else. She had no one she could talk to, having so few women friends. She wanted to discuss this almost physical ache for a child. Friends had never played a big role in her life. Now she regretted it. Having left school early, she'd gone to work, then studied to improve herself until Mr Watson gave her the chance of developing Babylove. The company had become her substitute child, demanding her almost full-time attention and nurturing during the first years of its existence, even more as the company grew. Her pride in what she had achieved was just as strong as a mother feels for a well-adjusted child, but it was not the real thing.

Robert had never wanted a child with his first wife. To begin with, Ruth suspected he might not be able to have children, later maybe that the fault was hers. Visits to doctors had simply resulted in advice to be patient as there was nothing wrong with either of them.

She tried patience, watched her periods, and if not too tired, would suggest sex when she was at her most fertile. But nothing happened and she had decided to talk to Robert about IVF whenever they found time for their delayed Nile cruise.

Occasionally, Ruth would see some old school friends pulling prams in Crawley and she had absolutely nothing to say to them. She would make some cooing noises as she looked into their prams, trying to find something complimentary to say about their babies and hoping she would not burst into tears as she once had, when seeing a tiny baby in the arms of a former Babylove employee. The tired-looking mothers, no doubt thinking, "I could have been her, if I hadn't become pregnant when I was twenty."

Some of the girls from her school now worked for Babylove, proud to make some money of their own as their children started school. Ruth never invited any school reminiscing or intimacy. And as for children, she simply did not know any at all. Sirita had none, nor her friend Marcia. Was it too late? Had she missed out? Did Robert feel he had missed out? He seemed to feel guilty for having pressed Mandy to have an abortion, but could it also have been sadness for having lost his chance of fatherhood?

The thoughts whirled around as she was waking up, that soft hour when she could not control her mind. She promised herself to speak to Robert, to make sure they'd make an appointment with an IVF clinic as soon as the Pink's deal was done. Forget about the Nile cruise. Yes, that's what she would do.

Robert slowly woke up, with red-rimmed eyes and a cloudy voice.

"Didn't get to bed until half past one. I must say Luke can put it back, we probably drank almost two thirds of that brandy bottle. I like him, I didn't expect that. I always thought he was some sort of poncy public school toff from what you told me, but he is just a normal guy and with a great sense of humour. No, I really like him."

Ruth kissed his cheek, grateful that he had accepted her choice of first husband. Still, it felt awkward that Luke was down the corridor, in her house. She wanted him out as soon as possible; needing a clear demarcation between her former and present life.

"I've an early meeting in the office so it'll have to be a quick breakfast if you want me to drive you two to that Indian restaurant."

Robert nodded, crawled out of bed and limped into the bathroom with a groan. "OK, Ruthie. I'll wake Luke in a minute, let me just have a shower."

He closed the bathroom door and Ruth could hear the water gushing. No, it was better if she woke Luke up. She remembered how much Luke hated mornings and how it always took him about half an hour before his mind was awake, even if the body was up and about. It was never any use talking to Luke in the mornings, not if you wanted an answer.

She knocked at the door of the blue guest room. She knocked again this time harder. No response, so Ruth opened the door and saw Luke fast asleep with the bedclothes all tangled up. One foot was sticking out, his clothes in a pile on the floor. How different from Robert, who was always meticulous about hanging up his clothes, putting his trousers in that silly trouser press he had insisted on buying as soon as he moved into her house. She also remembered how upset she was when they were in the first throes of passion and he stopped kissing her to put the trousers in the press, as if his trousers were more important than satisfying her. He never noticed that she cooled when he turned back to her. He never knew how much she hated that press.

Luke stirred, a second foot shot out from the crumpled duvet and there was a low groan.

"Luke, time to wake up. I've got an early meeting at my office. If you want me to drive you to the Indian place to pick up your car, we must leave in twenty minutes. I'm going down now to make some very strong coffee. Are you awake, Luke, hello, open your eyes, please, *Luke*..."

He stirred, his eyes as bleary as Robert's. He murmured something that made no sense to Ruth.

"Are you awake?" she repeated and finally she got a response.

"Yes, and I shouldn't have had that last brandy. My God, your husband certainly knows how to drink. I couldn't keep up. Oh, my head. Have you got an aspirin or something before I start on that strong coffee?"

Without a word Ruth went into the bathroom, picked up a glass, filled it with cold water and found some aspirin in the cabinet.

"Here you are. Ten minutes to get ready and then just time for coffee before we set off. I've no bread or anything but might be able to rustle up an orange Jaffa Cake..."

"Oh, no, please, coffee will be fine." And with that he stepped out of bed, naked. For a moment Ruth stared, not knowing what to do or say. Luke smiled, with a smirk.

"Don't look so shocked, you've seen it all before."

And with that, he walked slowly to the bathroom as if to give her a chance to appreciate his still great physique.

It was past ten when Ruth finally arrived at her office. Both Robert and Luke had dawdled over coffee, which Robert had made extra strong. In the fridge he had found some eggs, insisting they needed some fried eggs to mop up the brandy still churning in their stomachs. Ruth had tried to hide her irritation as the minutes passed. She phoned Sirita and told her she would be late, "but I'll be there well before ten," she added loudly in the hope that Robert and Luke would hurry up.

Their cars were the only ones in the car park outside the restaurant apart from a van which proudly stated in red letters on the doors *Purveyors of Finest Curries for Your Delectation.* It confirmed Ruth's suspicion that none of the curries on the many pages of the menu was cooked on the premises.

Robert was first out of the car. He had insisted on sitting next to his wife and Luke with his long legs unfolded himself and crawled out of the cramped backseat of her BMW. She realised that it was the first time she had a third person in her newish car and how odd that she had chosen a car with hardly any room for a third person – just like her marriage.

Luke bent over and pushed his head in through the window and kissed her rather clumsily on the cheek.

"What a great evening and thanks for letting me stay the night. Let's talk soon, Ruthie, to get the ball rolling in Brighton. It's so good that Robert wants to join us in this project."

Luke turned to Robert. "Robert, I'm so glad we've met. I somehow knew Ruth would end up with a good husband, one she deserves. I'm equally glad that we're going to work together on the Brighton project." Luke grasped Robert's shoulders in something that looked like the beginning of a hug before he walked away to his own car with a slight wave.

Robert waved back but Ruth sat still. She knew she had to phone Sirita again to say she was on her way. Her fingers drummed on the wheel.

"See you tonight," she said as she closed the car window before Robert had a chance to kiss her goodbye.

There was an air of panic as Ruth returned to her office, telephones were ringing non-stop and Sirita looked harassed, something Ruth had never seen before.

"Thank God you're here, it's pure madness. There was something in the FT this morning about a possible takeover or merger, I can't understand half of it, but something about Babylove planning to merge with another firm called Pink's. Never heard of that either. What's all this about and why haven't you told me? I haven't a clue what to say. I asked them all to phone back at ten, and then you weren't here. Please tell me what's going on, please." Sirita almost whispered her last "please".

Ruth forgot all thoughts of coffee and instead asked Sirita to come into her office. "And close the door."

Even before the door was closed, the telephone started ringing. It was the London evening paper. "I never comment on rumours. If there were any truth in what you're saying I'm sure I would know before you did." There were two more calls, receiving equally abrupt replies to their questions before she turned her phone onto automatic answering and also disabled her mobile.

It took Ruth ten minutes to explain to Sirita what was happening and also to ask her not to repeat anything to the rest of the staff. "I'll do it when I have something to say but now it's only rumours and yes, there are negotiations going on but there have been so many twists and turns. It might not happen."

In the late afternoon, when things had calmed down, Ruth got a call from John Barley.

"Are you sitting down? I've just heard through a source of mine that that damned Parkin has agreed to restart their negotiations with Wonderdrug. I was also told that they're offering twenty fucking pounds per share, excuse my French. I don't think we can top that. Not without outside partners coming in, a hedge fund or something like that. I'm livid. Just knew one couldn't trust that man."

"So, what happens now?" Ruth did not know what to say. How would it affect Babylove, would everything go back to normal? And what would her board say?

"The only good thing about this mess is that the bank stands to make a nice profit on all those Pink's shares we bought for thirteen pounds each.

"Is that all you can think of, the bank's profit?" Ruth was almost spitting out the words.

"Well, my dear Ruth, if we didn't make a profit now and then how do you think we could finance deals like yours?"

"And your indecent bonuses," she responded.

"Now, now, don't let this temporary disappointment sour our happy relationship. The battle isn't over yet. If we don't get this prey, I'm sure I'll find us another take-over target very soon. You win some, you lose some. That's business. Chin up – and Ruth, remember, what it *did* show was that it certainly didn't help to see that Parkin chap without me."

Ruth swallowed hard, thinking that whatever happened, John Barley was never in the wrong yet he always made her feel she was.

"Call me back if you have any news," she said with ice in her voice and put down the phone.

Chapter 28

Next day the pandemonium continued. What could she do? The number of calls was rising each hour. Ruth needed help, and fast. She suddenly thought of Paul, charming Paul. He was, after all, a PR consultant who specialised in dealing with the media. She knew the PR firm which helped Babylove Foundation was not up to the task. At Christmas, Paul had talked about a pub chain caught between two prospective buyers. The press had a field day, scenting blood. Paul spent four days with hardly any sleep trying to dampen the rumours while still giving the journalists the available facts. In the end, he told them the deal was off. Both prospective buyers of the pubs had withdrawn as a white knight appeared in the shape of a well-known Italian hotel chain which bought all the pubs. The banks licked their wounds as they added up their fat fees. Surely Paul could help her now?

Paul was not surprised to hear from her. He too had heard the rumours of a merger between Babylove and Pink's. "I was just about to phone you and offer my services," he said with a laugh, "mate's rates, of course."

Two hours later Paul was installed in her outer office with a Welsh assistant called Megan. After Ruth had briefed them, they called all the journalists who had contacted her as well as those who had left messages with Sirita. Paul and Megan had little to say except promising the full story, if and when there was one. They also emailed links to Babylove's website as well as the one for Babylove Foundation.

"Charitable involvement has enormous PR value, just look at all those guys who end up in open prison for shady deals and insider trading, rather than in Brixton. They were all big on the charity circuit. I don't mean *you're* into any monkey business, but having a charity gives a varnish of respectability and that's always useful when it comes to the media," explained Paul.

It was eight at night when Paul and Megan stood up to leave. "We're off to have a drink at the nearest pub. Fancy coming with us?" For a moment Ruth was tempted. Paul's arm was around Megan's shoulders and they looked close as if the hectic afternoon on the phones had given them an erotic charge.

"Robert is waiting, I'd better go home. Thanks Paul, and you, too, Megan. You've been fantastic. I'm sure tomorrow will be an equally hectic day. God knows what will happen," Ruth added with a sigh.

John Barley had not been in touch since the day before, nor had he answered her call. Maybe he too was inundated by journalists? All Ruth knew was that she was tired – no, exhausted – but she had not given Robert or Mandy a single thought all day.

The drive home was slow. The traffic bunched up around Fulham making Ruth wonder if there was a football match on. Finally, she found a parking space a block away from the house and, by the time she reached their front door with its stained-glass windows, she could feel her knees almost buckle with exhaustion. She opened the door, surprised there was no light in the hall. They always left the light on to give the impression someone was at home. Several of the houses down the road had been burgled during the last year and a couple of months ago they had come home from a late dinner and found the back-door window smashed. The thieves had tried to break down the door and, when not succeeding, crawled through the broken window frame. Police found blood on the kitchen floor, useful for DNA testing, they said with glee. But they never found the culprits. Maybe they lost interest as all the burglars took was Robert's old computer, a digital camera and an unopened bottle of coffee liqueur – a gift from one of Robert's clients.

The house felt cold, uninviting. Robert's winter coat was not hanging on its usual peg in the hall, nor his colourful old university scarf. She regretted that she hadn't phoned him before leaving the office; he must be busy with a client. Her thoughts made a dead stop. It was almost ten o'clock. Surely, he would have phoned her? Ruth felt her insides churning; there could only be one reason for his unannounced absence: Mandy, bloody Mandy. She pulled out her mobile and speed-dialled Robert. No answer, only his voice politely stating he could not take the call at the moment. Ruth angrily pressed the "end call" button and then phoned again leaving a message asking him to contact her immediately. He should be with her, especially now, supporting her when the future of the company was at stake. Her company.

Ruth went into the kitchen, opening cupboards, then the fridge. Although she was hungry, she couldn't be bothered to make even a sandwich, and, anyway, Robert would probably phone the minute she sat down to eat. Instead, she grabbed a digestive from the biscuit tin, but found she had lost her appetite and put it back. Walking across the floor to the fridge again, she opened the door, closed it and walked back to the biscuit tin. She couldn't stay still and while walking backwards and forwards she looked at her mobile on the kitchen table, trying to stare it into action. "Ring, ring," she said in a loud voice.

It was close to eleven when he finally telephoned. "Sorry to be so late. I'm down at Hicks. I saw Luke again to have a proper look at our project. I wanted to meet the architect and the planner at the Council because things are really moving. There is another buyer sniffing around. You know, I really think we have a winner on our hands here."

"So why are you at Hicks?" There was a short silence.

"Luke and I went to a place near The Pavilion to meet the architect, Gavin Snell. Nice guy. Gavin suggested taking a look at one of the clubs which happens to be one of Brighton's top night spots. It turned out Gavin had designed the interior so the owner kept plying us with free drinks and suddenly it was late. I did phone your office *and* your mobile but all I got was voice mail. And you never phoned back, so I assumed you got my message until I got yours and that was only after I had come out from that club. So bloody noisy inside, I couldn't have heard a siren let alone a mobile. I'm too old for clubs, you know, but Luke loved it. So how was your day?"

She felt hot with anger. How was her day, indeed! How *was* her day?

"Fine," she snapped. "Talk to you tomorrow, now I'm going to bed." She turned off the phone before Robert had a chance to say anything.

Was he telling the truth, or had he spent the evening, after seeing Luke, with Mandy? And was Mandy now at Hicks? For a moment Ruth was tempted to jump into the BMW and drive down to Hicks, but she was too tired. All she wanted was a bath and then bed.

Ruth woke up in the middle of the night. Her eyes opened before she was properly awake. She was shaking, damp with sweat, her heart pounding. She had dreamt of Hicks. She was outside the front door looking in and she could see how Mandy had changed the interior. Ruth did not recognise it but she knew it was Hicks. She knocked on the door but she was not let in although she could hear Robert and Mandy talking inside. Just a nightmare, she told herself, but the images were burnt into the inside of her eyelids and the shaking did not stop. She forced herself out of bed to find a sleeping pill which she knew Robert kept in his bedside drawer. She opened his drawer and found an envelope. It was an ordinary, cheap C5 office envelope, but the contents would change her life.

Chapter 29

John Barley was tired; tired of seeing his deal unravel, tired of dealing with people who had no idea how much work was involved with setting up a profitable transaction. He thought of the research he had done, the annual accounts he had ploughed through, the long, boring chats with the analysts on the second floor, self-important gits who thought they knew everything just because they had got a first from some crappy university. You don't learn about banking at university, John thought, as he went to collect the fourth coffee of the morning.

Stitching up a deal is a bit like chasing a woman, he often thought, although he had to admit he hadn't been too successful in that area. Or maybe more like strategic warfare. You find out weaknesses and strengths, the right time to make a surprise attack and then the final conquest. John was proud of his achievements and he knew that the bank appreciated his go-ahead attitude, but lately, he noticed that several young Turks were coming up the ladder and snapping at his heels. They were talking about algorithms and computer-based models, somehow forgetting that most deals were dependent on people and personalities. Not just figures.

He thought he had all the pieces in place and then the Farringdon woman had interfered and as it turned out, to no avail. He did not really trust women in business, all those emotions and hormones, but Eric Parkin at Pink's was not one iota better. How could he talk to

Wonderdrug when he was at the closing stage of negotiations with Babylove? "And they say bankers are bad," he grumbled *sotto voce* to no one in particular.

At that moment his phone rang. John rushed to his desk almost spilling his coffee. It was his manager, Colin Jones. John straightened his back automatically.

"Barley, what's this I hear about Pink's? I thought the deal was done, but I had a call this morning from one of my friends at the FT. I had to hear it from *him*, not you, that the deal is dead and that Wonderdrug is buying Pink's. What the hell is all this about? Can you explain it to me?" His mock-American twang always irritated John. He knew it was an affectation and a way to show off that Jones had taken his MBA at Wharton. As he gained his degree at the prestigious American university he'd somehow lost his South London accent.

"Colin, I was just about to call you. I tried to talk to you last night but your secretary said you were at a reception at the Mansion House."

"Not a reception, a dinner!" For a second Colin Jones forgot his American accent. "The Lord Mayor is a personal friend of mine, an old banker."

"Anyway, I could not get hold of you and the Pink's deal is not dead in the water, negotiations are still going on."

"That's not what I've heard. Anyway, I've asked Johnnie Lofgren, that bright young Swede, and like me an alumnus from Wharton, you know him from the credit committee meetings. Well, I've told him to join your team and have a proper look at the deal. Give him all the help you can. We've spent far too much time on this deal and time is money…"

John Barley saw an opening.

"We're not going to lose money, Colin. We've bought so many shares in Pink's. Once we sell them, and it does not matter who buys them, Wonderdrug or Babylove, we're going to pull in much more than the value of the time spent on the deal, trust me."

"I am glad for your sake, Barley, but I'm still asking Lofgren to have a look at the figures and see what can be salvaged." The line went dead.

Ten minutes later John Barley phoned Johnnie Lofgren. He did not remember him from any credit committee meetings, but these were full nowadays of young men all looking the same. The same boring grey suits with Brooks Brothers shirts and penny loafers, even the ties were similar and they obviously all went to the same barber. For a moment John Barley touched his own freshly plugged scalp and felt a twinge of jealousy, "but I bloody well know how to dress with some style," he thought and looked at his Jermyn Street jacket with its lipstick red lining.

The young Swede had an accent John Barley could not place. There was an American beat but also a soft melodic intonation which he assumed was the Swedish heritage coming through his otherwise faultless English, the kind of English only foreigners can produce.

"Yes, of course I know who you are," said Lofgren. "Colin Jones has spoken to me about you and how you might need some help with the Pink's deal and..."

He did not have a chance to finish the sentence before John Barley snapped.

"I need no help, no help whatsoever, thank you. Colin thought you might benefit from actually seeing how we are going to turn this deal into a money-spinner, whatever happens. You're quite new at the bank, aren't you? Oh, over a year already and before that? Oh, Goldman Sachs in New York, I see." There was a sour grimace on John Barley's face. "Well things are run differently in London," he added and suggested a time they could meet to discuss Pink's. "In my office, of course."

John Barley did not usually leave his desk for lunch. He completely agreed with Gordon Gekko from that old film *Wall Street* that lunch was for wimps. And so was breakfast for that matter. For him it was a caffè macchiato to go before he joined the crowds in South Kensington Tube Station. He always made sure he carried his *Financial Times*, not in his briefcase but under his arm as a sign of being a man of importance. After the Embankment he got his favourite seat and could enjoy both his macchiato and his paper.

But today he felt like lunch. As he looked around the office landscape, he noticed the new girl at the reception desk. She did not look very happy, maybe Colin Jones had been at her as well? What was her name? Emilie, Amelia, something like that. She was not exactly pretty but she was well dressed, properly dressed, not one of those skimpy outfits where all the goods were on show. No, he liked that, a bit of class. Her long hair was tied loosely in a neat ponytail with a navy-blue ribbon matching her dress. I'll ask her to join me for lunch, he thought, she'd be good company.

Amelie, or whatever her name was, smiled as John Barley approached.

"You're new here, aren't you? Have you been looked after properly so far, met all the people in our department?"

She stood up and held out her hand.

"Oh, yes, everyone has been so nice and I know you're John Barley. We haven't met properly. My name is Anne-Marie, Anne-Marie Juppert. Yes, it's a French name but I am actually Belgian."

He let go of her cool hand after having held it just a little bit too long.

"But you have no accent at all," said John Barley, quite disappointed as he liked the French lilt.

"I've lived here since I was five. We moved here when my father came over to set up the London office of Geomax, the Belgian hedge fund."

Good news, right sort of background, he thought as he gave her one of his flashy smiles, usually saved for special clients.

"Now, Anne-Marie, what about joining me for a sort of welcome lunch? There's a very good restaurant, French as a matter of fact, just ten minutes' walk from the office."

Anne-Marie looked down at her keyboard before smiling back.

"That's very kind of you but I always bring my own lunch." And with that, she sat down and her fingers started flying across the keyboard. She did not even look up as he left her desk.

It was not John Barley's day. With a sigh of resignation, he walked out of the office and went straight to the pub, not for a wimp's lunch but for two pints of bitter.

Johnnie Lofgren turned out to look just as he imagined a Swede would: tall, blond and with eyes as blue as a northern lake. He obviously spent hours at the gym, and, yes, he had a grey suit, a pale blue Brooks Brothers shirt and US-style penny loafers, so even the Swedes wanted to emulate the preppy look of Wall Street whizz kids.

John Barley offered coffee, which tasted odd mixed with the mints he had chewed to get rid of the smell of beer on his breath. The Swede looked as if he had never had a drink in his life but he gulped down the coffee.

"We Swedes drink more coffee per head than any other nation apart from the Brazilians," he said and smiled with teeth so perfect that an orthodontist must have been involved.

"I thought you Swedes just drank Aquavit."

It turned out that Johnnie knew the ins and outs of the deal. He had even read the press articles about Ruth Farringdon. He seemed quite impressed by her achievements. They discussed what they could do to salvage the deal, and, if not the deal, how to make sure the bank got its fees.

"What do you say to a kind of reverse take-over?" asked Johnnie Lofgren as he stretched out his long legs and crossed his feet.

"What do you mean?"

"Obviously Babylove is not big enough to expand on its own. It needs the backup of a supermarket chain, or a chemist, see what I mean?"

John Barley did not see what he meant but hummed gently.

"Mmmm, tell me more, it's getting interesting."

"What if we suggest that Pink's takes over Babylove? Eric Parkin does not seem very keen on being taken over by Wonderdrug. He knows full well he would be swallowed like a worm on a fish hook by those Americans."

John Barley chewed his lips. This cool Swede had something there. A take-over like that would bring in very fat fees and it would be one in the eye for Ruth Farringdon.

John Barley nodded his approval.

"And who knows, once that deal is done," continued the Swede, "we might suggest to Wonderdrug that we've done the preliminary work for them and that the combined new company will be a far better buy than just Pink's."

John Barley wished he had thought about that, even fatter fees.

Chapter 30

Ruth held the envelope in her hands hesitating for a moment before she opened it. Inside was a grey and white blurry photo. She could not quite see at first what it was. It looked like a fish under water. At the top of the paper was the name of a clinic in Orpington and underneath it said Amanda Richards. Mandy.

It struck Ruth like a hammer across her forehead. It was a scan of a foetus. Why would Robert keep a copy of the scan of the baby Mandy had aborted all those years ago? The hammer struck again. The date was two weeks ago. This was NOW. The reason Robert had a copy was that it must be his baby.

She sat down on the floor by the bedside table, still holding the paper in her hands. "It can't be, it can't be," she muttered to herself as her eyes watered. She fell down, hitting the bedside rug with her clenched fists, screaming, "It can't be, it can't be." She picked up the scan from the floor. How old the foetus was when the scan was taken? The report gave a date two weeks ago; she read the rest of the text and saw it was a three months scan. The baby must have been conceived three and a half months ago. Her mind, usually so analytical, went into a spin; did that mean that Mandy and Robert had been lovers since before Mandy came down for Christmas? How could that bitch stay at Hicks, eating their food, drinking their wine and sleeping in a bed that Ruth had chosen. It made Ruth's stomach heave and her anger bubbled like boiling milk. At the same time, she felt belittled. Mandy must have laughed at Ruth being so house proud, with her damask linen and silver rose bowl, when Mandy had what Ruth thought she would never lose: her husband.

The baby changed everything. This was something Robert could not deny. The proof was in her own clammy hand. No, she would not wait until tomorrow before speaking to him, she needed to talk to him now, this very minute. There might be an explanation, maybe as Mandy's friend he had been given this photo? No, it did not seem credible. There could be no other reason for this scan to be kept in his bedside drawer. It was his baby, as simple as that.

In the bathroom she washed her tear-smeared face. Looking at her red-rimmed eyes in the mirror the sight was so pathetic she stared crying again, sobbing into the soft fluff of her towel. "Robert, Robert," she whispered as she wiped her tears.

She would phone him now. She looked at the bedside clock and saw that it was just after four o'clock. So what, she said to herself. She had to think and for a moment she could not remember the number to Hicks. Her mind was frozen.

There were about five rings before Robert answered with a sleep-drunk voice.

"Hicks Manor."

"Robert, it's me, Ruth…"

"Has something happened? It's very late – well, it must be the middle of the night. Are you OK?"

What a silly question, Ruth thought. "No, I'm not. I just happened to find a scan of a baby in your bedside drawer, a baby which must have been conceived some three or four months ago. It's not your baby, is it?" Her voice softened. "Tell me it isn't, please." Ruth started crying again and for every second Robert didn't respond to her plea her sobbing increased.

"Ruth, this is not the time nor the place to discuss this. And what the heck were you doing in my drawer?" His voice was sharp and Ruth stopped her sobbing immediately.

"Well, why the hell do you put a photo like that in your drawer? I think you wanted me to find it, that's what I think. And it is your baby, isn't it? It means you were having an affair with Mandy before you asked her to come down to Hicks. What a bitch. I welcomed her with open arms and even bought her a bloody Christmas present. How could you, how could you?" She started sobbing again. There was silence at the other end, but she thought she could hear a cough in the background.

"Is Mandy there now? In our home? In our bed?"

"Ruthie."

"Don't Ruthie me, you bastard."

"Ruth, you're upset and now is not the time to discuss this matter. I promise you I'm on my own. Listen, I'll be up in London tomorrow and we can talk tomorrow night."

"No, no, I want to talk about it now and I want you to come here. Get out of that bed and come to London now."

"That's not a very good idea, Ruth, it's twenty past four in the morning…"

"I said NOW!" she screamed. "Or you'll regret it. And kick that bloody whore out of my house, NOW!" She slammed down the phone into its holder and started pacing the floor. Two minutes later the phone rang.

"Ruthie, I'll be there tomorrow morning. I am not sure I'm sober enough to drive."

"Fine, then I'll drive down to Hicks. You'd better organise a taxi to Orpington for your mistress. I'll be there as soon as I can."

"I told you she's not here. You're paranoid." With a sigh, Robert ended the call.

It had never occurred to Ruth that Robert could be unfaithful. He was there for her; in return, she pulled in the money, made sure that he had the latest car, fancy holidays and a wealth of cashmere sweaters. She had worked hard so that he could enjoy the freedom of being his own master. Was this not what they wanted out of life? A fantastic house in the country, all mod cons. most of them chosen by Robert. A wife he could be proud of, did all of this mean nothing to him? And what about the baby they both wanted, the child that would anchor their lives?

And what could that mousy woman offer him? Was she not a clerk or secretary or something, always having problems with her colleagues?

The hopelessness and chill she had felt when opening the envelope were replaced by white-hot anger. She had done everything for him, everything and this is how he repaid her, by running off with a boring bint.

She threw off her nightie and went to the wardrobe. She rejected her office suits and her leisure wear jeans. What did a woman wear when confronting her husband with his infidelity? A shadow of a smile graced her face for a second. "Black, it has to be black," she thought as she picked a pair of plain black trousers and her favourite polo-neck.

It was dark and the Fulham street was deserted. The newsagent had a dim light on, hardly visible behind the tightly meshed iron grill set up to deter burglars. "No wonder I want to move permanently to Hicks," Ruth thought as she started her car. Then she remembered Mandy might be there at this very minute, probably waiting for a taxi. Mandy in their bed, with her pillow-mussy hair, no, she would have to change the sheets. Had Robert and Mandy made love in her bedroom, her beloved bedroom? She saw images in front of her eyes and almost hit a bollard. She had to concentrate, be clear in her mind when she finally confronted Robert.

There should be no talk about divorce. Robert was her husband and that was that. By all means he could give some financial support for the baby, but that would have to come out of his own earnings, no way was Ruth going to pay for that child. No way. She bit her lip so hard it left a taste of iron in her mouth.

No, they would talk sensibly, how to help Mandy if she insisted on having the baby. Was it too late for an abortion? Yes, it will all work out and I must make sure we spend more time together. Ruth regretted she had cancelled the Nile cruise. Maybe she could arrange a new trip once this hullaballoo with the Pink's deal was over.

It was still dark when Ruth arrived at Hicks. The journey had been quick, less than an hour, as there was little traffic on the motorway, just lorries travelling to and from the coast. The hall light was on and Ruth felt immediately that she was home and everything was going to be sorted out.

She stepped out of her car and realised she had forgotten her handbag in the rush to leave and in it were her keys to Hicks. She stood outside in the cold and rang the doorbell. She could hear it echoing through the house. No one came and for a moment she remembered her nightmare. Were Robert and Mandy inside laughing at her? Then she heard footsteps and the clinking of the security chain.

"Sorry to keep you waiting. Had to turn off the alarm before I could open the door." Robert had his dressing gown on and Ruth felt over-dressed as she looked at his unshaven face and tousled hair.

"Robert, what is all this about?" she whispered as she threw herself into his arms. Slowly he put his arms around her and then patted her on her head.

"Ruth, could you not have waited till tomorrow? I said I was coming up. Well, you're here now. Come on in, I'll get some strong coffee brewing. We probably could do with a small brandy as well."

Ruth did not want to move, she wanted to stay in his arms where she felt safe, but he led her towards the kitchen. There were no signs of anything having changed since she was last down, everything looked normal. Robert put two cups on a tray with two shot glasses and a brandy bottle.

He then pressed the button on his espresso machine and the scent of coffee reminded Ruth that she had not slept for almost twenty-four hours. Her eyelids were drooping, but she knew Robert's strong coffee would wake her up. Neither of them said a word as Robert clattered with the machine, shaking out the dregs in the sink.

"Shall I light the fire or do you want to sit here?"

"A fire would be lovely, if you don't mind. I feel a bit cold, maybe because I haven't slept."

Politely they skated around what they knew must come. The truth about the baby. And now when the time had come, neither of them wanted to bring it up.

It took some five minutes for Robert to get the fire going and Ruth stared at his back as he crumpled newspaper to put among the logs. She had seen this procedure so many times, every weekend, even on cool summer evenings, because Robert knew how much she loved a fire.

Ruth felt calm, everything was going to be all right.

"A small brandy, just to keep the chill away." Without waiting for her answer Robert poured the two shot glasses with brandy. Was this the same brandy he had tried to offer Mandy at her first dinner here? The image of Robert offering it to Mandy jolted Ruth, as she now knew that Mandy had been his mistress already then.

Ruth sipped her brandy hoping the warmth would spread to her shivery limbs.

"Robert, I have to know. Is it your baby?"

"Yes, Ruth. It is. I am so sorry. What can I say?"

"You don't need to say anything. This is something we can deal with. I assume it's too late for an abortion, but I will say nothing more about this and I suggest you pay the poor girl whatever is considered a generous allowance for the child. I don't want to see that child, but I can understand if you want to see it now and then, to be some kind of father. Maybe I will feel different about it when we have a child. We will still try, won't we?"

"Ruth, I'm sorry but you don't understand. I want this child. I want it very much and it's going to be my child and I want it to grow up in a loving home."

"Well as I said, you can provide the money for the child's upbringing and I am sure Mandy will give the child a loving home." Ruth felt proud that she could talk about this child as if it did not hurt every nerve of her body to know that her husband had not only been unfaithful but also wanted this child to be part of his life. Well certainly not mine, thought Ruth as she took another sip of brandy.

"You don't get it, do you?" said Robert and looked at Ruth with something like pity in his eyes. "Poor Ruth." Robert leant forward across the table and grasped her icy hand.

"This is not just an affair. Mandy and I want to bring this child up together. I know this must come as a bit of a shock to you, but Mandy was my first love and I never understood why she left me after her abortion. Now I do, and I certainly don't want her to go through something like that again. This time I am taking responsibility for our child and also for her."

"What are you saying? I don't understand." Deep down Ruth knew what he was saying. She was still hoping she would wake up from this nightmare and that Robert would join her on the sofa and give her a hug. Robert did not move. His eyes were firmly on the brandy as if he could find an answer in the glass.

"Ruthie, I don't think you have ever understood what it was like for me to be Mr Farringdon" – his fingers made two quotation marks in the air – "the husband of The Businesswoman of the Year. No one even knew my name or cared for that matter. I was the one who drove you home after functions and carried your briefcase. My schedule was always prepared to fit in with yours and if we planned a holiday and work came in between, tough, there went our holiday. I knew you weren't keen on a family when we married and I thought I could cope with that, but as I get older, I do want a child, a proper family."

"We should have gone for IVF, but there has been so much on with Babylove and I thought time was on our side. There is nothing I want more than a child with you. You know that and it is not too late. Is it? You still love me, don't you?"

"It's more than just a child, it's about making a home, a real home not just one bought lock, stock and barrel from some department store. And I know that's what Mandy wants too, a real home."

"Mandy this and Mandy that. What about me? And what **I** want. Have you two ever thought about me?" Her tone was shrill.

"You have a very busy life, awards galore and everyone admires you. Business is in your blood. I can't see you sitting at home with a baby. Your baby is Babylove, even the name says it all."

"So am I going to have to put up with you spending more and more time with Mandy? Is that it?"

"No, Ruthie, that's not what it's all about. I love Mandy and I'm going to marry her as soon as we've sorted out our affairs. That's what it's all about." Robert did not look at her as he finished his sentence. He stood up and poured her another shot of brandy.

"Drink this now. It's almost morning and we have some busy days ahead of us. Do you want a sleeping pill?"

Ruth did not move. Robert's words echoed in her sleep-deprived brain. Like lightning her anger returned.

"You bloody shit. I'll make sure you get nothing out of this marriage, nothing and I ask you to leave Hicks now. Take what you need, but I don't want to see you here again. Ever." She stood up and left the living room, carefully carrying her cup and the empty glass.

* * *

When she finally woke up next morning, her digital alarm clock showed 10.32 and her mobile was blinking with unanswered calls. How could she have slept for so long? Then she remembered the three sleeping pills she had taken plus another three glasses of brandy, while Robert packed a few things into a suitcase. Downstairs, she found a note on the kitchen table.

Dearest Ruth

I understand that all of this must have been a great shock to you. Once you have calmed down, we can discuss details. I think it's best I move out as soon as possible both from Hicks and Fulham. You can always reach me on my mobile, any time.

Love

R

It all came back to her; nausea gripped her, made her retch. And then came the tears. A bleep on her mobile showed another message, but she couldn't be bothered. She went back to bed and pulled the pillow over her head sobbing until she fell asleep again.

Chapter 31

Mrs Green had spent the morning peeling Seville oranges in her kitchen when the telephone rang. For a moment she thought of letting it ring as her hands were sticky with orange juice, but she wiped her hands on the kitchen towel hanging on the oven door and answered the phone.

"Mum, can I come and see you?"

"What's the matter, dear? Everything OK?"

"Not over the phone, can I come now? I'm down at Hicks and could be with you in half an hour."

"Well, I'm busy today making marmalade, can we say tomorrow instead?"

"No, Mum, it has to be today."

"Has it got anything to do with the money you gave me?"

"No, Mum, we'll talk when we meet. Nothing for you to worry about."

Mrs Green did not feel reassured. Ruth's voice had sounded so different, almost pleading. This was so unlike her daughter, who was always in charge. She had never understood what made Ruth such a driven person. Ruth's father had never shown any ambition and she herself had always been happy enough at the Building Society, but Ruth, no, she always had to aim higher. The endless times Ruth had sent her clippings from the business pages or told her to watch the television for some interview. Had it made Ruth a happier woman, all this business malarkey? Mrs Green still regretted that the marriage to Luke Farringdon had not worked, such a charming man, but he wanted a family of course, while Ruth only wanted fame and status – money as such did not seem to matter to Ruth somehow.

She turned off the heat under the marmalade saucepan. She would deal with that later. "Frank, darling," she shouted. "My daughter's coming around, you'd better scarper. She said she'd be here within half an hour. I'll give you a ring as soon as she's gone. God knows, what she wants this time."

There was a grumble from the sofa followed by a sigh as the television was turned off. Mrs Green started clearing up in the kitchen. She would offer her daughter some bought biscuits, not the nice lemon drizzle cake she had baked specially for Frank. He deserved it having brought unexpected joy into her life. Frank Addleston had moved into a cottage on the other side of The Meadow some years ago and Mrs Green had watched him endless times through the kitchen window as he pushed his shopping trolley from the local shop. There was never any sign of a Mrs Addleston. One day, after Christmas, he had come across the snow-covered meadow and knocked at her door. Someone had broken into his cottage and got away with some cash and his beloved Leica camera. The police had shrugged their unconcerned shoulders and left him with a crime number. "Maybe one of your neighbours saw something," one of them said. "It was daytime after all." When Frank Addleston suggested the police should do a house-to-house inquiry, they smiled benignly and said, "We only do that for murders." And that was that, but not for Frank Addleston. He remembered there was a grey-haired woman who always looked out of her kitchen window, just opposite, maybe she had seen something.

She had not seen anything but she invited him in for tea and soon enough they were off to the multiplex in Crawley whenever there was a film musical on – and Frank had one of those wonderful TVs with a big screen and he often showed Marjorie Green the latest films he could stream. That was a word Mrs Green had never used and it turned out that Frank was pretty nifty with a screwdriver as well. He helped her change light bulbs and other boring tasks. And all this in return for a home-cooked meal now and then. Now he was over most afternoons and left after dinner. Frank was very correct, making his contribution to the food bills and bringing his own fine malt whisky, to which he was very partial.

Frank had recently mentioned a holiday together and Marjorie thought about a romantic cruise down the Nile. "We're going Dutch, of course," said Frank. "And separate cabins, I need my proper sleep," he added as he saw Marjorie's face light up. He was far too tired for sex, he had explained to her from the beginning, but he told her that when on holiday he quite liked a cuddle.

Marjorie Green had quickly found out that a cruise with a single supplement for one would cost over two thousand pounds. That's when she decided to speak to her rich daughter. All her savings had shrunk seriously since she started going to the hairdresser, buying new dresses and having her nails done. It was the reason she had decided to speak to her rich daughter. Now here Ruth was asking to come over for a chat. Maybe she could get another cheque, she could use some money for evening wear on the cruise they were planning. Frank liked her to look smart.

He had several times asked to meet "this famous daughter of yours" but Marjorie felt that the time was not right. She pitied Frank as he and his now dead wife had never had any children although his wife had acted as a foster mother to several youngsters. "Most of them seemed to be half-criminal, but it pleased Betsy to do some good and it filled her days."

They had agreed they would ask Robert and Ruth over for dinner once they were back from their planned holiday. They had even discussed moving in together; the cottages had two bedrooms and Frank's had a more modern kitchen and bathroom so that is where they planned to live. The money from Marjorie's cottage they could spend on holidays in the future. "Might even buy a small flat in Spain and spend our winters there," suggested Frank and that was an idea that really appealed to Mrs Green. Crawley was a miserable place in the summer but even worse in the winter.

With thoughts of holidays to come Mrs Green opened the door and let in her daughter followed by a gust of cold air. She looked across The Meadow and hoped Ruth would not stay too long. There was a film on this afternoon that both she and Frank were looking forward to, Young at Heart with Doris Day and Frank Sinatra. Mrs Green stopped as she saw the face of her daughter; her eyes were red-rimmed, her skin was ashen. She wore no lipstick, her daughter who was always so immaculate.

"Oh, Mum," Ruth sighed and her voice was almost a whisper.

"Come on in, I'll put the kettle on for a nice cup of tea. You look all done in. What's the matter, dear?"

Ruth took off her coat, kicked off her winter boots and followed her mother into the kitchen. Ruth had always loved the scent of the Seville oranges but the dominant smell was still from her mother's strong disinfectant. "Sorry about your marmalade."

"Never mind, you go into the lounge and I'll bring the tea, and I have some lovely lemon drizzle cake almost straight from the oven." Never mind Frank, she thought, I'll bake another one. Now it looks as if my daughter needs cheering up. She cut two generous slices.

"Now, what's the matter? I can see you're upset. Trouble at work?"

Ruth did not answer, her shoulders started heaving and she was snivelling, hiding her tear-stained face behind a wet handkerchief.

"It's Robert."

"Robert, is he ill?"

"No, he's leaving me. He wants a divorce so that he can marry that stupid woman, you remember her, Mandy. She spent Christmas with us."

"You can't be serious. What are you saying? No, you got that wrong. They were just old school friends or whatever. Didn't he say he knew her from Leeds?"

"They were lovers then and they are lovers again. It's been going on since before Christmas."

"Sweetheart, I can't believe it. What a bastard. Men are like that. They think they can get away with it. You just have to sit it out. Your father was the same. Saw any woman as his rightful prey. Ignore it and it will die out. You're the one with the money, remember that, he's just, what was it called again, a house-husband. He'll come crawling back when the fun is over."

"Oh, Mum, it's worse than that. Mandy is pregnant and he says he wants the baby. He is going to divorce me and marry her so that the baby grows up in a loving home."

Mrs Green was silent. What could she say? She had never really liked Robert. He was too quiet and he was half German, they say never trust a foreigner. He was always very polite, very correct but he never made her laugh. Not like Luke, now there was a man with charm – and he had a proper job and came from a proper family. But she had got used to Robert and he seemed to make Ruth happy.

"A baby, are you sure?"

"Of course, I'm sure. I've even seen a scan of the baby. It'll be born in six months. Oh, what am I to do?" The sniffles grew louder.

Mrs Green moved closer to her daughter and put one arm around her shoulder.

"I always told you that you should've started a family. Then this would never have happened."

Ruth turned her face to her mother and she almost screamed.

"Well, I can tell you we really tried. We've been to see doctors and specialists and they all said there was nothing wrong. We did try, we really did. And then he gets HER pregnant." The sobbing got louder.

Mrs Green took away her arm and looked out through the window. She could not see Frank's cottage from this window but she longed to be over there, not here with her hysterical daughter.

"I'll freshen up the pot. Are you sure you don't want a glass of sherry or something to eat? I have some sausages in the fridge."

She had never seen her daughter like this and didn't know how to calm her down. Yet, she knew that sausages were not the answer. She had run out of things to say and whatever she had to say would only make it worse.

"You should've learnt from your first marriage. Luke went on to marry a woman who gave him a family."

Ruth turned her face to her mother and said sharply, "She was pregnant, they *had* to marry and anyway, he's divorced again. So much for a happy family." Ruth spat out the last words.

Mrs Green stood up and without looking at her daughter went out to the kitchen and put the kettle on. Ruth waited for a few minutes then rose and walked to the hall and very quietly put on her boots and her coat.

"I'm off. Somehow, I thought you'd understand and I don't have anyone else to go to. If I had, I wouldn't have bothered you. You get back to your marmalade." The door slammed shut and Mrs Green went straight to the telephone and rang Frank.

Chapter 32

Sirita sighed, leaning over her keyboard. She had been trying all morning to phone Ruth, on her mobile, her Fulham line and finally to Hicks but there was no answer anywhere. Finally, she phoned Robert and left a message on his mobile.

Even Sir Rupert had phoned twice and in the end, his secretary left emails and texts with URGENT in very large capital letters asking Ruth to call him.

John Barley had also stressed the need to speak to Ruth. Next to Sirita's office, Paul Gallagher and his assistant Megan dealt with even more enquiries from the press. She felt something important was happening but there was no one she could ask. This was so unlike Ruth. The only time she had been late to the office had been when she had lunched with Luke Farringdon. Ah, Luke, maybe that's it, thought Sirita and quickly clicked through Contacts on the computer and there he was: lukefarringdon@farringdonestates.co.uk. She sent an email to him asking if he knew where Ruth was, by any chance, adding, "Nothing to worry about." But she was worried.

Within twenty minutes a ping notified an answer from him. "*No idea but please let me know when you hear from her. Saw her the other day and she was fine, maybe her mobile has run out of battery. Kind regards Luke*".

By lunchtime no one had heard from Ruth and the whole office knew something was wrong. They were discussing contacting the police when Robert phoned Sirita.

"Still no word from Ruth? I'm sorry to say we had a bit of a quarrel this morning, well, very early this morning down at Hicks. Have you tried there? OK, what about her mother Mrs Green in Crawley? I've got her number. I don't think it's likely she would have gone there, but it's worth a try. Let me phone Mrs Green, it'll save you time. If you hear anything, please let me know. Between you and me, she was in quite a state this morning."

Five minutes later Robert was back on the line.

"Ruth's fine. She went to see her mother about an hour ago and left some twenty minutes later and is probably on her way to the office right now. She might have turned her mobile off. Mrs Green doesn't approve of mobiles," he said. He did not tell Sirita that Mrs Green had given him a right dressing down calling him a bastard and saying she never wanted to lay eyes on him again – and how could he do this to her lovely daughter. He had not bothered to explain knowing Mrs Green would never understand anyway.

It was after three o'clock when Ruth finally did turn up at the office. Sirita saw at once something was wrong. Ruth looked as if she had not slept at all – her eyes were swollen and red. "I'm so sorry. Overslept, not feeling very well and forgot to charge my phone. Everything OK here?"

"Oh, Ruth, everyone has been trying to get hold of you. We've been so worried. There's a list as long as my arm on your desk with people wanting to talk to you. Sir Rupert is top of the list but also Robert, he's very worried, so start with him." Ruth started to shake. Sirita stepped towards her and put her arms around Ruth's trembling body.

"Are you all right? Can I get you a coffee or a cold drink? I've got some aspirins in my drawer. Or do you want me to call the factory nurse? Have you eaten anything? You look done in."

Ruth smiled but Sirita could see it required some effort.

"I'll be fine. I'd better get on with that list. Maybe you could just email Robert and say I'm fine."

"And Luke, he is worried, too."

"Luke phoned? How does Luke know I turned up late?"

"I contacted him. We tried everyone and Robert even spoke to your mother. I gather you saw her this morning."

Ruth smiled, without effort this time. She knew her mother would have given Robert an earful, a well-deserved one.

Ruth called Sir Rupert first and was told that he was still at a luncheon at his club, where no mobiles were allowed but he would call her as soon as he was back. It was important, his secretary stressed. John Barley, on the other hand, was at his desk – no fancy lunch for him.

"Where the hell have you been? We've been trying to get hold of you all day, well, all morning. There has been an important development. Are you sitting down?" There was a theatrical pause. "Pink's wants to buy Babylove. No, listen Ruth. Some bloody white knight has turned up on the battlefield with money from some hedge fund. They want to take you over."

He failed to mention that he had contacted the hedge fund and told them what a good fit there was. He had also told them how much money they could make as there was an even bigger buyer lurking in the background willing to take over the merged company. There would be no trace of the conversation, no papers signed, just a gentleman's agreement and a handshake, one worth several hundred thousand to the bank in fees.

Ruth tried to understand what John Barley was saying but the words would not sink into her muddled brain. It was as if her tears had clogged the neurons.

He repeated it to her very slowly as if she were a small child. "What am I to do?" she asked.

"I will present the outline of an offer to you from the prospective buyer tonight. Due diligence of course has to be done first before it becomes a final offer. Then it's up to you and your board to decide whether you want to accept it or not. If you want my advice, dear Ruth" – he still talked to her as if she were six – "I would accept the offer. You need money to expand, you need the contract with the supermarket and, of course, there are all the other advantages of being a larger company. You can cut down on your storage facilities as Pink's have plenty of that, as well as releasing some of your administrative staff."

Releasing staff meant sacking people, that much Ruth understood. She had always regarded everyone who worked with Babylove as part of the family. During her many years as managing director she had only "released" one member of staff. It was a man she had taken on in the sales department who was found falsifying invoices and pocketing sums of money received from customers. Even with the proof in front of her Ruth had felt sick to her stomach as she had to fire him. The man could hardly hold back his tears, talking about his young family and a sick child. For a short moment Ruth considered forgetting the whole sad affair but forced herself to go through the firing process. She promised him the firm would not take him to court but he had to go immediately. Later she found out that he had done the same thing at another firm – and there was no sick child.

She told John Barley that she would come back to him. As soon as she had put the telephone down, Sir Rupert called.

"Ruth, dear" – again someone sounding as if he was speaking to a six-year-old – "I've had lunch with my old school chum Eric Parkin today. He's never been to my club before. We had a confidential chat, it was his idea, and he told me that he wants to take over Babylove. He's got a firm willing to put up the money and I must say it makes sense, Ruth."

"How could this total turnaround of affairs make sense? It doesn't to me. Tell me." She could hear how whiny her voice sounded.

Sir Rupert repeated almost word by word the benefits John Barley had already given her.

"But what about our board, and may, I ask, what about my role?"

"Well, you two had come to some agreement that you'd be sharing the role of MD, but now, of course, after the first six months the post will go to Eric and I'm sure you want to remain in the new company as director of development or whatever title you may choose. The board will be merged with the board of Pink's and some board members from both sides will have to go, that's the nature of a merger. The best will remain. You'll be pleased to hear Eric has already asked me to remain chairman of the new board. Eric has some rather good ideas on how the merged company can increase profits. He's really fired up by the thought of all the benefits but best of all a chance of a listing on the Stock Exchange. Think of that Ruth, you could end up rich!"

"I don't want to be rich. I want to be in charge. It's my company, I built it up." Ruth swallowed hard. Sir Rupert had certainly changed his tune. Now it seemed that Eric Parkin, who earlier he had called a joke, had turned into a brilliant businessman.

She felt ambushed by Sir Rupert and did not know what more to say. If only she could talk to Robert, he would know what to do. The thought of Robert and his hasty retreat at dawn made her feel nauseous. She had no one to talk to. Her mother's response had not given her any comfort at all. It was Robert she needed. They were all ganging up against her. Babylove was her anchor and without it how would she cope? Her eyes welled up again and after a search through her desk drawers she found some tissues.

"Are you really OK?"

Ruth had not heard Sirita coming into her room.

"Not really."

"Tell me what I can do. You know I'll do anything to help you but you must tell me." Sirita sat down on the corner of the desk and put her hand on Ruth's arm. It was this unexpected gesture of kindness that brought on a new attack of hiccuppy tears.

"I don't know where to begin. Robert is leaving me. He's in love with some old girlfriend of his and now she's pregnant. There's nothing I can do. He's moving out. It's all come as a shock, I had no idea. Well, I suspected something, but not, not ever, that he would leave me. I've given him everything he's wanted and what do I get in return?"

"Are you sure it's not just a quarrel? These things seem to happen in marriages. I'm sure you and Robert can work it out."

"How?" Her voice sounded croaky as she sniffled into her hankie. "There's a baby involved."

"I don't know, but things usually sort themselves out. I had no idea this was going on. I thought it had something to do with the company as both John Barley and Sir Rupert have been so eager to speak to you."

"Oh, God, yes, there's that too. I really shouldn't mention it but it looks as if our company is going to be sold."

"Sold, but why? I thought you said there were plans to merge with another company, not selling out."

"Sirita, I really don't know what's happening. I feel as if I'm on a dark cloud looking down and seeing things change without me being able to do anything about it. I tried to speak to my mother, that's where I was this morning. She implied that Robert would never have looked elsewhere if I had spent less time in the office. It is all my fault." The sniffles grew louder.

Sirita patted Ruth on her shoulder. "I think I know what you need."

Ten minutes later (it felt longer to Ruth) Sirita came back with a bottle of brandy. "I borrowed this from Brian in accounts, he always has a bottle for emergencies. Now I suggest you drink a big glass of this brandy and then wash your face. I'm going down to the canteen to find you a proper sandwich. I bet you haven't eaten a thing today. No, no arguments."

Ruth had never thought of Sirita as a friend, but here she was, caring for her, more than her mother had done and certainly more than Robert. She sat up straight. She would cope, she knew she would cope, it was just a question of surviving day by day.

Chapter 33

Somehow Ruth managed not to cry for the rest of the day. The ham sandwich had tasted like blotting paper but it gave her some energy as did the sweet tea Sirita had insisted she drank. She had rejected the brandy, those three glasses at dawn had left a slightly acid taste in her mouth. The telephone calls, emails and discussions with Paul in PR and his assistant Megan, as well as with Andy in accounts, kept her busy and kept her thoughts about Mandy and Robert at bay. Paul had asked in passing about Robert but Ruth just ignored his question and he hadn't seemed to notice.

Ruth was certain there was something between Paul and Megan. Megan's eyes lit up every time Paul looked at her. Ruth envied her; how wonderful to be at the beginning of an affair, when everything was exciting and shimmering. When it was too early for disappointments or compromises. Would she ever have that feeling again or had Robert robbed her of that as well?

It was dark outside and the thought of returning to either Hicks or Fulham filled her with dread. Had Robert been up to London to collect his clothes and where was he? Had he moved in with Mandy in Orpington? She tried to imagine what Mandy's flat would be like. How could he give up Hicks for what she suspected was a dark and cramped flat in Orpington?

When she finally opened the front door in Fulham her heart sank. There would be no dinner prepared for her, no cheery hello and an offer of a glass of wine. The hall was dark and the air was cold. She put on all the lights downstairs and turned on both the radio and the television in order to drown the silence. She had never felt so alone and she knew that this was what her life would be like from now on.

She opened a tin of sardines. Their oily smell revolted her, but she forced herself to eat them straight from the tin. She found an opened bottle of white wine in the fridge and, without even bothering to reach for a glass, she took greedy gulps of the wine. With the half-full bottle in her hand, she walked into the living room and found yet another note from Robert.

Dear Ruthie

I've taken my clothes and some other personal belongings but will collect the rest at a later date when it suits you. I'm staying at a small hotel in Bayswater until things are sorted out and you can always reach me on my mobile.

Robert

Ruth rushed upstairs and opened his wardrobe. Nothing there but jangling hangers. His drawers were equally bare, even his summer clothes were gone. She stared at the space, before robot-like walking into their bathroom. His shelf was emptied. She could still see the mark left by his electric toothbrush, a whitish ring on the glass. Her finger touched it but she could not, would not erase it. If only there had been something left, something with Robert's smell. Then she remembered the laundry basket and there she found one of Robert's shirts. She took it out from the basket and held it to her face. It still had the smell of Robert, his body and his citrus-fresh cologne. Ruth threw herself on the bed and kept the shirt close to her face. And that's how she woke up the following morning, still clutching it.

"You look a lot better today," said Sirita as Ruth walked into the office. Ruth had slept in her clothes; when she woke up at six, she had a long, hot shower, rubbing her body with a loofah as if to erase the bad dreams of the night. Finding nothing to eat for breakfast she remembered that there was a small café next to the newsagent. She dressed quickly and bought a newspaper, in spite of having two delivered to her house. She needed human contact, to hear a friendly voice and Mr Patel had known her since she and Robert bought the house some eight years ago.

She had never been to the Café Vienna before although she had passed it several times, admiring the Art Deco interior with its dark panelling and with newspapers on sticks hanging from the wall. As she entered through the door, she realised that most of the people there were probably regulars. They all looked at her, as if assessing if she was worthy of joining their special club. There was a nod or two in her direction, so she sat down. The men, they were all men, talked to each other though they did not share tables. Occasionally someone would read out loud something he found amusing and there would be a gentle laughter from most of the tables.

A kind-looking woman, with a girth which showed that she had eaten far too many of the cakes on offer, asked Ruth what she wanted. Ruth hesitated. "Try Joan's full English, sets you up for the day," said a man sitting in a corner, half-hidden by his *Daily Telegraph*. Ruth smiled at Joan and nodded and within a few minutes a plate of freshly cooked bacon and eggs with tomatoes and mushrooms and a steaming cup of coffee were put in front of her.

"Haven't seen you here before, love," said Joan as she hovered between the tables with a large teapot. "Do you live in the area?"

"Yes, just down the road, number 47."

"Isn't that where Robert lives, George?" Joan looked at the man in the corner. "You know who I mean, the nice guy who comes here for lunch quite often or just a coffee in the afternoon." George nodded.

"You must know Robert? I'm afraid I don't know his surname, a man in his forties. I'm sure he said he lived in number 47, the one with stained glass panes in the front door."

"No, I don't know him," said Ruth and suddenly her throat constricted and she knew she was about to start crying. She bit her lip and quickly asked for some more coffee.

And with that first lie, she knew she would be able to survive.

The days continued. To Ruth they all seemed the same and there was some comfort in that. Early to work, frantic discussions with lawyers and accountants as well as with John Barley. She asked Paul and Megan to stay on to handle all enquiries from the press and also to help with the information that Pink's lawyers wanted. She noted with envy how their relationship was growing. They did not ask again if she wanted to join them for after-work drinks.

Every morning she went to Café Vienna where they had now accepted her as one of them. She gorged herself on bacon and eggs and very strong, almost bitter coffee. Joan made her sandwiches for lunch and at night in the echoing house she learnt to microwave ready-made meals, which she bought at the weekend. Her sole company was the white wine, which she also bought in bulk.

As her first weekend came she avoided Hicks, too full of memories. After two more lonely weekends she was pleased to hear from Marcia who phoned one evening to invite her and Robert over for a meal.

"We haven't seen you for ages. We drove past Hicks yesterday and saw none of your cars were there. Are you free for lunch next weekend? My roast is a joke," said Marcia with a laugh. "But Dick has some fine wines in the cellar to make up for it. I think Dick also wants to discuss with Robert this hotel deal in Lithuania or whatever it was. Do say that you can come."

"I'm afraid we can't." There was a pause. "Robert's away and I'm not sure when he's back."

"Has he gone to Lithuania? I remember him mentioning something about a trip to check the progress of financing the hotel and to meet the other partner. I'm afraid I don't really listen when Dick and Robert discuss business."

Marcia's friendly chatter gave Ruth time to think. She had hated her two lonely weekends, the café was closed on Sundays, and she could do with some company.

"But I'm free, if you don't mind, and I'd love to come and see you. I'll drive down from London."

Ruth noticed Marcia's pause before she exclaimed that it would be lovely.

"Will one o'clock suit you? I suppose Dick can always get in touch with Robert via email. I know there was something he wanted to discuss, some rumours he'd heard on the grapevine. You know what the City's like."

Ruth suspected that he had also heard about the rumours circling about Babylove. Marcia never read the business pages but Dick did. No doubt he wanted some inside information while chewing Marcia's overcooked roast.

During the rest of the week, several young men from an accountancy firm chosen by Pink's came to inspect the accounts. Ruth spent hours with them replying to endless questions about logistics, their research programme as well as the links to the Babylove Foundation. According to John Barley, an initial offer would be made to the Babylove board the following week.

* * *

On Sunday, Ruth bought an excessively expensive bunch of flowers having rejected the pitiful ones at her local supermarket. Where did Robert find those fine flowers that he always brought for the weekends at Hicks? And did a bunch really cost thirty-five pounds? She had also bought a bottle of fine brandy for Dick; it was as if she wanted to buy the Callanders' affection. Or was it just an excuse for her lying about Robert's whereabouts, she wondered.

Marcia met her at the door, elegant as always in navy blue trousers and a silk blouse in a lighter shade. She didn't look like a woman who had spent time in the kitchen. Ruth handed over the enormous bouquet and felt slightly ridiculous as Marcia disappeared behind the oversized blooms.

"Oh, you shouldn't. Come in and have a drink. It's such a boring drive from London, especially on a Sunday when every Sunday driver is out on the road." She put down the flowers, kissed Ruth on the cheek, or rather the vicinity of the cheek, and helped her out of her coat. "Dick's in the drawing room ready to take your order."

"A G&T? Or would you rather a glass of white wine?" Dick asked her before he even looked at her and then said: "Ruth, dear, you look tired. I've read all about the proposed merger in the papers and I know how tough these kinds of negotiations can be. You must be exhausted. Not the right time for Robert to dash off to foreign lands. Now my dear Ruth, what can I offer you?"

Dick poured a gin and tonic, adding ice and a slice of lemon. "This will see you right and also help your digestion. I'm not sure what Marcia is cooking but I find gin always helps." He handed her the glass and she took a deep sip, her lips shrinking from the cold.

"We can't all be good cooks like your husband. Oh, the fine meals we've always had at Hicks. Every one memorable." Ruth clenched her fists and tried to smile. Why wasn't Robert here with her?

They sat down on the sofa in front of the spluttering fire. The rest of the room was in semi-darkness. There were pictures in heavy gold frames on the mustard-coloured walls. Dick had never shown any interest in art but paid his annual subscription to The Royal Academy as Marcia loved the private views. Small tables were placed next to the sofas and easy chairs close to the fireplace. Silver ornaments, mostly animals, were everywhere. Marcia had once told Ruth that she gave a silver animal to Dick on every birthday as she never knew what he wanted.

"I felt I reached the end of my imagination and that of the jeweller's when I presented him with a silver squirrel last year."

Dick wanted to hear her views about the forthcoming – or maybe not – merger and Ruth stalled his all too invasive questions because John Barley had warned her that secrecy was vital until the contract was signed. Marcia's entrance stopped the questioning and her presence as well as the effect of the gin helped Ruth relax. She looked at her friends and wondered if their marriage had ever been at risk. She thought not – the two of them seemed so content in each other's company. Dick always looked at his wife with a hint of a smile as if they shared some secret. Marcia had spent her life making Dick a home, ensuring he was comfortable. Her only fault was not being perfect in the kitchen.

Ruth recognised the soup as one from the supermarket's ready-to-heat section, the lamb was overcooked, dry and tasteless, but the wine was velvety-rich and comforting. She realised with a jolt that during all the years they had known each other, she had never seen the Callanders without Robert. She could almost sense his presence at the table and she knew that he would have been able to compliment Marcia on one of her dishes – maybe the mint sauce or the potatoes?

Over coffee, prepared by a machine, Ruth thanked them both for the lunch and handed over the bottle of brandy to Dick.

"I know you're partial to a brandy after a meal. No, not for me. I'm driving, but I'd love another coffee."

Ruth could not muster the energy to leave. The thought of the empty house in Fulham, so dark and unwelcoming, made her depressed and she was not ready for Hicks, not yet. Marcia seemed to understand and suggested that they take a walk, it was cold but dry and the sun was getting low. Her idea was met with false enthusiasm by Dick, who had just started to enjoy his brandy.

They walked briskly for an hour and Ruth was physically tired for the first time since Robert had left. Her body ached pleasantly and she greedily accepted Marcia's offer of a cup of tea with hot crumpets.

It was close to six when she left Marcia and Dick standing in the doorway waving and asking her to come back soon to see them. "And next time we hope Robert can come, too," said Dick.

That night Ruth slept without dreams. She was ready for the working week – and to hear the offer from Pink's.

Chapter 34

Ruth was pleased to return to work on Monday morning. She had not heard a word from Robert for the past two weeks. She had forced herself not to telephone him, needing time for some healing before dealing with the formalities of splitting their possessions. It would not be difficult as she had paid for almost everything. Robert had paid for his books and records as Ruth seldom had time to read a book and she found his taste in music too serious. There would be nothing for her to miss. She envisaged no quarrels as they had two homes and therefore duplicates of everything – but then Mandy must have stuff as well.

It came as a surprise for Ruth when a lawyer called Friedman rang. She supposed it was just another lawyer from Pink's team, working on the deal.

"I'm phoning on behalf of my client, Mr Robert Nieder, your husband. He is applying for a decree nisi. We need to discuss the details of your finances and your two homes. As you must realise such a discussion is vital, especially as Mr Nieder is entitled to his share of your combined wealth."

"I'm afraid he's not," Ruth said sharply. "Most of what we own has been bought with my money. I am very willing to share things he wants from our two properties but that's as far as it goes."

"Mrs Nieder, or shall I call you Mrs Farringdon?"

"Mrs Farringdon, please. I have never used my husband's name."

"All right, Mrs Farringdon. This is not a matter to discuss over the telephone. May I suggest we meet for a consultation. You may wish to bring your own solicitor."

"I'm afraid I don't really have time now as I'm in the middle of some very important negotiations. Besides, I haven't even got a solicitor for my private affairs. Do I really need one? Can't my husband and I deal with this on our own?"

"It's always best if both parties agree, then there would be no need for solicitors, but as we're talking about quite a portfolio of assets: flats, some in Leeds I gather, then there is your home in London plus a manor house in Sussex. That's why your husband feels it's better for you both to have proper representation."

"Can I call you back next week as I haven't got a minute to spare right now? I will try to find myself a solicitor. Tell my husband he just has to wait. He'll understand."

Mr Friedman was willing to wait a week and said he would convey her thoughts to his client.

Did this mean that Robert was going to be difficult, having hired a lawyer? She had not even thought of that. When she and Luke divorced, they sold their flat and shared the money. He kept most of the furniture, which they had been given by his parents and that was it. She and Robert could sell the house in Fulham; she had never been very fond of it. There would be enough with her share to buy a small *pied a terre* in London, preferably close to Café Vienna. She was not going to give up Hicks, of that she was absolutely certain. That house represented everything she had worked for.

Ruth was still shaking when Sirita said there was a lawyer called Brent on the phone.

"It's all lawyers today, Ruth," she said with a laugh. This time it was from a major law firm in the City. Mr Brent said he had been asked by Pink's management team to set up a meeting to present their initial offer.

"Can't it be done by phone or email?" Ruth asked.

"No, definitely not. What about next Wednesday afternoon here at our offices?"

"That suits neither me nor my team. Thursday morning next week at our offices." Ruth felt like a fox defending her territory, it had to be on her terms. Mr Brent suggested a neutral venue. In the end they agreed the meeting would take place at the office of Sir Rupert in the City – but on the date Ruth had suggested. A small victory, one she thought John Barley would approve of.

The days ran away. Ruth forgot about her own need for a solicitor as she spent her time talking both to her company solicitors as well as Pink's. The board held an EGM at which it was decided that Babylove would accept any offer over 18 million. It would mean a real windfall for each member of the board and especially for Sir Rupert. Ruth would also benefit: the simple bedsit in Fulham she had envisaged could be turned into a proper house. Robert could not complain either, as he had secured some shares during the years, maybe enough to install a fancy kitchen wherever he moved.

Thursday morning the following week Ruth took a taxi from Fulham to Finsbury Square, where Sir Rupert had his office. She had only visited him once and been impressed by the marble entrance hall, the exotic jungle of orchids on the reception desk, which was manned by a young woman who must have been selected for her good looks, Ruth thought, rather than her office skills.

This time there was a different girl at the reception desk and even more exotic blooms to admire. Business must be good, thought Ruth as she was asked to sit down on a beige suede sofa. Just as she started turning the pages of *Investors' Chronicle*, her team arrived. John Barley with a tall blond man she didn't know, David Hofmeister, and Dan Higgins from the board of Babylove and Andy from accounts. All of them were carrying heavy folders apart from John Barley, who had his usual brief case.

"While we're waiting, may I introduce my young colleague, Johnnie Lofgren?" John Barley pointed to the tall man with pride as if he were his father. "Johnnie has been most helpful. He comes from Goldman Sachs in New York, where he specialised in big-ticket mergers."

No one took much notice, however, as at that moment the blond receptionist came over in very high heels. "Gentlemen, Mrs Farringdon, Sir Rupert is ready to see you now. His office is on the fifth floor." The eyes of the men followed her tottering walk back to the desk.

Another beautiful girl met them as they reached the fifth floor. Was there an agency specialising in these girls, Ruth wondered. The team was led via a soft-carpeted corridor to a spacious room with a large Victorian partners' desk, a single file laid on its leather surface. There was a heavy-footed table lamp in polished brass but no chairs for visitors. Sir Rupert rose from his desk and welcomed them to his office and the girl re-appeared, asking everyone how they wanted their coffee. At a table near the window there was a basket full of croissants and chocolate brownies. As on a given signal the door opened again and the Pink's team appeared. Ruth had not seen Eric Parkin since their odd evening at the Goring Hotel. He rushed forward and kissed her on the cheek with unexpected warmth. He then introduced her to the men in his entourage including Mr Brent, who turned out to be much younger than she had thought. As usual, Ruth was the only woman in the room, apart from the secretary.

Once everyone had given their coffee preferences, Sir Rupert opened two folding doors which led into an oak-panelled boardroom. "Yes, I know it looks out of place in this modern building but when I left the merchant bank which I used to run I asked the new American owners if I could take my office and boardroom with me. They were only too pleased to get rid of the old junk as they called it. The panelling is early 18th century and it cost a small fortune to have it moved and replaced here, but the Americans gladly paid. I also got two paintings from my office; one is quite valuable but as they wanted an open-plan office with hardly any walls, they were happy to let the pictures go, so everyone was pleased." Sir Rupert invited everyone to sit down around the large table, where they found note pads and pens both embossed with Sir Rupert's name.

"Let's not waste time. I gather that Mr. Brent will speak for Pink's." Sir Rupert pressed a button in front of him and suddenly one of the panels disappeared to reveal a white screen.

Mr Brent opened his laptop and after a few keystrokes the screen was filled with not only Pink's logo but also Babylove's love knot in blue and pink. "Let me show you how we see the future for the merged company," said Mr Brent as tables and diagrams kept appearing on the screen. Ruth found it difficult to follow Mr Brent's rasping voice. She wished she had been given all this information on paper, preferably beforehand.

His presentation took some twenty minutes, by which time everyone looked dazed. "I have copies here of my presentation for all of you. If you have any questions, please feel free."

David Hofmeister was first to speak. "We have now seen what the advantages of the merger would be for Pink's. As a board member of Babylove I would quite like to hear how the merger would benefit Babylove." Ruth wanted to pat him on the back. David was right, the whole presentation was seen through Pink's eyes.

For a moment there was silence before Mr Brent stood up again. He looked lost without his laptop to guide him.

"First of all, Babylove will be part of a larger organisation with all the benefits that entails. Nor will there be any further costly competition between the two; that is a saving in itself. We have calculated that Babylove can cut half of its delivery staff, and at least three staff from the administrative office. The cost of distribution and logistics could fall by some thirty percent as Babylove can give up their storage facilities in Reading. Pink's have depot space for both. We're talking enormous savings, all in all cuts worth a quarter of a million per annum. Add to that marketing costs which will be shared. We will also have a wider range of products, of which some could be produced at Pink's factories, others at Babylove. In this way we can spend more on research and find new products for our customers. We note that Babylove has already started with a new line of toiletries for adults such as soaps and bath products. This would fit in very well with Pink's wares – and, not to forget, we have our contract with the supermarket and I am sure we can expand and offer similar advantages to other supermarket chains. All in all, in monetary terms Babylove would not only get a decent offer for its shares, it would also be able to expand and cut production costs by at least two million per annum. Add to that all the other benefits and all I can say is that we have a perfect fit."

"And what about the management structure?" David Hofmeister was not giving up.

Now it was Eric Parkin's turn to speak. "I've already an agreement with Ruth that we should share the post of managing director for the first six months and then after that, just as I was willing to step aside if Babylove had taken us over, I'm sure she is willing to do the same. I suggest that Ruth takes over the role as director for corporate development and also the chairmanship of Babylove Foundation. Apart from that I see no real changes in the management structure for the time being. Sir Rupert has very kindly offered to remain as chairman of the new board. During the first six months after the merger, there will be negotiations about changes on the board. Ruth is of course offered a seat on the board as director of corporate development."

Ruth could hardly breathe. Which company would have to decimate its staff? Everything seemed planned to the finest detail. Now it seemed to be only a question of the price. There were a few more questions, mostly from Ruth's team regarding legal niceties. Suddenly Sir Rupert stood up and said that he had reserved a table at a restaurant nearby, which had a private room, "so useful for negotiations. Everything runs more smoothly after a glass of wine." With a sigh everyone stood up gathering their pads and pencils.

Chapter 35

The restaurant was only a few minutes' walk from Sir Rupert's office. It was clear to everyone from the obsequious bowing from the *maitre d'* that Sir Rupert was a regular. He led the assembled group up a flight of stairs to a light-infused dining room with a large picture window overlooking the square. The sun had broken through the clouds and suddenly Ruth felt a sharp sting of joy. Everything was going to get better. She would eventually get fewer responsibilities, enjoy greater involvement with the Babylove Foundation and get more money and, best of all, more time to spend with Robert at Hicks. It took two seconds before she realised there was no Robert to spend time with. The thought hit her so hard that she felt tears filling her eyes.

"Everything all right Ruth?" asked Sir Rupert who had placed her by his side. Paternally he patted her hand which rested on the table. "Fine," she whispered while feeling quite faint. The voices around her were loud and excited. It was difficult for her to make any sense of the noise. Sir Rupert lifted his glass of wine and looked at Ruth.

"This is an important day in the annals of Babylove and I think we should all lift our glasses to Ruth Farringdon, without whom this company would not exist today."

"Hear, hear," mumbled the people around the table.

"This must be like selling your child," continued Sir Rupert and glanced at Ruth with a benign smile, "but I can assure you that your child will be in good hands and you'll be there to see it grow and mature."

The fine Bordeaux, chosen by Sir Rupert, went straight to Ruth's head and she put the glass down and gulped some ice-cold water. She had no appetite and asked for a simple Caesar salad while the men all picked the dish of the day, a pheasant casserole. The two teams did not speak to each other, which seemed odd to Ruth. Why else were they here?

Sir Rupert waved away the bill with a swift gesture and then suggested that coffee was better served at his office where they could continue their discussion. Ruth stood up asking for the ladies' cloakroom – she needed a few minutes to herself, still feeling giddy after that single gulp of wine. All the men stood up as she left the room. Again, she hated the fact that she was the only woman.

The ladies' room was downstairs. She washed her face with cold water over the marble basin with its golden taps and immediately felt better. Her freshly applied red lipstick made her look less ashen; with her armoury in place, she returned to the dining room upstairs. The men had gathered their briefcases and coats and Sir Rupert was tapping his feet as she collected hers.

Back in the boardroom Mr Brent opened his laptop again and after serving up more diagrams and pie charts showing the financial structure of Babylove and Pink's, he finally presented the offer.

"Before proper due diligence has been done, we are prepared to pay fifteen million pounds for Babylove in return for a hundred percent of Babylove's shares, the majority of shares at present held by trustees of Watson & Rubens, The Progrow investment fund plus smaller parcels held by Mrs Farringdon, Sir Rupert, other members of Babylove board. These shares will be exchanged for shares in Pink's. We will pay half in cash and the other half in shares. We hope that within a year or two we can start to plan for a full listing for the merged company."

There was absolute silence. John Barley had already told Ruth that she should not accept less than twenty million, eighteen at the least and here was an offer of just fifteen.

Ruth stood up. "This is an unacceptable offer and on behalf of the management and the board I reject it." Everyone looked at Ruth, who noticed a just perceptible nod from John Barley. No one else said anything and the silence was only interrupted by Sir Rupert tapping his gold pen against his pad.

"We've heard what Mrs Farringdon has said and I suggest that Mr Parkin and his team think again. We should meet here in a week's time in the hope that the offer can be improved. Gentlemen, thank you for today." With that Sir Rupert stood up and opened the double doors that led to his office and invited the teams to leave but indicated that Ruth should stay.

Ruth looked at Sir Rupert and said, "Tell me, what does this mean? I thought there was a figure more or less agreed on. That's what I understood from John Barley."

"It's all part of the game. Next week they will increase their offer, don't worry. Just relax." He patted her shoulder gently. "If I may say so, Ruth, you look a bit under the weather. Can't you take some days off, spend some time down at Hicks in peace and quiet?"

"Thank you, yes, I do feel a bit run down. I might just follow your advice."

In the taxi back to Fulham Ruth wondered who had paid for the expensive lunch. It certainly was not Sir Rupert, who was well-known for his parsimony.

* * *

There was to be one week before negotiations were to start again. No doubt the bankers and lawyers would go through budgets and available accounts once more and see if there was any room for manoeuvre. It also gave Ruth breathing space. There was still no word from Robert but there was a further call from his lawyer asking if she had found a lawyer of her own. She had pushed that task further down the agenda in some vague hope that it would not be necessary. She still imagined Robert would wake up realising it was all a mistake.

She noticed when she came home one evening that he had taken all his papers and his office computer. Was he now working from Mandy's flat? He had left no note but there was a slight change in the air. Maybe it was just a hint of his aftershave? It bothered Ruth that he still had the keys to the Fulham house and felt he could walk in and take what he liked, when he liked. Should she change the lock? No, that seemed too drastic.

She didn't want to ask if any of the board members could recommend a lawyer specialising in divorce, it was too personal. Nor did she have any friends to ask. Then she remembered Dick Callander. He was, after all, a lawyer in a biggish firm – and he might also have heard something from Robert as he was Dick's financial adviser. That evening, after two glasses of wine and a half-eaten microwaved lasagne, she phoned Dick. It was a cheerful Marcia who answered.

"How lovely to hear from you. We were just talking about you, wondering if you were away on some exotic holiday. Weren't you planning a Nile cruise? I know Dick's not been able to get in touch with Robert and I think he's getting a bit worried. Has Robert gone off somewhere? I can't remember the name of the country they have invested in, wasn't it Lithuania?"

"That's one of the reasons why I'm phoning. I've not seen or heard from Robert either for some time." Marcia interrupted her with a voice full of worry.

"But Ruth, that's horrible. Have you been in touch with the police? What could have happened? Oh, you must be so worried."

"It's a bit more complicated than that. He's left me." Just saying the words thickened her voice.

"Left you, no, it can't be. Are you sure? I can't believe it. I always looked upon you two as an ideal couple."

"So did I." There was a short pause for Ruth to gather her thoughts, should she mention Mandy? "But I was wrong. Do you remember Mandy, who spent Christmas with us?"

"Yes, of course I do. Sweet, rather shy girl, didn't say a lot. Wasn't she an old school friend of Robert's?"

"He's left me for her." Ruth could not decide if the sound she heard from Marcia was a derisive snort or a laugh.

"I don't believe it. Are you sure?"

"She's pregnant and the baby is his. He wants that baby more than he wants me."

"Are you absolutely sure?"

"And that's why I'm phoning. Robert has got himself a divorce lawyer, who's told me that I need one, too. I don't know anyone I can turn to and then I thought about Dick."

"But Dick's a commercial lawyer. No, wait a minute, his cousin is a divorce lawyer and is meant to be quite a good one. He dealt with one of those Russian oligarchs, so if he's good enough for one of them, he must be very good. Just wait a minute, I'll get Dick to speak to you. I've only met the cousin on social occasions. He seems a very decent man and I like his wife, that's a good sign," said Marcia with a short laugh. Ruth could hear how Marcia called Dick to the telephone and then there was a minute or two of hushed conversation before she finally heard Dick's voice.

"I can't believe what Marcia's just told me. Is it true? Poor Ruth, this must've come as a great shock. Did you have any idea?"

"No, I still can't believe it, Dick. I need your help."

"Of course, my dear. I'll get in touch with my cousin. His name is Archie Arnold. He's a very good lawyer specialising in family matters. You can trust him completely. He'll make sure you get the best advice possible. I'll phone him tomorrow and ask him to contact you directly. Do you want him to phone you at work or at home? On your mobile, all right, I'll tell him. I can't tell you how sad we both are. Must be terrible for you. I just can't understand it, Robert always appeared to me to be such a well-balanced man – and so deeply fond of you. I've also been trying to get hold of him as I haven't heard anything about our hotel investment. A friend of mine, who is in the know, said that the Baltic countries are like the Wild West, so I need to be reassured. But here I am talking about my worries. First of all, we must sort you out."

Marcia came back on the line and asked if Ruth would like to come down for the weekend. "We have, as you know, plenty of space and it would be lovely to see you. I can't imagine you want to be alone at Hicks. Come down on Friday night, no, I won't take no for an answer."

Ruth acquiesced, pleased not to have to face another weekend alone but said she would be down on Saturday at teatime. Without Robert she now had to run all errands on her own.

The next day she received a phone call from Archie Arnold and Ruth felt relieved that she now had a name to give to Robert's lawyer. She fixed an appointment with Mr Arnold at his offices in Bloomsbury for the following week – after the meeting with the Pinks' negotiating team. She could not deal with two such important changes in her life at the same time, she explained to Mr Arnold. He said he understood perfectly well and added, "the outcome of that negotiation will of course have an impact on the maintenance you will have to pay your husband."

"Maintenance? What do you mean, maintenance? I don't intend to pay my husband any money at all. He left me, not the other way around."

There was a pause, then Mr Arnold cleared his throat.

"Mrs Farringdon, I'm afraid that there will be a question of maintenance as you're the main breadwinner. But let's discuss all that when we meet. I'd be grateful if you could bring your bank statements to our meeting and also a list of your other assets like houses, flats etc. I gather from Paul, my cousin, that your husband is a self-employed financial adviser. He must have copies of his tax statements as well as yours, so please could you also bring those."

Ruth was shocked. She had hoped for a civilised separation. He had his own income, she had hers so what was there to quibble about? She had paid for the properties, all of them and that included the student flats in Leeds, which they had bought to let. It had never occurred to her to make sure that the properties were put in her name. She had left all the investment decisions to Robert. She had trusted him completely, but now she wondered. Then she realised she could not check the documents as he had taken all the files with him.

Ruth's heart started to beat faster. She could not think about it now. She had to concentrate on the business.

Chapter 36

The next meeting with the team from Pink's took place the following Friday. It had not been a happy week for Ruth. She'd had a rather stern note from Robert's lawyer stating that he had not received the name yet of her solicitor, "and my client stresses that it is urgent that this matter is dealt with as quickly as possible." Ruth had completely forgotten her phone call with Archie Arnold, in spite of getting a very polite note from his secretary reminding her of the appointment they had agreed on. She asked Sirita to contact Henry Friedman, Robert's lawyer, to give all the details as she already felt harassed by him and did not want to speak to him.

During the week after the inconclusive meeting with Pink's, Ruth had spent quite some time with her board especially with Andrew Miskin and David Hofmeister, both with experience in mergers and acquisitions. They had agreed that eighteen million pounds was the absolute minimum they could accept. "Just the properties, the factory, the offices and the warehouse depot are worth at least ten and add to that the acres behind the factory, they would be worth quite something with building permission. Then there's the good-will as well as the cash in the bank. Hold out for twenty," was the advice from Andrew Miskin.

They met again at Sir Rupert's offices and the girl at the reception remained as unsmiling as on their last visit. Her face seemed frozen. It made Ruth feel uncomfortable, as if the girl already knew something about the outcome of the meeting. David Hofmeister led Ruth to the lift and put his hand on her arm. He must have felt her discomfort.

The Pink's team was already there, ready with their coffee cups as Sir Rupert hurried Ruth and her colleagues in. Her team ignored the coffee table and went straight into the panelled boardroom. There was no polite chitchat before they all sat down on opposite sides of the large table with Sir Rupert alone at the head of it.

Mr Brent nodded, looking at Eric Parkin before he stood up.

"Our team has considered this deal with utmost care and we find that there's no way we can increase our initial offer of fifteen million. We are the ones taking a risk. You must admit that Babylove is a young company without much of a track record and with a very narrow product range."

Ruth swallowed and looked at David Hofmeister and also shot a glance at John Barley. Both were stony-faced. John Barley, in a rather sober suit today, looked at his open laptop and very slowly stood up.

"Gentlemen, if this is your final offer, I have nothing more to say, nor does the board of Babylove." He closed his laptop as if to stress that the discussion was equally closed.

There was a minute of silence and then Eric Parkin said that they might be willing to increase the offer with a further half a million but that was as far they were willing to go.

John Barley looked at David Hofmeister who shook his head. "The minimum we could even consider accepting is eighteen million pounds."

Sir Rupert cleared his throat. "Gentlemen, would it not be a good idea if Mr Parkin and his team and Mr Barley used my outer office for some privacy in order to discuss the level below which Babylove will not accept an offer? Let's say we meet back here in ten minutes' time." He looked at Ruth. "And that will give Ruth and her other colleagues time to have a cup of coffee."

The Pink's team and John Barley stood up and left, leaving Ruth and Sir Rupert alone to talk. "Do you think they will agree?"

"I really hope so. It's a bloody good deal for them at any price. But somehow, I sense that they have got cold feet. I can't put my finger on it, but there is something there that has changed. Have you spoken to Mr Barley?"

"Well, we've had one or two telephone discussions and I somehow get the feeling that he's lost interest in Babylove. I thought it was just the indecision that got to him, but now I'm not sure. Would you be very upset, Rupert, if this deal did not go through?"

Sir Rupert smiled. "No, Ruth, I wouldn't. In my banking career I've seen so many good deals fall by the wayside and some really rather bad ones go through – leaving the shareholders to pick up the pieces afterwards. Of course, I would love to be chairman of an enlarged Babylove, whatever the new name would be, but not at this price. What about you Ruth?"

"I was happy as it was. I feel strongly that Babylove has a future without Pink's. I only got interested when we discussed merging with Pink's because Eric Parkin wanted out, then things changed and suddenly they want to take us over. The only thing that worries me is what the rest of our board will say. And how the media will react, they've been on our tail ever since the first rumours started."

"Dear Ruth, don't you worry about the media. They'll write whatever they feel like, usually rubbish, and then the next day it'll be forgotten. The financial journalists today behave like vultures circling over a dying body, not caring one hoot whether they tell the truth or not as long as next day there is something with their by-line in the paper. They have no idea how a company, or a bank for that matter, works. I remember the good old days when you could have a discussion with a journalist and brief him about deals and trust him or her not to divulge plans before they became official. And they trusted you, because you talked to them directly, not via some polished PR expert. And as for the board, I shouldn't worry. Anyway, who knows, they might up their bid."

Sir Rupert put his large hand on Ruth's and smiled, but she noted that the smile did not quite reach his eyes. "So, what about that cup of coffee, my dear?"

At that moment the double doors to the boardroom opened and John Barley and Mr Brent walked in followed by the rest of the Pink's team.

It was Eric Parkin who spoke. "We have decided not to increase our offer. We do not share your view that Babylove is worth at least eighteen million pounds and therefore we withdraw our offer unless you can meet us at fifteen and a half million."

This time it was Sir Rupert, who stood up, almost a head taller than Eric Parkin. He looked at him as if his old school chum had been caught red-handed cheating at an exam.

"In that case, there is nothing more to say. I now declare this meeting closed."

Ruth said goodbye to Sir Rupert, who seemed remarkably happy at the outcome.

"Never trusted that man. I did ask around and it seems Parkin was never liked at school. He was seen as a buffoon by those in his house."

Together with David Hofmeister and Andrew Miskin, she walked down the corridor to the lift. There, waiting for her, was John Barley. He also touched her hand as if in commiseration. "There will be a new suitor along soon enough, or maybe there'll be someone *you* might want to take over. Johnnie Lofgren and I will keep our eyes peeled."

It was a long journey back to Babylove's office and neither David nor Andrew had a word to say.

The weekend at the Callanders turned out to be more difficult than Ruth had anticipated. They could not have been nicer and maybe that's what made it so hard. Dick hardly mentioned Robert, maybe out of embarrassment, but he did say that he had heard from him and that Robert was investigating some claims that the Lithuania hotel business might be some kind of a scam.

Marcia fluttered around Ruth all weekend as though she were a delicate invalid. Some neighbours were invited for Saturday dinner and the discussion over another overcooked roast flowed like treacle. The Callanders had obviously told their neighbours that Ruth had just been deserted by her husband for a younger woman. The rather dumpy wife of the neighbour watched her husband like a hawk, fearing that it might be contagious.

However, it gave Ruth a welcome break from the empty house in Fulham. She still had not plucked up the courage to go to Hicks. It was too full of memories of the last night with Robert, not to speak of all the love they had lavished on their home. She had tried to explain to Mrs McCleeney that they were spending some time abroad and not to worry but to keep on cleaning and to take her money from the pot, which was there for essentials. Mrs McCleeney had harrumphed in her usual manner but not asked any questions.

On Monday morning Ruth took a cab from the house in Fulham straight to Archie Arnold's office near Bloomsbury Square. The building did not look impressive and she felt nervous as she stepped into the hallway. No fancy reception area, just a simple brass plaque on the wall. He obviously did not work with a large firm as the plaque only gave his name. There was no lift so she walked up to the first floor where there was a reception desk behind a glass door. She entered and found herself in a modern office with walls in a muted colour showing off some abstract paintings and some rather expensive-looking leather furniture in the waiting area.

"Mr Arnold is expecting you. Please let me take you to his office," said a welcoming middle-aged woman with clothes matching the taupe walls. She led Ruth to another staircase which led up to a mezzanine with two doors. One was open and a large man with a mop of grey hair stood in the doorframe.

"Mrs Farringdon, I'm Archie Arnold. Do come in. Do you want some tea or coffee? Or I can even offer you a glass of dry sherry. I know it's early but it tends to relax clients at their first visit." His smile made Ruth feel at ease and she asked for a coffee, not because she wanted one, but because she needed the distraction.

His office was large with a mahogany desk with a worn leather top and an old-fashioned swivel chair. In front of the desk were two tweed-covered chairs. He pointed to one of them as he asked his secretary to get two coffees. "Milk and sugar?" he asked and Ruth nodded.

There were no signs of his personal taste, no photographs on the desk or the walls only some insignificant watercolours in heavy gilt frames. Yes, she could see that he was related to Dick Callander.

"It's always a sad time when a marriage breaks down. Our role is to make sure that it is done without harm to your relationship. May I ask how you and your husband are approaching this divorce? I mean, have you in principle agreed on how your assets should be divided?"

Ruth put down her cup with the sweet coffee, she felt she had to take a spoon of sugar having agreed to it, if even only with a nod.

"Tell me a bit about your financial affairs, put me in the picture as far as you can," Mr Arnold smiled benignly.

Her voice thickened and she coughed in order to collect herself. "Robert, my husband, has always looked after our affairs. He is an independent financial adviser and an accountant by profession. During the years we've been married I have always been the main breadwinner. We agreed early on that, as I earned so much more than he did, he should try to make a career as a self-employed financial consultant. I'm afraid I have no idea how much he earns but I guess it can't be all that much as he only has a few clients. I have a feeling that most of his time is spent looking after our assets, which consists of three student flats in Leeds, and a couple in Manchester. We're not talking high-end properties here. They are all let and without mortgages but I have no idea what they are worth. You have to get that information from my husband via his lawyer. We have a house in Fulham worth just over 2.2 million and our house in the country, Hicks Manor is worth probably quite a bit more than that. I'm sorry but I really have no idea. I noticed the other day that he's moved all his files away from his office in our London home so you'll have to get the information from his lawyer. Our shared bank account is more or less empty as my husband has made a recent investment in Lithuania and my own bank account is about to be emptied as I am investing in a project in Brighton, in which my husband is also interested."

"Well, until we have all the information there is very little we can do at the moment. Have you and your husband made provisions for pensions? Oh, I see, you have a company pension through Babylove, but what about your husband? Not as far as you know. Well, that must be taken into consideration and also some form of either an outright payment or maintenance as you are, and have been for many years, the main breadwinner."

"What do you mean? How can I be forced to pay him when he has his own income?"

Ruth felt the blood rushing to her cheeks and she wanted to scream. She was *not* going to support her errant husband and some new family that he intended to start with that woman.

"He's talking about re-marrying. Surely, I cannot be asked to pay for him to support his new wife, that's mad."

Archie Arnold leant forward, his jowls shaking slightly as he looked at Ruth.

"You are *not* paying for him, nor for his new partner. You said he gave up his job in order to assist you in your demanding role as managing director of a fast-growing company, and you have indeed been very successful. Yes, I do read the business pages, and he has the right to share some of that success as your partner. While you've been working, he has looked after your financial assets…"

"Whose lawyer are you, his or mine?" Ruth's smile had turned into a scowl and she banged her spoon against the saucer.

"Of course, I represent your interests Mrs Farringdon, but I don't want you to think that it's just a question of you keeping all the assets. You must prepare yourself for letting some of your flats and houses go, either to be sold or handed over to Mr Farringdon."

"He is actually Mr Nieder, N-I-E-D-E-R. Farringdon is my first husband's name."

"Oh, I see. So, you have been through a divorce before?"

"Yes, and there was no question of me having to pay for my first husband."

"But maybe the situation was different, maybe more evenly balanced when it came to earnings and assets?"

Ruth nodded. She did not really want to speak about Luke, nor was she discussing entering into a business deal with both her past and present husband. She thought that would confuse the gentle Mr Arnold too much.

After discussing a timetable and fee structure, Archie Arnold stood up and again assured Ruth that he had her best interests in mind. "But I can't really make any plans until I have access to the full information about your combined assets and your respective earnings. No doubt your husband's lawyer will get in touch with me to provide me with that as soon as possible. I gather that Mr Nieder is in a hurry because of the impending…"

Ruth coughed and cut him short.

"We all want this over and done with as soon as possible. At present I'm very busy with some important negotiations which concern the future of my company."

He took her hand, just for a second and, as if on a secret command, his secretary turned up at the door and gave Ruth a very professional smile.

"Let me show you out. It's such an old building with many nooks and crannies," she said as she led Ruth down the short staircase. Ruth wondered how many heartbroken, soon-to-be-divorced people she had smiled at during her career. There was no wedding ring on her finger, obviously she had seen and heard too much of failed marriages, Ruth thought as she stepped out into the damp morning air.

Chapter 37

Later that afternoon, Sirita told her that Robert was on the line. "Do you want to take the call?" For a moment Ruth couldn't think clearly, thoughts whirled in her head. Was he finally coming to his senses? Had Mandy had an abortion, would the nightmare be over and life return to normal again?

"Yes, yes, put him on," she said and felt positive for the first time in weeks.

"Ruthie?"

"Robert, darling, so good to hear from you." Her voice was soft. "Everyone has been asking about you. Where are you and how are you getting on? There are so many questions. And we must discuss the Brighton project. Has Luke been in touch? I gave him your mobile number."

"Ruth, as things are standing now, there's no way I can afford the Brighton project. You go ahead with Luke if you want to. The reason I'm phoning is because, as you know, I'm staying at this small hotel in London but in order to save money I'm going to move in with Mandy soon. Maybe next week. There are some things I need though. I thought we could meet up this weekend at Hicks and go through the things that I might take and…"

Ruth felt winded but took a deep breath.

"No, there's no way we're going to start divvying up our possessions. And I don't really want you at Hicks without me. I can see that we might have to sell the house in Fulham and split the proceeds but I want nothing done before we've talked it all through with our lawyers. My lawyer has been in touch with yours today in order to get access to our financial files, bank statements and a list of all our assets. I see you've taken all the files with you. Until we have reached an agreement with the help of our lawyers, nothing is taken from Hicks or Fulham except purely personal belongings, is that perfectly clear?"

"There's no reason to be so aggressive. All I want is some stuff from the kitchen and my outdoor gear and, if you don't mind, my golf clubs, that's all."

"So you'll have time to play golf now, do you? If I were you, I'd start sorting out your affairs first. I gather from Dick Callander that he's very worried about the Lithuanian project. How's that coming on?"

"Too early to say, but that's another reason why I don't want to invest in Brighton anymore. What has Dick said exactly?"

"He's heard rumours that the Lithuanian project was a scam, run by financial crooks and that there was a risk of losing all the money of his that you've invested in the project. This can't be true. Or is it?"

"I've been to Lithuania trying to sort it out. It'll take time."

"You took the money from our joint account. How much are we talking about?"

"I can't quite remember just now. I'll give you all the figures with the rest of the financial statements."

"I sincerely hope you don't make any more transfers from our account until we have settled our affairs. Can I have your word on that?"

"Yes, you can. I'm using my own private account but, with the hotel bills, my resources are coming to an end. I'm waiting for some money from Paul Gallagher, for work done. Then there's some fees from some of his colleagues as well, but it's a bit tight at the moment, so I would be grateful if you could help me by letting me have a couple of thousand pounds on account until we split our assets."

"Can't the lovely Miss Mandy sub you?"

"Ruth, let's be sensible about this. I don't want us to fight. We are, after all, grown-ups."

His words hit her and Ruth could hear her own whiny voice, so full of bitterness. How could Robert ever come back to her, if she treated him in this way. She had to be grown-up, as he said.

"All right, Robert, I'll transfer two thousand pounds to your private account today. I'm sorry I snapped. It's been a hellish few weeks for me with this planned merger. Sometimes I don't know if I'm coming or going. And I miss your advice, you know someone I can talk to and trust."

"Ruthie, you know that I'll always be there for you" – there was a short pause – "with any kind of advice you might need. And thanks for the money. I'll wait with picking up the golf clubs. You're probably right, I won't have time to play in the near future anyway. Bye-bye."

"Bye-bye darling," she whispered but by the time she got to "darling" he had already put down the phone.

She called Sirita who rushed in to hear what Ruth wanted.

"Sirita, is there a way you can find out where Robert's call came from?"

"Simple," said Sirita with a smile. Two minutes later she was back in Ruth's office.

"Yes, here's the number and I even googled the prefix 01689. It's a number in Orpington in Kent. I know it's not the number for Hicks."

Ruth gripped the rim of her desk so hard that her knuckles turned white. A small hotel, he'd said. Yet another lie. He was with her. Mandy.

* * *

Andrew Miskin was a successful management consultant and had helped Ruth with advice for several years. She appreciated his calm demeanour and he seemed to enjoy dealing with a business so far removed from his other clients, all in hi-tech. He had a young family, as he had married late, and maybe having become a father in his fifties, he was interested in everything dealing with children. Andrew had impressed Ruth when he had discussed the advantages of the new rubberised plastic for their Babylove dummies. "It doesn't crack no matter how hard the baby sucks," he told her as they discussed the new range of dummies and it was Andrew who suggested that they should attach a thin plastic chain with a clip at the end, so that the dummy could be fastened to a blanket or a piece of clothing. "I don't know how many times I've picked up the dummy from the floor after Rosie's spat it out."

She always had time for Andrew. Now he wanted to see her and she welcomed his visit after her disappointing call from Robert.

"Coffee?" Ruth gestured for him to sit down in her pink visitor's chair. Andrew sat down looking more solemn than she had ever seen him before. Something must be wrong was her first thought. His family?

"Ruth, I've come to speak about Babylove. You know how much I love this company. My two little daughters have literally grown up with Babylove."

"How are the girls? I'm so fond of them both, such lovely and lively girls." She tried hard to remember the name of Rosie's younger sister, something romantic, but her mind wouldn't work.

"Fine, Ruth, thank you. But coming back to Babylove. I've had a chat with John Barley and also that young assistant of his, Johnnie something, and they are determined that in order to make Babylove grow we must either buy a company or merge with a larger one in order to benefit from a wider market place. We also need a larger range of products."

"But we are extending the range. The laboratory is working hard on soaps and a few other toiletries. You know that and I do keep the board informed."

"I've also spoken to the board and they agree with John Barley."

"You've spoken to the board? Without my knowledge?" Ruth's voice sounded shrill. "Why, tell me, why?"

"Well, we know you're under stress due to some of your personal problems. I don't want to pry into your private life, but we all think that the negotiations with Pink's could've been handled better."

"But you were with me, you were there all the time. What could we have done better?" Ruth stressed the word "we".

"We should've allowed more room for negotiations. You slammed the door on them and I don't think they'll be back."

"You told me to hold out for twenty million pounds, that's what you said. Remember? So that's why I wouldn't accept an offer of fifteen and a half million. I listened to your advice."

This was not a discussion she wanted, nor had the energy for. If the door was closed, why bring it up now? Something was not right. She looked at Andrew, his strong face with just enough grey hair to look dignified rather than old. His face was tanned, she knew he spent two weeks every winter skiing and always proudly showed photos of his two daughters who seemed more stable on skis than on their young legs.

"Ruth, we have to look at this coldly, without emotion. I know that you look at Babylove as your own baby and, of course, it is. You have built up a well-run and profitable company from next to nothing. That takes a special kind of management ability, but you need quite a different one to bring a company to the next level."

Andrew smiled at her, but it was not a gentle smile. It was one warning her that the discussion would turn less friendly.

"I know you're under stress, no doubt due to problems at home." Ruth put up her hands to stop him.

"You know nothing about my private life, and even so, why should that interfere with my work?"

"Well, to be honest Ruth, it already has. We've all noticed how distracted you have been and sometimes we've not been able to get hold of you, which is vital in times of negotiations. And when you're here, you're not always here, if you see what I mean." That sickly smile was there again.

"No Andrew, I'm afraid I don't. I have listened to you and John Barley and taken your advice all along and now, when the outcome is not what you want, you blame it on me and my so-called personal problems. I'm afraid I think it's *you* who's not very professional."

"Think what you like, Ruth, but when I contacted the board there was a suggestion that we should have an extra board meeting in light of these latest developments. I think we have to go back to Pink's and see if we can come to some conclusion. If not, maybe we should speak to Wonderdrug. According to John Barley they've been sniffing around looking for a company to buy in exactly our sector. The baby market is growing fast and they want a stronger presence in the UK."

"Is that the way you feel about the future of Babylove? Are you really proposing a gunshot marriage with an American company, famous for breaking their promises as soon as they have the company in their clutches? You do realise they'll sack half of the staff here?" She broke off and allowed herself a smile. "And they'll probably kick you off the board as well."

"I can see that you're not in the mood for a discussion at the moment," was his curt reply as he stood up and gathered his papers, stuffing them unceremoniously into his briefcase. "I'll have another chat with John Barley, that is if you don't mind, and I'll also prepare a paper for the meeting. We should all meet as soon as possible."

And with that he left the room without even saying goodbye.

Chapter 38

Two days later Ruth had a call from her lawyer, Archie Arnold. "I have just received the financial statements from your husband. I'm having a meeting with his lawyer tomorrow to see what we can do in order to speed things up. This is a request from your husband and I think we should oblige, don't you, Mrs Farringdon?"

"By all means," she answered but she raged inside. She had other worries now, with the extraordinary board meeting coming up. John Barley had been at her as well, saying that he agreed with Andrew Miskin about approaching Pink's again. She had no one to turn to, she was so used to discussing any problems at work with Robert. He always managed to calm her down, suggest a solution. Luke had telephoned several times hoping to finalise plans for the Brighton project, but she had stalled him. At one moment she had almost felt tempted to tell him about Robert and also about the happenings at Babylove, but Ruth remembered how her mother had reacted when she had told her, and, anyway, it seemed as if everyone knew about her and Robert without her having said a word.

"I hope we can come to some agreement very soon and I suggest we apply for the decree nisi as soon as possible," said Archie Arnold.

"But we haven't come to an agreement at all," Ruth snapped, which she immediately regretted. He was after all on her side.

"Mrs Farringdon, this is just to save time. It would help to have an agreement if it comes to court." He spoke to her so calmly, paternally that she cooled down. Of course, he was right.

As soon as she had put the phone down, Sirita called to say there had been a call from Ian Shield, the director of the Babylove Foundation. Ruth phoned him back.

"Ruth, I've just had a call from Andrew Miskin and I'm a bit worried about this meeting. Before I reply to his report, I'd like your view."

"What are you talking about? Which report?" She almost screamed at Ian.

"You've not seen the report? That's odd. I'll scan it and send it over immediately. Lucky I phoned, isn't it? Anyway, he suggests that you should be made director of the Foundation – the man has not even had the courtesy to discuss it with me. After all, I am the director of the Foundation," he added with both anger and hurt in his voice. "Then he suggests that you should become some sort of Babylove Ambassador, whatever that means."

"But who is going to run the company?" Ruth sounded incredulous but somehow she knew the answer.

"Sir Rupert Cherlow, our beloved Chairman," said Ian, and his contempt gave an icy ring to his words.

"I can't believe it," said Ruth, close to a laugh. "I thought you'd say Andrew or maybe even John Barley."

Ten minutes later she had printed out the report. It said above the heading that it had been circulated to the whole board. She looked again at her computer. There was nothing there from Andrew. Her cheeks reddened with anger. What was he up to? She called him and after a hardly civil "hello" asked him what the hell he meant by not including her in the distribution of the report.

"I asked my secretary to send it to the whole board," was his reply. "I'll speak to her and come back to you."

A few moments later he phoned again. "I'm terribly sorry, it's my secretary's fault. Usually, your secretary sends out all the papers before a board meeting and she had just used your circulation list, which does not include you. So sorry, just a simple mistake. Have you got a copy or should I send you one now?"

"Don't bother, Ian Shield has sent me one already. I'll come back to you once I have had time to read it. And I'll be there for the meeting – of that you can be sure."

She looked at the report again and then at the distribution list. He was right, her name was not on it but Sirita's was. She always included her own name on whatever board document she sent for her own computer files. Yet Sirita had not received a copy of the report either. Ruth felt there was no one she could trust.

Then Ruth remembered her call from Archie Arnold. He had told her that he had received the financial statements from her husband. The flats in Leeds and Manchester had been mortgaged – this had happened quite recently as well as the house in Sussex. Their joint bank account was more or less empty, the two thousand pounds she had remitted to Robert had gone from her private account to his personal account.

She phoned her bank and after the usual security questions she was told that Mr Robert Nieder had taken out a loan and used the properties as guarantee for it.

"The properties are after all in his name, Mrs Farringdon, and he has always looked after your joint affairs. We didn't want to trouble you. He did the same when you bought your Sussex property, used the student flats as security for the loan – now repaid, of course."

She was livid and phoned Robert who calmly explained that he needed the money to sort out the Lithuanian affair. Part of the money went to lawyers, but the majority had gone to repay Dick Callander, who had threatened to sue Robert over the mismanagement of the hotel project. "You'll get it all back, I promise, but just now I'm in a fix. I've got the best lawyers in town to deal with the Lithuanians and I'm sure to have the money back quite soon."

Ruth froze. What could she say? And now she had to deal with Andrew's machinations, it was just too much. She put her elbows on her desk with a deep sigh. Everything seemed to be against her.

That night she drank half a bottle of wine on an empty stomach. She had lost her appetite. The pre-cooked meals she bought all tasted the same whatever she chose. There was never anything on the television she wanted to see, and this night was no exception. She had brought the report home to go through again but reading it only made her even angrier. In it, Andrew stated that an opportunity had been missed to merge with Pink's and reiterated all the advantages a merger would have brought. He did not say straight out that Ruth was responsible for the collapsed deal, nor did he mention his own supporting role in the negotiations. He also made suggestions that "due to personal reasons", Ruth Farringdon should be relieved of her present duties for the time being and that Sir Rupert Cherlow was willing to step in temporarily. She threw the report back into her briefcase and went upstairs in search of a sleeping pill. She swallowed two with the rest of the wine, now warm and with a sour taste. Sleep came late and Ruth woke up at dawn with a swollen tongue and a hammering headache.

* * *

"Darling Ruthie, how lovely to see you. You look as great as ever." Ruth looked at Luke across the table and knew that even he must have realised that his lie was obvious. That morning she had looked in the mirror and seen her sunken face. Her skin tone was almost grey and under her red-rimmed eyes were dark shadows. No, she was not looking great, but she appreciated his lie.

They were sitting in a small Italian bistro in Fulham. He'd phoned and asked if they could meet for lunch, but her day-time diary was packed with meetings. She'd phoned each board member to set up a time to speak to them personally, knowing that she had to convince at least half of them that Andrew Miskin's report was an insult and that his suggestions should be ignored. Everyone had sounded embarrassed when she phoned but they'd all agreed to a private meeting. She had busy days ahead, so instead she asked if Luke was free for dinner and she suggested the bistro not far from her house. She had read about it in a Sunday paper but had never been there. She and Robert seldom went out during the week as Robert's cooking was better than most restaurants.

The bistro was half full when she turned up and Luke was already at a table near the window. His smile was lightening up his face as he stood up with arms outstretched to welcome her. There was a bottle of Pinot Grigio in an ice bucket on the table. After his welcoming lie about her looks, he pointed to the bottle.

"I hope you didn't mind that I ordered some wine, I remember you used to like Pinot Grigio. I can change it if you want something else, they haven't opened it yet." And there was that lovely smile again, the smile that made her love him all those years ago.

"No, it's absolutely fine."

Luke called the waiter who pulled out the cork with such theatrical flamboyance Ruth felt he expected an ovation as he poured the wine with one arm behind his back. Having had the nod from Luke he filled Ruth's glass.

"So, how's life?"

Ruth did not answer, she took a deep slug from the large wine glass as the waiter handed over an imitation parchment menu. All the old favourites were there, no modern fusion dishes, just honest Italian home cooking. She sighed with relief.

"All my favourites, I don't know what to choose. It's just the kind of food I like."

She pretended to read the menu because she didn't want to answer any questions about her life. It was all in such a turmoil.

They discussed their menu choices, talked about a speech the prime minister had given about the worsening economy, sipped their wine and welcomed each dish as it arrived, but she knew that she would have to explain to Luke about her changed finances which, like the British economy, had not improved.

"There's something I need to tell you," she said as she crumpled her napkin on her lap. "Robert and I are getting divorced and everything's a right old mess. We're trying to sort out our finances, and it's not fair of me to keep you waiting because it looks now as if it'll be some time before I have access to my money."

"What do you mean? After all, it's your money and Robert said he was willing to invest in the Brighton project as well?" It surprised her that he didn't mention the divorce.

"Yes, I know, but he's got himself involved with some hotel project in Lithuania and it's all gone belly-up and lawyers are involved. God knows how long it'll take before it's all sorted out. I only found out the other day that he's mortgaged our Sussex house as well as the student flats we own in Manchester and Leeds. He told me he needed the money to repay an investor or else he would have been sued. The investor was a close friend of ours, so it's all, as I said, a right mess. I'm sure it'll all sort itself out but just now there is no money. I'm sorry, Luke."

Luke didn't say a word but put down his coffee cup so hard that it made the saucer jump.

"But what about your house in Fulham?"

"We've got quite a hefty mortgage on that as it is."

"You talked about your nest egg, the one Robert did not know about, what about that?" There was a slightly hysterical tone to his question. "Surely, you being so bloody well-paid you must have some money of your own?"

"Luke, I am getting divorced and my lawyer has been told that Robert is going to insist on half our assets as well as asking for money."

"Money? Is that guy mad?"

"I'm only telling you what my lawyer has said."

"What am I to do with Brighton? You know I can't afford it on my own. You and I had an agreement." She remembered how his cheeks used to get blotchy red when he got angry. They were bright red now.

"We never had a formal agreement, as you well know." Her voice was steady, the voice she used every day at work. "And, as I said, I'm sorry, very sorry, but I didn't count on a divorce and I hope you will understand that just now I have other problems on my mind than your project."

His eyes were cold. She tried a smile, but he turned away and called for the waiter.

"Well, there's not much more to say then, is there? You go your way and I go mine."

When the bill arrived, she picked it up and threw her credit card on the silver platter. He made no movement, nor did he thank her for the dinner. He pulled out his chair and then stood behind her, ready to pull hers out. Always such good manners, she thought as he draped her coat over her shoulders.

Outside it was cold, bitterly cold and she shivered in her coat.

"If things change and you want to be in again on the project, give me a ring," he said turning away without looking at her.

Chapter 39

Andrew Miskin had not waited for the extra board meeting. Like Ruth he had contacted everyone on the board after they had received his report. Only three of the board members had phoned or emailed Ruth to tell her that Miskin wanted private meetings with each member of the board before the EGM. Bill Bradshaw told her that he had refused and accused Miskin of being disloyal both to Ruth and Babylove. Ian Shield of Babylove Foundation had also refused. "You have my total support," he assured Ruth. Sir Rupert had also been in touch but, as usual, he was guarded in his comments and said he had agreed to meet Miskin because he wanted to hear what he had to say. The fact that so few of the eight-member board had been in touch worried her. Even more so when David Hofmeister sent an email cancelling the date for their meeting. "After all, we'll discuss the matter at the EGM."

Paul Gallagher and his assistant Megan were still dealing with press enquiries, preparing press releases to still the appetite of the news-hungry journalists. In confidence, she told Paul about the pending divorce. Like the Callanders he was shocked. "I always thought you were so well suited. Robert seemed to worship you, always said how proud he was of what you have achieved. I don't really know Mandy but she's not in your league, can't even be compared with you. But then I thought my wife and I had a happy marriage until she told me she was off with someone else. One never knows these things," he added with a sigh.

Paul added he had seen Robert as he had come around to ask for his fee for the financial consultation he had given him. Robert had looked harassed but Paul thought it was due to a cash flow problem nor had he mentioned a word about a divorce, just grabbed Paul's cash.

Ruth turned to Paul.

"I need your advice on how to deal with the board members. What do you suggest?"

"You're doing the right thing talking to them each individually. Yes, I know you said some have cancelled the meetings you have set up, but talk to the rest. You must not go into that EGM next week unprepared. Your enemies can scent it. You've got the two members from the company on your side as well as Bill Bradshaw and Ian Shield but you need a few more. You must make it perfectly clear that you're capable of running the company. Remember you built it up from nothing. Come to think of it, now might not be a bad time to have a chat with your chum at the BBC, see if he can organise an interview with you on Good Morning or any of those chatty news programmes. That will give you a chance to put over your views. Megan and I can also send out press releases and offer interviews to the business editors of the major nationals. Remember not to talk about any deal, as it's not out in the open, just show what you have achieved so far. Woman's Hour might do an interview as well. I know one of the producers. I'll give her a ring now. And, Ruth, don't worry, it'll be all right." He smiled at her, nodding encouragingly.

Her meetings with the board members who had agreed to see her did not go well. Apart from Bill Bradshaw and Ian Shield they all mumbled something about waiting to discuss the matter at the proper board meeting. Only months earlier they had told her what an achievement it was to be chosen as Businesswoman of the Year. Now they couldn't look her in the eye. Ian told her that he had gone along to the meeting with Andrew Miskin to hear what he had to say, which was that Ruth could not lead the company forward as she was unable to negotiate and had no idea of business at a higher level. Even Sir Rupert thought so according to Andrew. He had also told Ian that Ruth seemed more interested in sorting out her personal problems than dealing with the offer from Pink's.

"I can't understand this," Ruth said to Ian. "He was with me all the time during the negotiations, and a fat lot of help he was." Here were the people she had trusted, who had been on her side and cheered her on as the company grew. Now they thought her incompetent. What had gone wrong?

Paul managed to get her some interviews with the financial press and Charles Butterworth pulled a few strings getting her an interview on Woman's Hour. But first up was a programme where she was placed next to some comic on a TV sofa at eight in the morning. She knew immediately she was not at her best. She answered some rather lame questions from the silver-haired interviewer who was more interested in looking at himself on the monitor. The comic made some stupid joke about women and dummies, which Ruth felt forced to laugh at. The TV interview contained a snippet from the *In Depth* programme Charles had done and Ruth watched herself appearing so self-confident as she took Charles through the factory. How it had all changed. Now she had lost her husband and the confidence of the board. Ruth enjoyed the Woman's Hour interview, about five minutes long with another businesswoman who had founded an underwear company and become a multi-millionaire. "But it cost me my marriage," she confessed in a Northern twang to the interviewer. Ruth wanted to stretch out her hand in sympathy but stopped herself in time and they went back to the question of the eternal glass ceiling.

* * *

When she returned from the TV studio Sirita told her that she had been fantastic and that she had made the comic look totally inane. Ruth knew she was lying but smiled and accepted the compliment. After a quick sandwich at her desk Ruth's mother phoned, something that did not happen often.

"I saw you on the telly this morning, you're not looking well. Are you eating properly? I'm just asking."

"Yes, mum, I had a proper lunch and a very fine breakfast of bacon and eggs" – it was not true, she had not had time before she was ferried to the studio for the make-up session – "so you don't need to worry about me. What can I do for you?"

"Well, you're so busy. You never get in touch. But I have some good news. I know you'll be pleased. I'm getting married. I should have told you when you came to see me, but you were in such a heap over this affair of Robert's I couldn't tell you then. Anyway, his name's Frank Addleston, he's a widower and lives just on the other side of The Meadow. He wants to meet you. Is there a date in your busy diary to see us? I also thought I might ask you if you would like to host our wedding reception at Hicks."

Ruth shook her head as if she couldn't understand what her mother had said. It was too much. A boyfriend after all these years. Robert had been right. But marriage? And at Hicks, no, that would not do.

"I am free this Friday if that suits you, what time would you like to see me?"

"Why don't you take us out for a meal? What about Honington Manor, so we can celebrate our engagement in style? Frank saw you on the telly this morning. He says you don't look like me at all and that I must be very proud of you." There was short pause. "I suppose I am. So Honington Manor on Friday. Will you book and pick us up at seven here at my place? Neither Frank nor I like driving in the dark."

Ruth did a quick calculation. If she organised the dinner maybe she could get out of having the reception at Hicks. Who would they ask anyway?

Chapter 40

Ruth didn't sleep very much the night before the board meeting. On the day before she had a long meeting with Paul and Bill Bradshaw during which they discussed tactics. Paul had been a great help. He had been in touch with the trade press and thanks to his efforts there was a half-page interview in *The Financial Times*, a shorter one in *The Daily Telegraph. The Evening Standard* had sent a reporter down to the factory to interview not only Ruth but also some of the staff, who all praised her. In all the interviews Ruth mentioned that as a growing company Babylove was always seen as a takeover target.

"There are sharks circling around us all the time." Ruth had stressed that the company could pay for its own expansion. "And expand we will," she said and mentioned the new lines to be introduced later in the year. Paul had also updated her social media account and given links to her more than 700,000 followers to watch all the media coverage. Sirita had made copies of all the press cuttings and also a recording of the Woman's Hour interview. The Good Morning sofa chat, in his view, was to be mentioned but not shown.

Sirita laid out all the notepads, the cuttings and the agenda; there were also copies of Andrew Miskin's report on the table. The tape recorder had been tested and Ruth felt it was a good radio interview as it was mentioned several times that the two women had both been chosen as Businesswoman of the Year and that they had both been successful in businesses aimed at women. The interviewer had actually said that they had an advantage over male bosses as they had a deeper understanding of their markets.

"That's something Andrew Miskin can't change," Sirita said with a laugh as they listened to the interview again.

Larry Fender had produced reams of statistics showing how the profit had increased year by year and the forecasts showing both a higher profit and a much higher turnover for the next year. Sirita's contribution was some very expensive chocolate eclairs from the local bakery. "Chocolate makes people feel happy and that's what we need today."

The security staff had made a space for Sir Rupert's car in the car park and everything was ready, but Ruth still felt her nerves bunching up in the pit of her stomach. "I used to love these board meetings as I got nothing but praise. I always felt stimulated as we kicked ideas around. Now I just want to have it over and done with. I do feel quite nervous," she admitted to Sirita, who was placing bottles of mineral water on the table. Ruth had never before said anything as private as that to Sirita, but now she looked at her as a friend.

As always, Sir Rupert turned up last when everyone was already sitting down and eyeing the chocolate eclairs while pretending to read the agenda. There was no small talk. Andrew Miskin also looked nervous, which Ruth saw as a good sign. Sir Rupert's face had the vivacity of a marble bust, nothing showed on his face. Bill Bradshaw tried to catch Ruth's eye but she was also busy reading the agenda as if she had not seen it before. Sirita busied herself with organising coffee.

Like a priest beginning his sermon, Sir Rupert intoned, "We have gathered here today to deal with an unexpected problem. There has been some disquiet about the way the negotiations with Pink's were handled. I assume you have all seen the report from Andrew. I therefore suggest we hand the floor to him."

Andrew Miskin cleared his voice and looked without blinking at Ruth. "What I have to say will probably upset some of you but it has to be said. I was present at the negotiations and I must say that I was disappointed by the way Ruth has handled the whole affair with Pink's.

Almost all of us were against Babylove buying Pink's at the beginning but we trusted Ruth and she convinced us that it was a good deal. We agreed on a budget but then suddenly the price for Pink's shot up, so new budgets were prepared and again we trusted Ruth and her bankers. What happened then? Suddenly we find out that Pink's wants to buy Babylove. Talk about a ride on a merry-go-round. Again, we were told that it would be a good thing for Babylove, synergy effects galore and a listing on the Stock Exchange eventually. We trusted Ruth yet again, and what happens? Nothing, absolutely nothing. After all these twists and turns, I must admit I have lost my confidence in Ruth as managing director of Babylove. I therefore suggest that she is moved from her present role and becomes director of development and chairman of the Babylove Foundation."

Ruth looked around the table. No one met her gaze, they all had their eyes on their notes, only Sir Rupert stared back at her with his impassive face.

"I think we should hear what Ruth has to say. We've read your report, Andrew, and heard your views."

Andrew smiled. "Before we listen to Ruth, I'd like to say that I know she's going through a tough period in her private life, which is probably the reason why she's not kept her eye on the ball. We might even regard her move sideways as a temporary measure."

"Thank you, Andrew. I'd rather we kept my private life outside this discussion," Ruth said angrily. "And yes, I do have something to say. I find it absolutely extraordinary that Andrew, who was present at all these negotiations, now suddenly blames me for failing to reach an agreement with Pink's. He advised me before and during the negotiations which price would be acceptable, that the value of our company was close to twenty million and we should not even contemplate accepting a price below eighteen million. And I followed his advice and now that is now seen as incompetence. I did what I thought best for Babylove, just as I have done all through my years here."

"Excuse me for interrupting." Andrew rose up from the table. "I have since spoken to some analysts in the City and they produced some rather more interesting figures than those laid on the table today. They show your forecasts are far too optimistic and with the new lines we will need to invest in expansion of the factory, new machinery and also a strong marketing campaign. I see very little of those substantial costs in your forecasts. In plain language we need money to grow and Pink's would have provided that money as well as saving millions in synergy effects. We'd also have had the chance of finally getting our foot inside a major supermarket. I therefore suggest that we re-start negotiations with Pink's and under the guidance of Sir Rupert, who has kindly offered to step in as an interim managing director."

Sir Rupert allowed himself a quick smile but, at that moment, Ian Shield banged his fist on the table.

"I must say I find this unacceptable. No one has even had the courtesy to confer with me about my role as chairman of the Babylove Foundation and now I find that my position might be handed over to Ruth as some form of a consolation prize. I've spent seven years as its chair during which time we've donated close to seventeen million pounds to good causes. The Foundation has achieved a high profile thanks to the work I've done during these years and I will not be fobbed off. As for Ruth," he added, as if he suddenly thought of her, "it was not all that long ago when we praised Ruth for her achievements of which one is being Businesswoman of the Year. I think Andrew's suggestion is both unprofessional and unethical. I will therefore not vote for any changes."

"Hear, hear," said Bill Bradshaw. "I agree with every word of what Ian has said. I also speak as director of our local Chamber of Commerce. What Ruth has achieved is remarkable, she has become the face of Babylove. Without her drive and energy this company would simply not exist. So, Andrew, I will not vote for any changes either."

Ruth nodded gratefully to Bill. Things were going her way, this nightmare might soon be over, she thought. Then Dan Higgins stood up.

"Let's not be personal. We all know that Ruth has built this company from next to nothing. But, and it's a big but, as an accountant with some thirty years' experience, I have seen too many companies fail because the original founders did not grow and develop at the speed of their companies. I have a strong feeling that we have reached this point now. Like Andrew I find that the forecasts are not as robust as they should be. In the next year or so we will need to spend millions in order to cope with the expansion the company needs to survive in a very competitive environment. Our share of the growing baby and toddler market has remained static, and in order to cope with increasing costs it's vital to expand. Ruth will still be involved in the development of the company, maybe as a Babylove ambassador, but I vote for a change, be it temporary or permanent. I believe that Sir Rupert with his experience of high-level negotiations can push Babylove forward, if not to a merger with Pink's, then maybe eventually to a listing on the Stock Exchange."

David Hofmeister nodded all through Dan Higgins' speech. "I speak here as a lawyer and I must admit that there are other reasons for a change at the top. During these negotiations there were times, and every minute is vital during a period like this, when I could not get hold of Ruth, sometimes for several days. Ruth was not forceful during the negotiations, yes, I was there, and it could have been handled much better. There was not only the question of price but also niggly details about who should lead the company after the merger and Ruth showed no or little flexibility in these discussions. However, if we vote for a change, I want to assure Ruth that her new role will in no way change her financial position as regards her salary and pension. The same goes for Ian, who is approaching retirement age anyway."

"Well, no one told me that I could retire with a full pension," said Ian Shield, relief visible in his face.

There were more discussions about the proposed change and its consequences, as if the change had already been approved. Ruth felt like she was the accused in the dock just waiting for her sentence. And when the vote was taken, she knew even before Sir Rupert gave his vote, that she had lost. The change would take place with immediate effect.

The men couldn't wait to leave the room, nodding towards Ruth but not saying anything. What upset her most was that Ian Shield had voted for the change, so much for his loyalty.

As Ruth and Sirita tidied up in the boardroom, it hit Ruth. She had been sacked from her post as MD. Not sacked as such, but shown to be unfit to run *her* company. Weeks of bad nights and busy days had taken their toll. Ruth gulped before weeping quietly, tears running down her cheeks without her even noticing them dripping onto her collar.

Sirita put her arms around Ruth's shaking shoulders.

"I'm handing in my notice tomorrow, unless I can continue to work with you, Ruth, in whatever post they give you. I will NOT work for Sir Rupert. Never. A real snake, that's what he is."

Chapter 41

Ruth wondered later whether it was Sirita's staunch loyalty and her threat of leaving that led her to her decision. Immediately after the meeting, when the sadness had been replaced by red-hot anger, she sat down and composed a letter to Sir Rupert. It was very short and to the point. In return for not taking the board to a tribunal for constructive dismissal, she would leave at once in return for two years' salary and pension payments.

"There is no need to have me hanging around here when there is no real executive post for me. In that way Ian Shield can keep his chairmanship of Babylove Foundation, a job he loves and performs well, until he retires.

As for Sirita, if she wishes to leave, I would insist on her getting the same settlement, i.e. two years' salary payment to our respective company pensions. She has worked for many years with me and deserves a proper pay-off."

She emailed a copy of her letter to Sir Rupert's office and within two hours she had a reply.

Dear Ruth

It is with great sadness we accept your resignation. During your stewardship the company has grown from a small chemical business into a market-leader. You are closely connected to the brand and will be hard to replace.

Your requests will be met in full as soon as you have signed an agreement that you will not discuss the reasons behind your resignation with anyone. This is perfectly normal in a high profile case like this as any unguarded comments can affect further negotiations with Pink's.

As for Sirita, if she leaves, the same applies to her and we will of course reach a settlement with her as per your request.

May I, on behalf of the board, yet again thank you for all you have done for Babylove.

I wish you all the best for the future.

With kind regards
Yours sincerely

Sir Rupert Cherlow
Chairman and Chief Executive
Babylove Ltd

Ruth smiled when she saw his new title, only hours old but already part of his email signature.

Before she had time to discuss the agreement with Sirita, Paul came into Ruth's office.

"What the hell is all this about? I've just had a phone call from Sir Rupert telling me that if there are any inquiries from the media, they should be referred to his office and there should be no contact from us at all. What's happened?" Paul threw himself down on the pink visitor's chair and pulled his fingers through his reddish hair. "Tell me, because this is not the way I work."

"I have just resigned, actually an hour ago, and Sir Rupert is now taking over as chief executive as well as chairman of Babylove."

"But why? For goodness' sake, why? I need a reason. You owe me that."

"It's personal and I am about to sign a gagging clause; that's all I can say."

"Is that it? Come on Ruth, you can tell me."

There was nothing Ruth would have liked more than to tell him but she had to sign Sir Rupert's gagging clause in order to secure her settlement and she needed the money. She was not sure she would be able walk into another job just yet.

"Sorry, Paul. I've nothing to add and I'm leaving this office at the end of today, I just need to pack a few of my belongings and say goodbye to some people. Do tell Megan, and let me say Paul, it's been a pleasure working with you and I hope to see you again, whatever I do in the future."

Paul rose, shook his head in disbelief, and took Ruth's outstretched hand and pulled her to his chest. "Whatever has happened, which you can't talk to me about, I will find out sooner or later. Do remember in my eyes you'll always be *the* Businesswoman of the Year."

Leaning against his chest Ruth felt the tears burning, but she stopped herself. She was not going to cry, certainly not, that would somehow give power to those who had voted against her.

Back in her office she looked in the mirror and noticed streaks of mascara under her eyes. Freshly made up, Ruth walked out to Sirita's office and told her about the resignation.

"If you're going, I'm going. I don't want to stay." Sirita looked fierce and her brown cheeks reddened. "Resignation! Bah. I know why you're leaving. Why should you stay in a company that you have more or less created as some kind of, what was it Dan Higgins called it, Babylove ambassador, wasn't it? Such nonsense. I suppose I have to work for the three months stipulated in my contract, but as soon as I can I'll leave."

Ruth told her about the offer from Sir Rupert and a big smile crossed Sirita's face. "Perfect. I'm off today, like you, and I'll sign anything Sir Rupert wants. I think I'll have a gap year like all those students, maybe a visit to India finally, yes, that's what I'll do." She gave Ruth a hug. "Thanks for organising such a good settlement for me. Hey, maybe you want to go to India, too?"

"Who knows, who knows? But, first of all, I must sort out my private affairs, but thank you Sirita for all you've done and for your loyalty. You are a real friend."

* * *

There were very few personal belongings in Ruth's office; some spare make-up in one drawer, which she threw away, paper hankies went the same way and on her desk was a silver letter opener with her name engraved. It was a gift from Robert when he had left Babylove to set up on his own. She had never used it as all letters were opened by Sirita but she enjoyed its elegant sleek design. With a flourish she sent it flying into the waste paper bin, yet realising that one day she might regret it.

She only managed to fill one small box with her tax papers from the company and some letters from satisfied customers she wanted to save. The only other person, other than Sirita, she wanted to say goodbye to was Larry Fender. He had worked so hard to prepare all the statistics and forecasts for every meeting and he had always supported Ruth with an almost doglike admiration.

When Ruth told him she was leaving and at the end of that very day, he crumpled in front of her and for a dreadful moment she thought he would cry. He coughed and lifted his hunched shoulders. Like Paul, he asked, "Why, what's happened?"

She tried to explain it was a personal matter, hinted at her pending divorce, but Larry did not look convinced. "Tell me where you're going next and let me know if they need an accountant, will you at least promise me that?"

Ruth had to push her nails into her fist so as not to cry. At that very moment a courier arrived with the agreement from Sir Rupert to sign. Looking ominous in his black leathers and a dark helmet he waited in Sirita's office, where she also signed her resignation documents.

When he left, Sirita came in with her medicinal bottle of brandy. "Let's drink a toast to happy memories and to a brighter future," she said as she poured the amber liquid into two mugs.

Just as Ruth was leaving with her small box, the phone rang. It was Archie Arnold, her lawyer.

"I have received the papers from Mr Friedman, your husband's lawyer. I think we need a meeting as soon as possible. It seems your finances are in a far worse state than I was led to believe and Mr Nieder is not only asking for maintenance and half of your assets. He also suggests selling your house in the country. I must say it's a good thing that you have a good job with a steady salary, Mrs Farringdon."

To which Ruth had no reply.

Chapter 42

It was the same painted receptionist as last time when Ruth had been there with Luke. She welcomed Mrs Green, her fiancé Frank and Ruth to Honington Manor without the enthusiasm she had shown Luke. Her mother was wearing a new dress, very similar in style and colour to the brocade she had worn when they celebrated Ruth's engagement, an evening Ruth would rather forget. Frank wore a rather fusty dinner jacket and his trousers had slipped down under his protruding belly. "I blame it on your mother's excellent lemon drizzle cake," he said patting his tight shirt as he noted Ruth's glance. Ruth immediately liked him, he seemed honest and straightforward, but the events of the last few days made her wary of trusting anyone. "At least he can't be after her money," she thought to herself.

A waiter, also in a dinner jacket, led them to their table and Ruth noticed how her mother straightened her back and her vowels as the waiter called her Madam. The wine list was handed over to Frank, who immediately gave it to Ruth. "My soon-to-be step-daughter, Mrs Farringdon, is our host this evening," he said, looking relieved he did not have to deal with it. "I'm a whisky man myself but I'm sure Mrs Farringdon knows her wines," he added. Frank and Mrs Green discussed the menu and neither one was sure what all the kitchen French really meant. Ruth had to step in and explain that *carre d'agneau* was not a lamb curry but a rack of lamb.

Over the lamb, Mrs Green told Ruth that they had picked a date and would the second Saturday in May be all right for a reception at Hicks? They planned a simple wedding at the Crawley registry office, "in spite of those ghastly carpets but it's a bit silly to have a church service at our age." Frank nodded, as he did to most of Mrs Green's comments.

Ruth had hardly touched her lamb. She knew she had to tell them what had happened two days ago.

"I'm not sure I can promise you Hicks for your reception. I don't know where we will be, come May. It's all up in the air for the moment. But why not here, at Honington? It's roughly the same distance from Crawley, and I know they have some function rooms."

"No, no, it's far too formal. Hicks is much nicer. Well, Frank hasn't seen it yet, of course. Maybe we can come down for a Sunday lunch and have a look?"

"Mum, as I said, it's all up in the air for the moment. I haven't been there myself for some time. But let me think about it."

The waiter came to clear the table giving Ruth a much-wanted respite.

"I don't think we're asking too much. Don't you agree, Frank?" Frank looked down on his napkin and smiled. "I leave all the arrangements to you two girls."

Suddenly Ruth thought about her former mother-in-law, who had dealt with all the preparations for Luke's and her wedding and how Ruth's mother had been left out. Of course, Ruth would help her mother, but please not at Hicks, she could not bear it.

"Now, who's for pudding?"

"I don't want any pudding, but some ice cream would be nice," said Frank and gulped down the last of the very expensive Burgundy, still the cheapest one on the long wine list.

Sipping his coffee Frank, now with a Burgundian glow, leant over and said to Ruth how proud he was soon to have such a famous woman in his family. "I thought you were excellent last week on the Good Morning Show, you really put that clown down. Now tell me, is there really money in dummies?"

"Dummies?" Ruth looked perplexed.

"Isn't that what you call those things babies suck?" Frank said

"Oh, dummies! Yes, as a matter of fact there is. Together with other products we have a turnover of almost 40 million pounds a year." Ruth stopped herself. What was she doing talking about Babylove and saying "we", when it should now be "they".

"Actually, I have something to tell you. It'll be all over the papers this Sunday or on Monday. As a matter of fact, I have resigned. I left the company on Thursday."

"You what?"

"Resigned, I'm no longer with Babylove."

Her mother's mouth opened and closed.

"But why? Are you going somewhere else?" Her voice rose in anticipation of some good news, no doubt with a better pay.

"I'm not going anywhere else. I'm going to take some time off and then decide what I'll do, but first I must sort out my personal affairs in the light of the divorce."

"I knew it, it's all Robert's fault. Never liked him, I told you Frank, didn't I. Oh, I could kill him, ruining your life, that's what he's done. It's not fair."

Frank put down his coffee cup and looked at Ruth. There was pity in his eyes.

"I'm so sorry. This must be a most difficult time for you and here we are prattling about weddings and receptions." He took her mother's hand. "Now, Marje love, I think there's quite enough on your daughter's plate at the moment. Let's fix the details for the wedding ourselves, I mean it's only about five or six people we want to invite."

"Why, Frank, why shouldn't we be at Hicks? My daughter paid for it, after all. And it's me you should worry about, what if Ruth can't continue with her payments to me, now that she hasn't got a job? I'm counting on that money. How could we otherwise afford a proper honeymoon?"

Frank put a calming hand on hers. "Now, now," he said. "Time to say thank you to Ruth for a magnificent dinner."

Ruth bowed her head and waved at a passing waiter to get the bill. She was exhausted and she had the long drive back to Fulham. She could not yet face staying at Hicks only a few miles away.

"I'll continue the payments for as long as I can, I promise that." But then she remembered that she might also have to pay alimony to Robert which might blow her budget, but it was too early to worry her mother about that. "Now, let me drive you back to Crawley, I've had a long day."

Chapter 43

Archie Arnold looked more jovial than last time Ruth had seen him and this in spite of the bad news.

"I had no idea you were leaving Babylove. How will this affect your earnings, may I ask?" He told her that he had read reams of newsprint in the Sunday business pages and the news had also been discussed on the BBC and ITV. The papers all stated that Mrs Farringdon had left the company in order to pursue other interests. There were pictures of a smiling Sir Rupert, not sitting in her old pink office but in his dark panelled room in the City. No doubt he would spend most of his time there, while heading new negotiations with Pink's, Ruth thought, as she saw the photos.

Some of the reporters knew about the failed negotiations but drew their own conclusions that it was Babylove wanting to buy Pink's. Her role in the negotiations was not touched upon but they all mentioned how Ruth Farringdon had created a multi-million company from almost nothing. There was even a photograph in *The Daily Telegraph* of the original founders, Mr Watson and a smiling Mr Rubens, long since dead. Mr Watson had given a statement praising Ruth for her determination and good business sense: "I saw her potential when I first laid eyes on her, she's a cracker of a girl with a fine head on her shoulders." Ruth had not answered any calls or emails from scoop-hungry reporters, only when she saw the name of Charles Butterworth on her mobile screen did she answer.

"I can't talk to you, Charles, because I'm not quite sure what I'm going to do yet, but as soon as I've made up my mind, you'll be the first to know. I need some time for personal reasons and that's all I can say at this moment."

Ruth had not even had the courage to inform her own lawyer that she had been demoted and that this was the real reason for her resignation. Archie Arnold somehow seemed to sense that there was more than she was telling. He stood up and opened a small cabinet next to his big book case and pulled out two glasses and a bottle.

"Here, have a small sherry, my dear, I think you might need it. I had no idea of your changed circumstances but I have been in touch with your husband's lawyer and explained what has happened. He had of course seen it himself and so has his client. Have you heard anything from Mr Nieder?"

"No, not one word," said Ruth, who for some moments had forgotten all about Robert and Mandy, but now she realised how odd it was that he hadn't been in touch.

She sipped her sherry, far too sweet for her own liking, but she enjoyed the slight burn as she swallowed. Mr Arnold was right, she did need a drink.

"The news is not good. I have gone through the statements given by Mr Friedman. I can tell you that your husband is insistent on half of the rented properties as well as half of the properties you live in, that is your house in Fulham and the one in the country. And the future value of your holding in Babylove. He also has the right to maintenance. The sum he's asked for is of course based on your earnings at Babylove. May I ask if you were given a settlement?"

"Yes, two year's salary including pension contributions. But what about my husband's own earnings as a financial consultant?"

"According to his tax returns we're talking small beer, less than twenty thousand last year, while your salary is more than ten times that figure plus very generous bonuses. He also points out that he has worked as an unpaid consultant to you and Babylove and he has included an agenda from one of your board meetings which shows that one of the points on the agenda is the question of a retainer for Mr Nieder in light of the services he provides for the company. Is that correct?"

Ruth just nodded. How had he got hold of the agenda? How long had he planned to leave her? Even before he knew that Mandy was pregnant? She took another gulp of the sherry and then put her ice-cold hands on her flushed cheeks.

"Can you put a value on his services as an annual estimate? Did he provide any reports?"

"No nothing like that at all. He was my sounding board as simple as that. We would talk about the business over dinner, that's all. He knew the company well, as you might remember he worked there but left when we got married to set up on his own. I trusted his advice and wanted to show my appreciation by offering him a small retainer. My board turned it down as they had no idea what he did for the company. It was a flat refusal. Apart from being my sounding board, he would sometimes drive me home after late meetings or business dinners. But isn't that what any good husband would do?"

The lawyer put a plastic folder in front of Ruth and told her to look at the figures. All Robert's expenses were detailed including the money he had spent on living elsewhere while she had insisted on her right to stay in both Hicks and Fulham. What about him staying in Orpington, she wondered. The last sheet was a demand for thirty thousand pounds a year plus half of all assets. And that all assets should be sold as soon as possible. There was a value on both houses, it showed that Robert had recently taken estate agents around both properties in order to get up-to-date valuations. The flats in Leeds and Manchester were valued separately. All, apart from the house in Fulham, were re-mortgaged and quite recently.

"And what happened to that money? I haven't seen a penny of that."

"Most of it was invested in a hotel project in Lithuania, which came to nothing, I gather. The investment was done with your approval and he has a document signed by you to prove it. He also mentioned your account, one which you had not told him about until recently and that seems to be all the cash there is available. His account and your joint investment account are both more or less empty. After the sale of all the properties there will be enough to buy each of you a property with a value of some eight hundred thousand and no cash or you might choose a cheaper property and more in cash. There will also be some hefty tax liabilities on the sale of the investment properties plus your second home. Your private account must also be halved."

"But that's money I got from selling the flat when I separated from my first husband, surely that can't now land in my second husband's pocket? That's madness."

He stood up and poured her another sherry.

"I'm afraid it can. Mr Nieder gave up a well-paid job when he married you and you two came to an agreement that, as you earned far more, he would stay at home, cook, shop, pick you up after meetings, in essence act as your housekeeper. He also looked after your investments…"

"…And a fine mess he made of that!" Archie Arnold cut her off. "As I said, he did all this and for no payment as far as I can see. Is that correct?"

"But I paid for the houses, put the money into the investments, gave him a new car every second year and expensive holidays, doesn't that count for anything?" Ruth knew what the answer would be even before she had finished her sentence. It counted for nothing.

The two sherries had made her feel slightly giddy and as she stepped out in the street she felt anger rising in her and she cursed not only Mandy but also Robert, who had gone behind her back and organised valuations of the Fulham house and Hicks, her beloved Hicks. This was one step too far. That blasted bitch had ruined her life and she was not going to tolerate it.

Chapter 44

As Ruth stepped into a sunny Bloomsbury Square from the narrow and gloomy Bury Place, Robert was slowly waking up in the far too narrow bed in Mandy's flat in Orpington. He stretched out his hand but Mandy's side was cold. He slowly opened his eyes and saw that the greyish curtains with yellow stripes were half opened. It must be later than he thought and turning to Mandy's bedside table he noted that it was already close to ten.

Mandy had left hours ago to get to her office in London on a packed commuter train and she would not be back until after seven when she expected a light supper. She had got over the early morning sickness but she could not deal with a heavy meal at night. Nor could she join him for a glass of wine and last night Robert had finished the bottle of Burgundy he had opened to go with the chicken salad he had prepared. He had also knocked back two glasses of brandy. He needed the drink because of the bad news from Lithuania. He had spent over twenty thousand pounds on lawyers' fees just to be told that the Lithuanian developer with whom he had set up a partnership had gone into liquidation and there were no assets at all. His telephone conversation with Dick Callander to confirm this had not been a happy one and he had promised to restore as much of Dick's investment as quickly as possible, but had to admit to an anxious Dick that it all depended on getting his part of the assets now in Ruth's hands, "and at the moment she's not playing ball."

Robert was not a man to look back and once Mandy had disappeared out of his life more than fifteen years ago, he had not given her much of a thought. He had wondered why she would not see him after the abortion she had those years ago but at the same time he remembered how relieved he had been that there was no responsibility, no baby to tie him down. He had suspected at the time that Mandy's parents had had a role in forcing her to stop all contact with him. It was only now, when talking late one night recently, Mandy had confessed that her parents did not even know about the abortion. She had mentioned a school friend's hen-party in London as an excuse and her parents believed her when she told them that she had drunk far too much tequila; the reason for looking so wan. She told him why she did not want to see him again was simply that she had realised that he did not love her. If he had loved her, they would have coped somehow. "I set you free all those years ago. I didn't want to make you feel trapped and then start hating me," she said and she looked at him with those sad eyes that made his innards soften. That is why he wanted things to be right this time.

Mandy needed him, she was there for him and listened to him. Ruth never had the time and besides it was his given role to listen to her. She never asked about his work, never wanted to know about his clients and, ever since he left Babylove, just before they married, he knew that he was only useful to her as a sounding board. To begin with she had really listened to him but as the company grew, he was pushed into the background. He thought of all the nights he had been sitting in his car outside fancy restaurants in the West End when she was dining with major retailers or suppliers. He had to wait for her call on the mobile to say she was ready to leave. He was never introduced to her clients as they parted in the doorway of the restaurant. He might as well have been wearing a chauffeur's cap, but he got used to it. The expensive smell of leather in his BMW, the fantastic sound system made him feel comfortable and he knew that he could never afford such a car on his earnings.

After these meetings Ruth would sometimes sit down in the back seat, tapping out emails to send next morning to Sirita about the orders taken during a wine-fuelled dinner and not a word would be said to Robert apart from a sigh following "Oh, what a tiresome evening." She would never mention what food they had eaten, that was of no interest to Ruth, she just wanted to butter up the clients. Robert would always cook himself a steak on these nights, regretting that he could not accompany the fine sirloin with some good wine, as he was always expected to be stone-cold sober when he picked her up.

He missed the camaraderie which he had enjoyed at Babylove, the drinks after work. All that stopped when he started his affair with Ruth. And how did it start? Looking back, Robert could not remember falling in love, it just slipped over from a couple of drinks one evening into some fumbling in the back of her car. They had both complained about their failed marriages after having shared the latest office gossip. He had always admired Ruth. She fought like a lioness for Babylove, dealt with the banks, the retailers and the technical people in the lab without blinking. Of course, he had admired her, but loved her? After that first kiss in the car, they had their trysts in small hotels away from London and Caterham and he had longed for those weekends away, the excitement of it all with no one at the office knowing. It made him feel special. His first wife had run off with an up-and-coming musician, unfortunately one with a tin ear, so the affair did not last long, but Robert was happy to be rid of her and the divorce had been amicable, well, as amicable as it could be as there were very few assets to share.

Had he proposed to Ruth? Robert could not remember how or when. It seemed as a natural progression after some months of their secret affair. He wanted everyone to know that Ruth, the boss, had picked him, even though it meant that he had to give up his job. Proud, yes, he was proud. He wanted to show off his bride at a big wedding but Ruth wanted none of that. He always suspected that she was slightly ashamed of him. He was not a Farringdon, there were no cut glass vowels just a slight Leeds accent and there was no inherited money, just a dead émigré father and his Polish mother who never got to grips with the English language. Robert had never wanted to discuss Luke Farringdon. He knew he could never be at the same social ease that Luke enjoyed with his private school education and upper-class parents, but having met him he had to admit Luke was a charmer and he could see why Ruth had fallen in love with him.

And now he was in love. It had hit him so suddenly. He enjoyed the softness that enveloped him when he looked at Mandy as she undressed and gently patted her slight bulge. He longed for their private moments. Their baby, their son, would soon be part of their lives. Robert had never envisaged that the prospect of becoming a father would mean so much to him; pride, excitement and love most of all. "We're a family," he whispered to Mandy as he held her in his arms.

He had been surprised when Mandy had first contacted him early last autumn. When she said her name, it did not register to begin with, but then her voice brought it all back. His regret not having seen her after her return from London. He wanted – no, needed – to know why she had left him. In the recesses of his soul there was still an empty space, which was once filled by Mandy, his first love. Ruth gave him security, financial stability and a certain pride that she had chosen him to follow in Luke's footsteps. He had not asked for more, until he met Mandy again.

As soon as they met up at Victoria Station, he guided her around the corner to an almost deserted bar in the railway hotel. The carpets were threadbare, the lights dim and the bartender looked bored as Robert ordered two glasses of Sauvignon Blanc. He knew instinctively that he had picked the wrong place and they both hurriedly finished their glasses of wine without saying much. Mandy looked tired and slightly embarrassed as if she regretted that she had arranged the meeting and Robert felt uncomfortable in their silence. Then he remembered a small place nearby in Elizabeth Street and, as they stepped inside the door of this small Italian restaurant, they both relaxed.

Over a simple pasta and some wine, memories flooded back at the speed the bottle emptied. Mandy smiled at his descriptions of the house he shared with Ruth in Sussex. "It's like stepping into a furniture showroom. Everything matches and if I put a blue towel in the green guest room, I know there's hell to pay. Everything in its right place. This is the way Ruth wants it. I never wanted to live in the country, I was happy in Fulham but Ruth was brought up in the country, well Crawley actually, and that is about as rural as Fulham. Ruth found this monster of a house and I tried to persuade her not to buy it but she fell in love with it and now I rather like it. Well, I like being down there as Ruth can finally relax away from work."

"I saw your wife on television some months ago, she's so elegant and so bright. Don't know how she does it, running a company like Babylove. You must be very proud of her."

Robert did not want to talk more about his wife with Mandy; he felt he was unfaithful to her by just mentioning her. "Tell me about you, what are you doing? Married? Children?"

Mandy told him about her job, with a firm of accountants in London. She did not get on with the senior partner and wanted to leave but she had nowhere to go. "No one wants a woman of a certain age; they all want dolly-birds in their offices and my qualifications are rather outdated now. I act as company secretary and help some of the clients of the firm. My clients like me and I suppose that's why they haven't fired me or why I haven't left. The firm is small and there is no way for me to be transferred to another department, so I must lump it."

Robert felt so sad for her. The job was not well paid and all she could afford was the rental of a smallish two-bedroom flat in Orpington. "I took it because it has a balcony, so I'm able to grow some plants. All right, it's only in pots but at least I have some greenery to look at when I come home."

"You must come down and see us at Hicks, we're surrounded by acres of wilderness. Gardening has never appealed to me. I relax by cooking."

Mandy had a train to catch. "They're running only a few trains per hour," she said as he paid the bill discreetly.

At Victoria Station he bent forward and kissed her on the cheek. He struggled against his sudden urge to hold her tight and kiss her properly. "Let's meet again," he said as he escorted her to the ticket barrier. "Soon, please." Mandy nodded but her eyes were already focused on the train.

Chapter 45

When Mandy was down at Hicks for Christmas, he realised it had been a mistake to kiss her under the mistletoe but he had yearned for her all evening. She had been much more relaxed with Mrs G. there and Paul Gallagher oozing Irish charm. He had even made Mrs Green girlishly giddy. It was so unlike Mandy's first visit to Hicks, when she had been wound up and ill at ease. Ruth had not been very welcoming at that time. Mandy had heard the comment about lame ducks which had not helped. He remembered their first kiss after one of their secret meetings. Had that kiss changed everything? Robert could not remember when he had last felt such a volt of electricity surge through his body. It was not purely sexual, it made every nerve in his body react and he had found it difficult to look at Mandy after that. He somehow imagined that his thoughts were there for everyone to see, etched on his face.

It was after her first visit to Hicks that he had phoned her up. He hadn't really planned to ask to see her again, just wanted to make sure she had got home all right but when he heard her voice, he had wanted to see her so badly, and without anyone else present. That was when he started to go to Orpington. Her flat became their own private place where Ruth was never mentioned.

Ruth had never been very interested in sex. There was always a reason why she said no: a paper to read or a contract to be checked. "To-do" lists were another excuse. Their first secret months had been exciting, but once they were married and everyone knew about their relationship it was as if her interest fizzled out, but she did keep a check on her fertile periods and their sex became more of a duty than pleasure. Mandy, just as he remembered from their first years in Leeds, hid behind her quiet demeanour a fiery and joyful sexual appetite. She liked to seduce him, and he loved it.

The pregnancy came as a shock to them both and Mandy told Robert that this time, she was not willing to have an abortion. At the age of thirty-seven this was probably her last chance to have a child. She promised to make no demands, emotional or financial, but she was determined to have this child.

Robert had often played with the idea of becoming a father, now it was a reality. Ruth and he had tried for years but nothing happened, so in the end he forced himself not to think about it. The older he got, he had to admit, the more he liked the thought of a child. He told Mandy he would help financially and take some part in the child's upbringing. But as the bump grew, he realised that he didn't want to be a part-time father. He wanted to be there as Mandy's partner, sharing all the excitement and responsibility of parenthood with her.

Could he leave Ruth? Ruth had given him so much; a life with no money problems, something he had never experienced before. His own meagre earnings as a financial adviser would not enable him to pay for those exotic holidays he had enjoyed with Ruth. Could he really give all that up? Then he remembered the last few years, how lonely he had been and how his expensive car and luxurious kitchen at Hicks were nothing but consolation for his loneliness. His eager shopping had become a way of filling empty days. He was happy in Mandy's kitchen, cooking without fancy gadgets; all he had taken from Hicks was his set of knives and his blender. Mandy made him feel relaxed. He could leave his trousers on the bedroom chair without a comment and nothing, nothing matched in the flat and that made him feel strangely at ease.

Ruth was so busy with her Pink's deal she hardly noticed Robert's absence. He spent more and more time with Mandy. He hated lying to Ruth but anyway she took very little interest in his doings. One evening, he remembered, she had tried to get into his side of the bed but he could not even touch her, she was suddenly repugnant, and he had turned away. Many times, he had felt tempted to tell her about Mandy, but Ruth was in such a state about the business, that he never found the right moment.

When Mandy gave him the scan of their son, he knew he had to talk to Ruth and ask for a divorce. He put the envelope with the scan in the drawer of his bedside table hoping for courage. Ruth then found it and once she knew about Mandy, Robert started planning his exit. He got an estate agent to value Hicks, worth far more than he thought; the house in Fulham, according to their agent had also risen in value. Added to that were the student flats in Leeds. Yes, there would be enough to support Mandy once she left her job.

He counted on a share of their assets. Of course, he should be paid, he had after all given up his job to support Ruth in her career. That was a decision they had taken together as Ruth earned so much more than he could ever hope for. He wanted to be a proper provider for Mandy and their son, find a bigger flat somewhere, but first he must sort out the Lithuanian mess. Dick Callander had threatened him with a lawsuit and it was only because he knew of the impending divorce and the sale of the Fulham house he agreed to wait. Now Robert had just found out that Ruth had left Babylove and for a moment he suspected she had done it out of spite, to deny him a decent pay-off. His guilt at hurting Ruth changed into a feeling of hate, sometimes frightening him with its intensity. Ruth's lawyer had been pestering him and his lawyer and it seemed the sale of the houses had been held up again, there always appeared to be some reason to do with more papers to be signed.

Robert had hardly seen his clients. Paul Gallagher had finally paid the fee he owed but his colleague for whom Robert had done some tax planning was not returning his calls. The money from Paul had hardly covered his outstanding personal bills and he was waiting for the banks to advance the money of the properties in Leeds and Fulham. The thought of money, or rather the lack of it, followed him every day and again he blamed Ruth for only having given him a paltry two thousand pounds to help him out. He needed large sums of money to pay the bills from the lawyers he had hired to sort out the Lithuanians. He had Ruth's signature on the Lithuanian deal so she would have to share the costs of the lawyers. One thing was sure, Ruth would have to pay – and pay dearly for the years he had given her.

Chapter 46

Mandy once asked if Ruth had any friends. Strangely enough it had never occurred to Robert that it was odd that Ruth did not have any old school friends or never made new ones through work. Ruth liked Marcia, but it was not as a friend. Apart from the Callanders they saw very few people. There were no cosy dinners or shared holidays with friends or colleagues. Ruth hated the thought of mixing her private life with her work. Yes, she got on well with Sirita, but they never saw each other outside the office. It struck Robert that even he had not been a friend of hers, not really. She never told him her thoughts apart from those that had to do with her work. Sometimes she even listened to his advice. Only now as he was leaving her did he realise that she was going to be very lonely.

Mandy, on the other hand, had friends and after Robert had moved in, not officially as per his lawyer's advice, he met them and found he loved the evenings over food and wine in her cramped flat in Orpington. All her friends admired his cooking skills and the quality wines he served. And they all seemed so happy that Mandy had finally found her man – and wasn't it romantic, many of them sighed, that they had been lovers in their early twenties.

Everything he did for Mandy was met with thanks and kisses, even picking her up at the station at night after a long day at the office. She never took anything for granted and this made him feel more and more generous. He would pick out food in the supermarket he knew she liked, buy her flowers, serve her breakfast in bed, something Ruth had never approved of as she disliked crumbs in bed. "That's why we have a breakfast table."

He realised how lonely he had been. He remembered how he once asked Ruth if they could get a dog. She flatly refused. He asked once again and promised that he would look after it. Again, she said no. He told Mandy about his plea one evening. They had just eaten a simple salad; the television was on but the sound turned down and she touched his cheek and said, "You will never be lonely again."

He also told her about the time when Sir Rupert Cherlow had invited Ruth to a Christmas party at the Royal Academy, dinner with a private view of the current exhibition. The engraved invitation stated Ms Farringdon with Partner. "It's a business event," Ruth said as she put the date in her diary. Robert had said he would love to see the sell-out exhibition, but Ruth had just closed her diary saying she wanted to go alone as it would be easier for her to chat with the other guests.

"All those pin-striped chaps would bore you to death. No, you'll have a better evening at home." Of course, he drove her there and picked her up at midnight.

He could not wait to have his life sorted out, his and Ruth's possessions divided so that he could start his life as a husband and father-to-be. Mandy never asked about the impending divorce. For her it did not matter that they might not be married by the time their son was born; the child was proof enough of their love and their future together. In Mandy's world Ruth did not exist, that was her way of coping with any guilt she had for breaking up Robert's marriage.

Robert had brought his clothes to her flat and he had to admit it was cramped compared to Hicks. Mandy had cleared out her wardrobes but Robert owned much more than she did. Her pine chest of drawers was now full of his sweaters, hers were moved into a box under the bed. His computer and files crowded the dining area and his wine "cellar" was a couple of cartons in the corner of their bedroom.

She had lived in her flat ever since she left Leeds. She could have moved to a larger one as there was enough money saved but the effort was not worth the extra space – until now. Robert wanted her to move to a bigger flat or house, one that they chose together, with a room for the baby, but she was not in a hurry. For the time being they stepped around the boxes with files and cartons of wine knowing that it was only temporary.

Mandy would not mind staying in Orpington. It was easy to get to London and she knew the people in the building. A young artist called Ollie had the flat opposite and would often come in for a weekend coffee and a chat before Robert moved in. Now he often shared a beer with Robert as both were at home during the day. Ollie did not sell many of his paintings and in order to survive he set up web-sites for small companies. And downstairs was a young couple, who had just had their first baby and was looking forward to Mandy having her son so they could share pram-walks in the park. There were four flats in the building, an old Victorian detached house which was built for one family. Mandy's living room was large and must once have been an elegant drawing room with its large French windows with a small balcony looking out over the garden, which belonged to the basement flat.

The four flats had a common entrance and each had their separate door leading from the upper landings of the main staircase. The carpet on the stairs was worn and the table in the hallway was cluttered with unclaimed junk mail. The door bells had handwritten cards, Mandy's just said Flat No.2, while Ollie had a colourful card with his name in italic script. The front garden had long since been dug up and the landlord had concreted it over to provide each flat with a parking space clearly marked with the number of the flat. This was one of the things that had attracted Mandy, as she had been given a company car when she moved to London.

They were hoping that one of the larger flats in the building g would become free. But in the meantime, they looked at some flats and even houses in the area. Nothing had appealed to them and it was always with a sigh of relief they returned to Mandy's flat, where they felt at home. Robert had even got used to the small kitchen and found that its smallness made no difference to the quality of his cooking and he missed none of the gadgets he had left at Hicks.

They were cosy and safe in their haven in Orpington.

Chapter 47

Ruth had looked up the address on Google Maps. She knew it was a fifteen-minute walk from the station. The rain was soft but gave her an excuse to pull her hood over her woollen hat. Her dark hair was completely covered and her polo neck was hidden behind a red scarf wound around her neck and lower chin. She wore no make-up; somehow it had not seemed fitting to look at her best as she was going to ask that woman to leave Robert alone. Just a gentle chat. That was all.

She walked some dreary streets with old Victorian villas and suddenly she was in front of Mandy's house. "Just what I expected, so typical of Mandy," Ruth murmured as she looked at the cracked forecourt with its four parked cars. Ruth recognised Robert's car in the space marked 2 and pressed the bell marked Flat 2. There was a short pause and then a click. Ruth pushed the heavy door open and stepped into the hall. It was quiet and dark, the one window on the landing gave a shard of grey light. She waited and finally a door on the left side of the upper landing opened; there was Mandy, dressed in a pale pink dressing gown, obviously late in getting up as it was Saturday. There was no sign of Robert.

"Ruth, what are you doing here? I didn't know you were coming." Mandy sounded flustered and pulled the dressing gown tighter around her belly. The shape was there to see. Ruth shuddered.

"I've come to talk to you, just a friendly chat. Can I come up?"

"Well, I'm not dressed as you can see. And Robert's not here, he's gone shopping but he'll be back soon. Give me five minutes. Did you come by car?"

"Yes, I'll wait in the car and I'll come back in five minutes, if that's OK."

"Fine, I'll get some coffee going. See you soon then."

Ruth stepped out into the rain and wondered why she had said she'd come by car. The lie had just flown out of her mouth without any connection with her brain. Afraid that Mandy might be watching out of a window, she quickly walked around the corner looking at her watch. The minutes moved slowly but she waited seven minutes before she crossed the forecourt and pressed the doorbell again.

Mandy was dressed in an ill-fitting denim skirt with a loose tunic in dark blue, had combed her frizzy hair and put some lipstick on. She gestured to Ruth to step into the flat and there was a faint smell of yesterday's cooking in the air.

"Come into the living room and I'll get us some coffee. Milk?"

Ruth saw Robert's computer at the dining table and while Mandy was clattering in the kitchen, she rifled through the pile of papers beside it. There were several letters from Robert's lawyer Henry Friedman. She also noted some buff envelopes from her lawyer. Her eyes caught a note from an estate agent stating that they were happy to receive instructions to sell Hicks – and that they already had a couple showing interest. Ruth felt as if she had been hit. Hicks? No, Hicks was not going to be sold and that was it. She felt her chest contract. She had to take a deep breath to calm down as Mandy entered from the kitchen with a tray laden with a coffee pot, mugs and a plate of ginger biscuits.

Mandy busied herself laying out the mugs and a sugar bowl in white and blue china. She poured the coffee very slowly as if she did not want to hear what Ruth had come to say.

"I think you know why I'm here. It's about Robert's incredible claims on our common property. I thought I might be able to talk sense with you."

"It's all dealt with via your respective lawyers. I have nothing to do with your divorce."

"Nothing to do with our divorce. How can you say that? You are the reason for this divorce." Ruth's voice was strident and her hands were shaking as she lowered the coffee mug.

"Your marriage was broken long before I entered the scene."

"You know nothing about the state of our marriage, nothing at all. Robert only felt pity for you, and so did I. And that's why we invited you to Hicks, even for Christmas and how did you repay our hospitality?"

Ruth stood up and pointed an angry finger at Mandy. "You repaid our kindness by seducing my husband, making sure you got pregnant, so he would be forced to get involved one way or other. Is this your bloody revenge for the abortion he forced you to have all those years ago? It is, isn't it?"

Mandy stared at Ruth. She just shook her head, as if trying to gather her thoughts.

"No, no it wasn't. We happened to rekindle our love. Believe me, the baby was not planned. You must realise that. I told Robert from the moment I knew I was pregnant I would make no claims. He was free to leave me, but I insisted on having the baby this time. Now I know that he wants our baby as much as I do." Her voice sounded stronger, as if she was reassuring herself.

"I know he always wanted a child and we have tried for years. Now here's a baby on its way showing him that he can be a father. I'm still sure you've tricked him into this. I'm willing to take him back. I bet he didn't tell you that I threw him out. Did he? But he didn't want to go. Now I'm here to tell you that we're both willing to make sure that you're helped financially if you want to keep this baby. But we don't want to break up our marriage, especially not now, as I've just left Babylove in order to spend more time with my husband." Ruth stressed the last word.

"Really? I thought you were sacked, that's what Robert says. And have you asked him if he wants to spend more time with you? You must realise, Ruth, that he has already left you, all he wants is a divorce. That's the truth. And if you can't see that, there's not much to talk about. I am sorry for what has happened to you, especially as you already have a failed marriage behind you…"

"Don't you have one failed marriage as well? Or doesn't that count? You picked Robert, an easy prey considering his guilt about the abortion. Pity, that is all he feels for you. Pity!"

"Ruth, I think you'd better leave. Robert and I are going to get married as soon as the divorce has come through. We'll have our child and there is nothing you can do to change that." Mandy stood up.

Ruth opened her handbag and with clammy fingers she shook the silk scarf and the filleting knife fell with a tinny sound onto the coffee tray. Ruth saw Mandy's eyes widen with fear which egged her on. She took the knife and moved towards Mandy, who put her arms across her swollen belly.

"Ruth, be sensible, come on, put that knife down." She almost squeaked.

"You bloody cow. You've ruined my life and I will not have it. It is me he loves."

"Then why is he here, living with me?"

"You forced him with your pregnancy, that's all."

"We love each other and you'd better get to grips with the idea. He is not going back!"

Ruth felt that she could not breathe. Her anger was boiling inside her, her body temperature rose. She felt feverish, as if she wasn't really there. A white fog spread in front of her eyes. She was out of control.

"I trusted you, you're nothing but scum." And in that moment Ruth moved forward and without knowing what she was doing she thrust the knife into Mandy's face, again and again.

Blood was spurting all over the tray and the sugar turned pink in its bowl. Mandy was screaming and clutching her face. She managed to get up and run into the passage. Ruth followed her, still with the knife in her hands. With blood-slippery fingers Mandy opened the front door of the flat and screamed at the top of her voice.

"Help, help, heeelp."

The effort seemed to have exhausted her and her voice turned into a whisper.

Ruth stood at the open door and watched Mandy drop down on her knees. Blood was pouring from her face and neck. Ruth took a step closer and just then the door opposite opened. A man in his thirties with a rust-red beard appeared and looked first at Mandy and then with horror at Ruth holding the bloody knife.

"Oh, my god, Mandy. What's happened? You need an ambulance," he said his voice hoarse with horror.

He looked at Mandy now half-conscious on the floor and then again at Ruth, who was frozen in the doorway. With a leap he moved towards Ruth and kicked her in her lower abdomen. She curled up in pain and dropped the knife. Before Ruth even noticed it, the man had picked up the knife. He pushed her into the open door of Mandy's flat and closed it with a bang. She could hear him moving a table from the landing and wedging it under the door handle.

Ruth crouched on the floor behind the closed door and heard him phoning the ambulance and then the police. And at that moment there were running steps in the hall. It was Robert, she could hear his voice through the closed door.

"Oh, no. What's happened? Darling Mandy, don't worry sweetheart. Hold my hand. There. Ollie has called the ambulance and the police are also on their way. It's going to be all right. Oh, darling how could this have happened? Now, you're going to be fine it's just surface wounds. For god's sake, Ollie, tell me. Tell me it isn't my ex-wife who's done this? Mandy phoned me ten minutes ago and said that she had turned up unannounced. She asked me to come home and I took a taxi from the supermarket. Somehow, I didn't want her to be alone with Ruth – oh, my god. And where's Ruth?"

Ollie must have pointed at the closed door as there was no answer from him. Ruth crawled away from the door still in pain from the kicking. There must be a way she could escape before the police arrived. Her handbag was open on the floor next to the sofa and blood had spattered its pale leather. She opened the French window, stepped out on the narrow balcony and threw down the handbag which landed with a thud on the patio. Ruth looked down and knew she would break something if she jumped, but she had to get away. She turned around, saw the sofa cushions and quickly carried them one by one out onto the balcony. She threw them down to the patio. One fell on a garden table, but the other two landed just beneath the balcony.

Ruth had never had a head for heights. She hesitated and pushed one leg over the iron railing. She could not do it. She fell back on the cold balcony floor, curled up as in a shell and closed her eyes. She had no idea of how long she was there. In the background she could hear sirens but the sound held no significance for her. She only opened her eyes when a policewoman shook her gently. There were three officers and Ollie who watched as she was handcuffed and brought down to the police car. All Ruth could feel was the bitter cold which made her shake. The memory of what had happened was erased by her fear.

Chapter 48

Marjorie Green was not an early morning person nor did she know anyone who would call her at seven, so it was with a mixture of anxiety and anger she lifted her receiver while looking at her clock radio. It was showing 6.58 am in a ghostly blue light. "It couldn't be Frank, it mustn't be Frank…" she thought as she answered with a morning-husky voice.

"Mrs G. it's Robert. I'm sorry to phone so early but I have some bad news."

"Bad news, what do you mean? Nothing's happened to Ruth I hope."

Mrs Green sat up in bed and turned on her bedside light. She had hoped never to hear from Robert again but here he was on the phone.

"I'm afraid Ruth is in prison. She attacked my fiancée early yesterday with a knife and it is serious. There's a risk Mandy might lose her sight in one eye, not only that, she is also badly cut up."

"What? What are you talking about? It can't be Ruth. Are you sure it was Ruth? She wouldn't hurt a fly and you know it. Your fiancée you say, that's the woman I met down at Hicks? If that is the case, I can understand my daughter. Ruth invited that woman into her home and made her feel welcome, but I still don't think Ruth could attack anyone. Say it isn't true." Her voice faltered.

"I'm afraid it is true. I just wanted to let you know before you read it in the papers. Because of Ruth being who she is, the media has jumped on it. Those scandal-hungry journalists might try to speak to you. They even tried to speak to Mandy in the hospital. Whatever you do, don't say anything. It won't help Ruth. She'll be up in court later this afternoon but she'll have to remain in custody until the trial, whenever that will be."

"I can't believe it. Well, thank you for letting me know. I really can't believe you, it is not at all like Ruth. But, if it is true, you must also know that this would not have happened if you had treated my daughter with some respect. When I think of how much she has given you during all these years. Ask yourself, where would you have been without her?" Her voice rose. "And this is how you've repaid her, by running off with another woman. It's all your bloody fault."

Mrs Green was shaking as she slammed the phone down in its dock. She could not stand listening to Robert anymore. An hour later she heard the letterbox clatter as her daily paper was delivered. *The Daily Mail* had *"Boss attacks rival"* on the front page and under it was a photo of Ruth receiving her award from the Duchess. Inside there was a whole page devoted to Ruth's arrest, with a picture of the factory in Caterham as well as a photo of Mrs Green's house, "where Ruth Farringdon grew up". *"The Queen of Babylove in attempted murder enquiry"* was the headline.

Mrs Green dropped the paper. All she could think of was how to tell Frank. What about the wedding reception at Hicks? She went into the kitchen and looked over The Meadow to see if Frank had opened his curtains. To her relief they were still closed.

Then suddenly she realised that she hadn't asked Robert where Ruth was incarcerated. Was there something she was meant to do? Well, what could she do? She picked up the paper from the floor, spread it on the kitchen table and wept.

Chapter 49

Nine months later.

The Times

Businesswoman of the Year jailed for jealous rage.

Ruth Farringdon will serve 30 months for the vicious attack on her husband's lover. Sentenced to jail after a sensational ten day's trial Mrs Nieder, her married name, gasped with relief. The jury had cleared her of attempted murder and causing grievous bodily harm with intent.

Ms Amanda Richards, the victim of the knife attack in April last year, said that she was not happy about the outcome. "Mrs Farringdon will only spend a further two years in prison and with good behaviour can be out by the end of next year. That is not enough to compensate me for the agony, both physical and mental, that I have gone through these last months. But I suppose I have to respect the jury's decision."

Mr Robert Nieder also stated that the sentence was too lenient. "Amanda almost lost our baby in the attack and that was not taken into account." Their son Leo was born four months after the incident.

Judge Charles Collins said in court that this was a tragic case. "Here is a woman who has made a glittering career with many awards to prove it. I can only presume that losing her job in the company she built up which became a market leader under her direction and at the very same time as she was going through a painful divorce which must have exposed a fault line in Mrs Farringdon's character. There are many victims in this sad case, not only Ms Richards but also Mr Nieder and Mrs Farringdon."

Algarve, Portugal

Ruth put her foot down on the painted tiles on the terrace. She jumped as the heat burnt her toes and she stepped back into the shadow. The intense midday heat of Algarve still surprised her even though she had now lived in the villa for six months. Her plans were still unclear. She had spoken to her mother about a delayed gap year explaining she was still thinking about what to do. She did not tell her mother that she had contacted most of her business associates and even John Barley about possible openings but they had sounded uncomfortable talking to her just as her co-prisoners had been.

She would not speak to anyone about her time in prison. She was called Lady Lah-di-dah by the other prisoners, even the wardens did not seem to like her apart from one, but then she had pushed her knee between Ruth's legs while trying to kiss her. Ruth had slapped her and the warden threatened to report her – "And that will put an end to your early release for good behaviour," the warden had said with a smirk. After that Ruth kept herself to herself. Her mother talked to her on the phone once a month, "I wish I could come and see you, but I can't. I wouldn't know what to do with myself in such a place."

Ruth understood, no one else came apart from Frank Addleston who brought homemade biscuits from her mother. Archie Arnold came once asking her to sign the final divorce papers. He confessed that he had never seen the inside of a prison before. "Divorce clients usually don't end up in prison," he said with an embarrassed smile.

Ruth spent her free time in the library, an area avoided by the other prisoners, where she read legal and business books, never having been interested in fiction. She worked hard at the prison office where she folded junk mail into envelopes. This gave her enough pocket money to spend on luxuries like a decent soap and newspapers. She still trembled when she opened the business pages. She remembered how distraught she was having read an interview with Sir Rupert after the successful merger with Pink's. The fact that Andrew Miskin had taken over as managing director of the merged company, now called Pink's, made her so upset, she could not sleep for days. She would never forget his disloyalty but worse was the fact that the name Babylove had more or less disappeared. It was only retained by the Babylove Foundation. All Ruth's work erased by some signatures on a contract.

Ruth finally left prison. Her sentence halved taking into account her good behaviour. As both Hicks and the Fulham house had been sold, she was homeless. She stayed for a while in her mother's empty house. Marjorie had finally married Frank and they now lived in his house, hoping to buy a small holiday property in Portugal as soon as Marjorie's house was sold. It was Frank who suggested they should pool their resources with Ruth's and buy in Portugal. They would look for a house suitable for them to share. The idea was for Ruth to stay there until she decided what to do.

She had hated staying in her mother's house as she left prison. It made her feel as if all the Babylove years were just a distant dream. She thought of Luke and how he had saved her from the mean walls of the cottage. One evening, after maybe a glass too many she contacted Luke and asked if there were any jobs going at his company. "Yes, if you're planning to invest," was his answer before telling her that his outfit was a one-man band.

Yes, going abroad had been a good idea. Her plan was to start afresh after maybe six months in Portugal. Through an agent she had found a small house for them near Faro; a main villa with a couple of bedrooms and a small pool house, to which she could retire when Frank and her mother came to stay.

The house was part of a large estate of villas of different sizes. Most of the people staying there were retired and had chosen this area because of the many good golf courses in the neighbourhood. She bought the house in her maiden name, Ruth Green, but it did not take long before someone recognised her, all those television appearances now regretted. The neighbours turned their heads the other way when Ruth met them in the shops or at the very English pub, where she occasionally had a drink.

She changed her habits and shopped early in the mornings, when the neighbours were sleeping or out on the golf course. She had bottles of wine delivered rather than going to the pub. In a moment of generosity Babylove had allowed her to keep the company car; driving was now her only pleasure. Ruth made at least one excursion a week trying to find a new restaurant or a hidden beach.

Apart from a weekly call from her mother she hardly spoke to anyone. Her Portuguese was non-existent but she enjoyed a chat with a café-owner or a shop assistant during her forays. There no one knew her and for a short moment she felt normal, a human being not a convict.

Money was tight. Her signature on the Lithuanian deal meant that she had also reimbursed Dick Callander in order to avoid another court case. That had taken care of almost all the money from the sale of the houses. Robert still received half of the income from the student flats and her money from Babylove was slowly being whittled away. She had paid more than half of the price for the villa, in spite of Frank's protests. Her mother, however, thought it was right as Ruth was more of a permanent resident.

Ruth knew she had to find another job, but what and where? She played with the idea of becoming a waitress at the golf club, where most of the players were English, but she couldn't pluck up the courage to ask. The Anglo-Portuguese Chamber of Commerce had no suggestions either; "learn the language" was their advice.

Her only company in the dark evenings was a bottle of wine. Food did not interest her. Once a week on her excursions she would eat a good meal, but in her villa it was simple salads or ready-made meals. The wine put her to sleep and when she surfaced in the morning from her dreamless sleep she would think of Babylove and her marriage but never ever of Mandy.

Post scriptum

The call was unexpected. "It took some time to find you. Quite some detective work, actually," said Charles Butterworth. "I have an idea that I want to put to you."

Ruth sat down. This was the first time she had heard from Charles since the days of the merger negotiations. "I followed your story with great interest," he said. "And I think you would be perfect for a programme I have been commissioned to do for the BBC. It will deal with people who have gone through a tough time and come out on the other side. You'd be perfect. I want you to tell your story and how it affected you."

Ruth first said no, but Charles was adamant and being told that there was going to be paid expenses plus a week in a London hotel, she finally said yes.

The programme went out on prime time and caused quite a stir. Via the BBC's PR people she was interviewed by all the major papers and again on Woman's Hour. Suddenly she was seen as a gutsy survivor. And who could blame her for losing her temper with a woman she had seen as a friend? Especially as she had been treated so badly by her stay-at-home husband but also by the board of the company she had built up?

Through Charles she got an agent and together with a famous management guru who had managed a chain of retailers, now bust, she became much sought after as a lecturer on the profitable speaker circuit. When not speaking Ruth wrote a book, a strange mixture of autobiography and management tutorial, which became a best seller.

Ruth's relationship with her mother improved, mainly thanks to Frank Addlestone's intervention. Sirita left her job with a chemical firm in Birmingham and became Ruth's personal assistant. Ruth never spoke to Robert again, nor did the Callanders. The biggest surprise was the call from Sir Rupert, who asked If Ruth would be willing to act as temporary managing director of a small company, which he chaired. "The present director is going on maternity leave and I could not think of anyone better suited than you to take over the reins. Let's discuss it over lunch at my club."

"So sorry Rupert, but I'm not interested."

Ruth could not stop smiling as she turned the phone off.

Acknowledgements

My thanks go to the writing group I belong to. Helpful comments from Sue Gillie, Patsy Way and Tony Emerson have improved this novel enormously. We four are also grateful to the indomitable Maggie Smith who brought us all together.

I also thank early readers for their comments and encouragement: Colin Kaye, Karin Forseke, CBE, Dr Eva Du Bose, Katharine St. John-Brooks and Fred Emery.

The clever cover was designed by Nikko Hardrade-Grosz, my talented son.

Technical assistance, advice as well as layout was expertly done by David Firth.

My biggest thanks, as always, to my husband John.

About The Author

Pia Helena Ormerod is an international business journalist. She was invited to be the first woman to be a member of the 18-man Council for the Swedish Chamber of Commerce for the UK. Her talents for negotiating and creating business networks led to her being asked to be the first woman to lead the Chamber. Within the first year of her taking over as managing director she turned loss into profit. Ormerod has a unique insight into the challenges faced by women in the male-dominated world of business. She is a vociferous advocate for inclusivity in the higher echelons of corporations. She states: "Sadly, there has been no real change since I started. There are still too few women at the top of leading companies."

Printed in Great Britain
by Amazon

56760520R00158